OMAR & ALI:
THE KEY TO ORULENTHIA

by **Adil Bhatti**

First published June 2025

This novel is dedicated to my amazing son, Aslan Bhatti. Thank you for all the beautiful memories. May you have the healthiest life filled with happiness. I love you forever!

TABLE OF CONTENTS

CHAPTER 1
THE CLOCK, THE CRUSH, AND COUSCOUS.

Omar Jamali stared at the clock like it had personally wronged him. 2:53 PM.

The second hand ticked at the slowest speed allowed by the laws of physics. Somewhere at the front of the classroom, Mr. Edwards was giving a passionate lecture about the Industrial Revolution, but Omar's mind was miles away from steam engines and labor unions.

He was writing a letter.
A love letter.
Well... sort of.

Dear Lyndsey,
I know you probably think I'm just another guy in class who plays baseball and pretends to care about math homework (which is fair). But I just wanted to say...

Omar frowned. Too dramatic?

He tapped his pencil against the edge of his notebook. Maybe he should be more chill. Lyndsey liked chill guys. Or at least she laughed at their jokes during lunch.

He scratched out the last few lines and rewrote:

Hey Lyndsey,
If you're not doing anything this summer, maybe we could hang out? I promise I'm only slightly annoying in real life.

"Mr. Jamali?"

Omar snapped to attention.
Mr. Edwards was giving him *the* look—half-annoyed,
half-amused.

Omar blinked. "Can you tell us what effect the spinning
jenny had on the British textile industry?"

"Uh…" He glanced at the board, then at the book in front of
him. "It… made a lot of sweaters?"

The class burst out laughing. Mr. Edwards sighed.

"Close enough. That'll do for today."

The bell rang—*finally.*
Chairs scraped. Backpacks zipped.

Omar stuffed his crumpled letter into his hoodie pocket
and grabbed his bag. He was already halfway down the hall
when his phone buzzed.

Ali: *Meet u by lockers. Baba's here.*

Omar pushed through the crowd like he was escaping a
prison break. Down the stairs, past the cafeteria, straight
toward the row of blue lockers near the school's back exit.

Ali was waiting there—small, skinny, a head shorter than
Omar but packed with energy.

"Finally!" Ali groaned. "Did you get in trouble again?"

"Nope," Omar said, ruffling his brother's curly hair. "Just
suffered a near-death boredom experience."

"Did you give Lyndsey the letter?"

"Shut up."

"Whatever," Ali snorted. "You'll probably chicken out
again. You always do! Hahaha!"

"Yeah, well—" Omar was about to fire back when their
dad's car horn honked from the parking lot.

There it was: a clean grey Mazda CX-5, polished and in great shape. The same Arabic bumper sticker stood out on the back window: *"Masha'Allah."*

They jumped in.

"Salam, boys," Baba said, glancing at them in the rearview mirror.

"Salam," they said in unison.

Their father, an electrical engineer, always looked tired but focused—like his brain was still solving equations even after work.

The ride home was filled with Ali talking nonstop about a YouTube video where someone built a drone out of soda cans, and Omar zoning out—this time to thoughts of summer vacation.

Tomorrow, they'd be flying to Morocco. Not their first trip, but always something to look forward to.

"I hope Uncle Abdullah got the new football already," Ali said suddenly. "Last time we popped it on the second day!"

"He probably has like four of them waiting," Omar grinned. "You know he always goes all-out."

"And Grandma's gonna make those grilled kebabs again, right?" Ali asked, nearly drooling.

"Oh yeah. With the fries on the side. And the mint tea."

They both leaned back in their seats, daydreaming about Tangier's breezy beaches, the smell of fresh bread from corner shops, and late-night soccer games with all their cousins under the streetlights.

At home, the smell of couscous and lamb tagine hit them before they even opened the front door.

"Mama, we're home!" Omar shouted, kicking off his sneakers.

Their mother poked her head out of the kitchen, wearing an apron and a soft smile.

"As-salaamu alaikum, boys," she said warmly.

"Wa alaikum salam," Ali replied, already sniffing the air like a cartoon dog.

"Go wash up. Dinner's ready."

The kitchen table was already set: couscous piled high, with carrots, chickpeas, and zucchini tucked into the steaming mound. A giant bowl of lamb tagine sat in the middle, the sauce glistening like gold.

Omar and Ali ate like they hadn't eaten in a week, barely stopping to breathe.

"Slow down," their mother laughed. "You'll choke."

"We're carbo-loading," Omar said with a mouth full of couscous. "International travel requires strength."

Later, as the sun dipped behind the rows of suburban rooftops, the boys tossed a baseball back and forth in their tiny backyard.

Ali threw wildly. Omar missed. The ball bounced off the fence.

"That was a terrible pitch," Omar said.

"That was your terrible catch," Ali snapped.

"You throw like a chicken."

"You run like a camel!"

They wrestled in the grass for a bit before collapsing side by side under the sky, their breaths syncing as they stared up at the first stars peeking through.

"You think Grandma made your favorite cookies yet?" Ali asked.

"If she didn't, I'll cry," Omar said.

That night, after brushing their teeth and fighting over who got the top bunk, they finally lay in the dark, whispering across the room.

"Do you think we'll go to the beach the first day?" Ali asked.

"For sure," Omar replied. "Uncle Abdullah always takes us to that spot with the goal posts. You better start practicing. You're way behind on your game, yo!"

Ali chuckled. "Just don't cry when I score on you."

"In your dreams."

Neither of them knew that this summer would be the last *normal* thing in their lives for a long, long time.

CHAPTER 2
THE TRIANGULAR TALISMAN.

The terminal at Newark International Airport buzzed with noise—announcements crackling over loudspeakers, travelers wheeling luggage, and lining up for overpriced coffee. The Jamali family sat clustered near their gate, passports in hand, waiting for their flight to be called. Their trip had officially begun.

Omar had his hoodie pulled up and his headphones on, bobbing his head slightly to the beat of Kendrick Lamar's voice echoing in his ears. His playlist was queued with all his favorites—a mix of chill tracks and hyped anthems to keep his nerves at bay.

Next to him, Ali was curled into his seat, fully absorbed in his Nintendo Switch, thumbs moving quickly across the buttons. A boss battle was in progress, and from the look of sheer determination on his face, victory was near.

Their parents sat nearby—Baba checking his phone for boarding updates while Mama flipped through a travel guide, highlighting places she wanted to visit with her sister-in-law in Tangier. Every so often, she'd point something out in the book and smile to herself.

By the time they boarded the plane, it was already dusk. The flight to Paris took off slightly later than expected, and the boys dozed on and off, occasionally waking to sip ginger ale or stretch their legs. Omar drifted between sleep and half-conscious thoughts, picturing the Moroccan coastline and freshly grilled kebabs. Ali mumbled in his sleep, clutching his Switch like a teddy bear.

When the plane finally landed in Paris, they had less than thirty minutes to make their connecting flight. The entire family sprinted across Charles de Gaulle Airport, weaving through crowds, dodging suitcases, and huffing through the hallways like it was an Olympic event.

"Go, go, go!" Baba urged, holding up their boarding passes like a baton.

Breathless, they reached their gate just as the final boarding call was made. Sweaty and panting, they stumbled into their seats, laughing in disbelief that they'd actually made it.

"Morocco, here we come," Omar said, slumping into his seat.

"Best cardio of my life," Ali groaned.

Three quick hours later, the plane touched down in Tangier, Morocco.

They were greeted by the warm sun and the cheerful grin of Uncle Abdullah, who stood waving beside his trusty white Renault van. Hugs and greetings filled the parking lot as the family piled into the van.

The van's windows were down. Dareeja music pulsed through the speakers as the coastal breeze whipped through Omar and Ali's hair. Both boys leaned their heads out, taking in the rolling green hills and the sparkling blue sea as the van wound its way up toward the hilltops of Rmilat, Tangier.

Uncle Abdullah's house was perched just high enough to offer a breathtaking view of the Mediterranean. The smell of saltwater hung in the air, mixed with the faint scent of wildflowers.

As soon as they arrived, cousins swarmed the driveway. There were hugs, high fives, and laughter. The backyard had been set up like a mini feast—grilled kebabs, platters of seafood, baskets of round Moroccan khubz bread, and tall glasses of mint tea.

The jet lag hit hard.

By 7:00 p.m., Omar and Ali were barely able to keep their eyes open. They collapsed into the soft cushions laid out in the guest room and were asleep within minutes.

The next morning, they woke refreshed and excited. After breakfast, their aunt took them to the old Medina—the heart of Tangier. Narrow streets twisted and turned like a maze, the walls painted in faded whites and ocean blues. Market stalls overflowed with colorful produce, woven baskets, and the scent of spices.

At one stand, they helped their aunt haggle over bright oranges and fat, shiny tomatoes. Another stall sold heaps of fresh olives in shades of green, purple, and black. A vendor with a wide smile let them sample one or two. Omar's mouth puckered. "Sour! Sour and so good!"

They stopped at a café tucked behind an old tiled archway. There, they sipped hot herbal tea brewed with sweet mint and munched on flaky *brewat*—pastries filled with spiced fish and vegetables.

After resting a bit in the café's shade, they wandered deeper into the Medina until they reached a quiet side street. A small, arched wooden door with carved patterns stood halfway open. A faded sign above read: *Tangier Antiquités et Curiosités.*

Inside, the shop felt like a museum.

Shelves were crowded with old brass lanterns, worn leather satchels, dusty ceramic plates, and faded maps. Antique swords rested beside ancient-looking books. A taxidermy owl stared from a perch in the corner. Everything had the scent of age—musk, leather, and old wood.

"Whoa," Ali whispered. "This place is awesome."

They wandered through the cramped aisles. Omar picked up a small compass that spun wildly no matter how he held it. "Think this thing works?"

"Looks cursed," Ali grinned.

They passed a shelf filled with ancient Berber jewelry—silver cuffs and necklaces with bright coral beads. A stack of antique teapots glimmered under a dusty beam of sunlight. They chose a pair to bring home for Mama, and next to them, a tiny brass hookah pipe caught their eye. It had strange engravings and a cracked wooden base. Omar turned it over. "Decor only," he said. "Definitely not usable."

Just then, Ali spotted something strange tucked into a corner behind a velvet cloth. "What's this?"

It looked like a music box at first, but it was triangular—not square—and made of smooth, silvery metal. Embedded in the center was a large red stone, also shaped like a triangle, with a deep luster that shimmered oddly in the light.

Strange symbols were etched along the sides—not Arabic, not Berber, and certainly not anything either of them recognized.

Ali held it up. "Cool, right? Check this out, bro."

Omar frowned. "What is it?"

An old man emerged from the back of the shop. His beard was long and white, and he wore a *djellaba* with a small green cap. His eyes were milky but sharp, as if they could see more than others.

"That," he said in a low voice, "is not for children."

Ali blinked. "Is it a music box?"

The old man shook his head slowly. "It has no music. And it's not a toy. Don't play with it."

"What's it for, then?" Omar asked.

"I don't know. It came to my store long ago. No one's ever wanted it."

"Because it's expensive?" Ali guessed.

"Because it feels... strange," the old man said.

The boys exchanged a glance. Of course, they wanted it now.

They tried to haggle. At first, the man refused. "It's not something I should sell. It's... different."

But eventually, after a long back-and-forth, he named a price. Equivalent to about seventy-five U.S. dollars.

"Deal," Omar said.

They paid, packed the artifact carefully in a small cloth bag, and left the shop with their other souvenirs.

That night, after another delicious dinner with family and watching the sun set from the terrace, they crashed hard.

And they both dreamed.
They dreamed the same dream.

In the dream, the triangular artifact hovered in darkness, suspended in a space that felt both infinite and enclosed. It glowed with a soft, pulsing red light, the stone at its center shimmering like fire trapped under glass. Strange symbols floated around it, rearranging themselves slowly like a language trying to speak. A distant hum echoed, low and rhythmic, like the thrum of a heartbeat—or an engine from another world.

Then it called their names. Not aloud. Not like a voice. But like a feeling. A presence.

Omar... Ali...

The air seemed to bend around the names, heavy with meaning. The boys floated closer and closer to the artifact, unable to look away.

They awoke the next morning, the sun streaming through the windows. Over a breakfast of boiled eggs, coffee, and bread with butter and honey shared with their uncle and aunt, both Omar and Ali felt a bit uneasy and unrested from the strange dream. They kept glancing at each other, unsure if they should bring it up.

"Did you... have a dream about the artifact?" Omar finally asked, voice low.

Ali nodded. "It was glowing. And I felt like it was calling us. Like—not with words—but like it knew us."

Omar frowned. "Exactly. It wasn't even scary, but I couldn't sleep properly after."

They exchanged a look of silent agreement. Whatever it was, it wasn't normal.

The dream stuck with them, like dust clinging to their thoughts.

They ran down to the beach to kick around a soccer ball. The sea breeze and salty air helped clear their heads.

After a few minutes of kicking and passing, Omar said, "I still can't stop thinking about that dream."

Ali passed the ball back. "Same. It's like the artifact wants something."

"And it knew our names," Omar added.

Ali paused, then nodded. "We already talked about this at breakfast, but yeah. It keeps echoing in my head."

They looked toward the house, where the artifact lay tucked in the corner of their room, silent for now.

The wind blew across the beach, and somewhere far away, a storm seemed to gather.

CHAPTER 3
WHEN THE LIGHT HIT JUST RIGHT.

The thirty days in Morocco passed in a blur of laughter, adventure, and memory-making. Omar and Ali had lived more in those weeks than in the entire year before. Their days were packed with sun-soaked fun—long afternoons swimming in the turquoise waters of the Mediterranean, building sandcastles, and kicking soccer balls along Tangier's golden beaches. At night, the air buzzed with energy as cousins gathered for open-air barbecues, smoky lamb skewers sizzling over coals while the adults told stories and brewed strong mint tea. Music and the scent of spices drifted through the warm breeze as the boys ran barefoot under the stars.

One weekend, they took the train to Marrakesh—a journey that felt like stepping into another world. The medina pulsed with life: snake charmers swayed with cobras to the sound of flutes, henna artists dotted the alleyways, and stalls overflowed with leather bags, lanterns, and colorful spices piled in perfect pyramids. Later, in the shadow of the Atlas Mountains, they rode camels into the rust-colored desert, gripping the saddles tightly and laughing as their camels grunted and shuffled through the sand. That night, they camped in tents beneath a sky so filled with stars it looked like someone had spilled glitter across black velvet. The stillness of the desert and the crackle of the campfire left an imprint on their hearts.

There was shopping—endless shopping. Hand-painted ceramics, embroidered scarves, knock-off sneakers, and tiny glass bottles of scented oil were packed into their suitcases. Omar snapped dozens of photos: mountain sunsets, city streets, goofy selfies with cousins, and even a perfectly lit shot of his tea glass at a rooftop café. He posted them all to Instagram and Facebook, earning hearts and likes from friends back home. When Lyndsey from New Jersey—his long-time secret crush—liked not just one but three of his photos, Omar nearly dropped his phone. His mind spiraled instantly: She likes me. She definitely likes me now. His crush deepened into full-blown obsession.

Eventually, the trip wound down, and the time came to leave. The family boarded a connecting flight in Paris, dragging their heavier-than-before luggage through the familiar terminals. The boys were quieter this time, gazing out the window as Morocco faded below the clouds. After a smooth landing at Newark Airport, they were welcomed by the cool, leafy calm of New Jersey. The drive back to Old Bridge felt dreamlike. When they finally pulled into their driveway, the sight of their house made Omar and Ali break into tired but happy grins. As much as they had loved the adventure, it felt good—really good—to be home.

A month passed. School was back in full swing, and with each passing day, the incredible Moroccan trip faded a little more into the background. The mysterious dream the boys had shared on the plane ride over was long forgotten, buried beneath homework, pop quizzes, and basketball games at the local park.

It was on one of those ordinary afternoons, after shooting hoops with friends, that things began to shift again. The late afternoon sun cast long golden shadows as Omar and Ali walked home side by side, laughing and joking. When they got home, Ali bounded upstairs to his room, digging through a drawer for his old Super Mario Bros. cartridge for the Switch. That's when he saw it.

The talisman.

The strange, triangle-shaped object they had stumbled upon in the antiques shop in Tangier. It lay nestled beneath a pair of rolled-up socks, its ruby-like stone catching a glint of light from the window. Ali stared at it, curiosity flaring again. Without thinking too much about it, he tossed it into his backpack. "Maybe I'll show the guys tomorrow," he mumbled to himself.

The next afternoon, after school, Ali was in the yard with a group of friends, showing off the strange object. His friends were unimpressed and began tossing it around like it was a frisbee.

"Yo! Chill, that's not a toy!" Ali shouted, trying to catch it mid-air.

But one of the bigger kids, laughing and teasing, grabbed it and hurled it with all his strength. The talisman soared high and far—spinning through the air—and landed somewhere beyond a line of trees at the edge of the schoolyard.

Ali's stomach dropped. He scanned the area and spotted Omar nearby, walking with a few kids.

"Omar!" he yelled. "They threw the talisman—it flew way past the trees! Let's go!"

Together, they ran toward the small wooded patch, leaves crunching beneath their sneakers. It didn't take long before they spotted the talisman—lodged high in the crooked arm of an old maple tree. Ali groaned.

"I'll climb," Omar offered, already grabbing a low branch.

He made his way up slowly, eyes on the prize, but just as he reached for it, the talisman shifted and dropped several feet—catching in a lower branch, just out of arm's reach. The sun, now dipping toward the horizon, sent a sharp beam of golden light straight through the canopy, illuminating the stone with pinpoint precision.

The moment the light struck the ruby-like gem, the talisman began to vibrate gently. A high-pitched hum filled the air.

Then, without warning, a black, oval-shaped portal shimmered to life in the air—hovering just a few feet away from the tree, directly opposite the talisman. It looked like a crack in the world itself, edges rippling, a strange wind whispering from its depths. Colors and shadows twisted within it, too blurry to make sense of, but clearly… alive.

Omar stared, wide-eyed. "Did that… just happen?"

Ali didn't answer. He was too mesmerized by the portal's eerie glow. The beam of sunlight continued to shine through the talisman, as if focusing its magic with laser-like precision.

Curious but cautious, the boys gathered a handful of small rocks from the ground. Omar tossed the first stone toward the swirling darkness of the portal. It vanished instantly—no splash, no sound—disappearing as if swallowed by the very air itself. Ali threw another rock, watching intently as it too disappeared without a trace into the void. A strange silence fell between them, broken only by the faint hum that seemed to pulse from the portal's edges.

Omar picked up a long, slender stick nearby. Holding his breath, he carefully extended it into the blackness, watching as the tip of the stick disappeared into the shifting void. Slowly, he pulled it back, expecting it to be scorched or crumbled by some unknown force. But to their astonishment, the stick emerged completely unharmed—its wood smooth and intact, as if it had passed through a mere shadow rather than a tear in reality.

The portal remained suspended in the air, its edges flickering like a living thing. It was just the right size for a person to step through, beckoning with a silent invitation. A chill ran down their spines despite the warm sunlight around them. Omar's heart pounded loudly in his chest, and Ali's breath caught in his throat. Neither spoke, but their eyes met—an unspoken mix of fear, excitement, and something deeper. Ali snagged the talisman and shoved it into his backpack.

What lay beyond? Was it a doorway to adventure or a trap waiting to snap shut? The air around the portal seemed charged with secrets, warning them to think twice—but their curiosity burned too fiercely to turn away now.

With a final glance back at the familiar world behind them, Omar and Ali took a tentative step forward—stepping not just through space, but into the unknown, where every shadow could hold a mystery, and every heartbeat could be the start of something far greater than they ever imagined.

CHAPTER 4
THROUGH THE RIP.

The moment they stepped through the portal, time seemed to unravel.

Colors they had no names for exploded in slow motion across their vision, stretching into tendrils of light and shadow that bent around them like ribbons in a storm. Their bodies elongated—arms, legs, even their fingertips—pulled outward in impossible directions, as if they were strands of spaghetti being drawn through the eye of a cosmic needle. Yet they felt no pain. No fear. Only a sharp, electric hum that buzzed around their skulls like a hive of bees vibrating in harmony with the universe.

Sound warped. The wind screamed and then whispered, syllables folding over themselves like water rushing backward, laughter echoing and reversing as if time had hiccupped. They saw memories—some theirs, some not—flashing through transparent folds of light. The forest, the beach in Morocco, a distant tower in the sand, a city made of glass—all flickering by like old film reels skipping frames.

And yet, within all that chaos, their minds stayed still. Perfectly still. No panic, no confusion. Just the quiet, undeniable understanding that the whole journey lasted less than a heartbeat. Their bodies said eternity; their minds said blink.

Then, everything went still.

With a bone-jarring thud, the boys hit the ground.
Omar groaned first, the breath knocked clean out of him. Ali lay nearby, curled into himself like a dropped puppet. The land beneath them was coarse and cold, like dry gravel or volcanic

ash. A metallic tang clung to the air—sharp and alien. Their limbs refused to move at first—drained, heavy, as though they had swum through gravity itself. Neither of them opened their eyes. Not yet. There was a strange ringing in their ears, and a bone-deep ache settled into their chests, like they'd just run a marathon with their souls.

Minutes passed. Maybe more. Neither boy spoke.

Finally, Omar stirred. His eyelids fluttered open, and a shiver rolled through him. The air was frigid. It wasn't just cold—it was wrong. Sharp and thin, like breathing in fog from a forgotten place. He sat up slowly, heart still thudding in the back of his throat, and turned to Ali, who was blinking up at the sky—or what passed for a sky here.'

They both watched in stunned silence as the portal behind them twisted like water circling a drain, shrinking rapidly into itself until it vanished with a soundless pop. The light was gone. The warmth, too.

Around them: darkness. Vast, unfamiliar darkness. The only illumination came from a strange bluish glow seeping through a line of crooked trees. The ground was rough and uneven, littered with sharp stones and patches of brittle moss. There was no sign of a road, a path, or anything human.

Ali's voice finally cracked the silence, barely above a whisper. "We're not home, are we?"

Omar shook his head slowly. "No," he said. "We're somewhere else. I don't like this one bit. Dear God!"

They rose unsteadily, legs trembling, as if the very gravity of this place pressed differently against their bones. Omar clutched his chest, trying to steady his breathing. Ali wiped grit from his palms and stared around, eyes wide, pupils dilated. The boys didn't speak. Words felt small and useless here. The silence wasn't empty—it was pregnant with watching. Listening. As though the air itself were alive and holding its breath.

Above them, the sky churned in crimson waves. A red giant star loomed impossibly large on the horizon, casting everything in a copper hue. The sky wasn't just red—it pulsed. Alive with moving shadows that weren't clouds. Wisps of something darker rippled slowly across the blood-colored expanse, like jellyfish drifting through a liquid sky.

Floating mountains—yes, actual mountains—drifted in the distance, defying logic. Their jagged undersides were webbed with glowing veins of light that pulsed like the heartbeat of the planet itself.

A deep, resonant hum vibrated through the ground, low and constant. It wasn't mechanical—it felt biological, as if the land was breathing beneath them. Sometimes it faded, then returned with a bone-deep tremor that made their knees wobble.

Strange plants, twisted and glassy, grew in unnatural spirals nearby. Some pulsed with internal light. Others leaned as if sensing them. The boys backed away slowly, unsure if they had roots or feet.

They crept toward the bluish glow filtering between the crooked trees. The forest looked burned—but not by fire. By something colder. The bark of each tree shimmered like black obsidian, and the branches curled as if recoiling from the sky.

Here and there, strange clusters of stones floated midair, spinning slowly, as if trapped in their own orbit. Whenever they moved too fast, the stones quivered—like something in this world was hypersensitive to sound.

Then came the whispers. Faint, curling through the air—not with voices, but with thoughts. Fleeting images, half-formed impressions, like someone—or something—testing the edges of their minds.

Omar clutched his temples, heart hammering. "Do you hear that?" he asked, barely able to breathe.

Ali nodded mutely. The presence was neither hostile nor welcoming. It was simply... aware.

They didn't see the figures approaching until it was too late. Tall and fast, cloaked in something that shimmered like mist, the beings surrounded them without a sound.

Omar tried to yell, Ali swung blindly—but neither made contact. Something thick and soft wrapped around them like velvet, blinding them in darkness.

They were tied quickly and expertly, arms pinned. Panic rose in their throats, but before they could speak, a cold voice entered their minds—not with sound, but with thought:

"Remain silent."

The world vanished into black fabric, and then movement—jostling, bouncing. They were being transported somewhere, on something that rumbled beneath them, but they could no longer see the world they had just entered.

CHAPTER 5
THE VOICE IN THE DARK.

The boys hit the ground hard—pain blooming in their elbows, ribs, and knees as they were unceremoniously thrown onto a solid, cold floor. Their arms and legs were still bound, and they remained shrouded beneath thick, velvety cloth that muffled every sound and sensation. Omar tried to twist and shift, but his restraints held firm. He could feel Ali breathing beside him—fast, shaky, panicked. Somewhere above, a barrier hissed shut with a resonant thud, and then all was silent again, save for their strained breathing and the distant hum of unknown machinery.

Moments later, as if signaled by a hidden command, the large metallic cuffs binding their wrists and ankles clanked softly and released. Omar moved first, yanking the heavy fabric off his head and gasping for air. Ali followed, blinking in the low light. They sat up slowly, taking in their new surroundings.

They were in a small chamber—sparse, dark, and strange. The walls appeared to be made of some kind of polished dark stone, though they shimmered faintly with motion, as if alive. The "door" was a wall of softly glowing red light—more forcefield than structure—and radiated a low heat. Omar picked up one of the released shackles and threw it at the glowing barrier. It struck with a dull, anticlimactic thud and fell uselessly to the floor.

They shouted. They screamed. Nothing happened.

Ali's voice cracked first, trembling and thin. "Omar... I want to go home."

Tears spilled down his cheeks, and he crumpled into a seated position, pulling his knees to his chest. His small frame shook with silent sobs. Omar, heart breaking, knelt beside him and wrapped his arms around his little brother.

"Hey... hey, look at me," he whispered, brushing Ali's hair back. "Remember when we were in Morocco? At Mama's cousin's beach house in Tangier? We ran barefoot through the sand until the sun went down. You found that crab and tried to keep it as a pet." He chuckled softly, though it was more ache than joy. "Baba told us stories every night. Mama made those sticky dates you love."

Ali sniffled but didn't speak.

"They're waiting for us. Mama, Baba... they're praying for us. They always said, 'Believe in Allah, and no matter how far you fall, He will guide you.' We're not alone, Ali. Not really."

Ali's crying softened to hiccups. He nodded faintly and leaned into Omar's shoulder.

The exhaustion finally overtook them both, and the two brothers slumped into sleep, curled together on the cold floor of the alien cell.

They didn't sleep long.

With a sudden, echoing clang, the forcefield buzzed and flickered—and something, someone, was hurled inside. The heavy sound of a body striking the stone floor jolted them awake. The boys scrambled back, hearts racing, eyes wide.

The newcomer groaned—a tall, spindly figure wrapped in a long black cloak, nearly eight feet tall even while half-kneeling. On his head was a towering, ridged hat that brushed the ceiling of the chamber. His limbs were wiry, angular, and his skin was pale like bleached bone. His face was humanoid but uncanny, with large, pupil-less black eyes that shimmered like polished obsidian. The whites of the eyes were completely absent.

The cuffs on his wrists and ankles clattered and unlocked, falling away like Omar and Ali's had before. The tall being looked up—and screamed. A high, echoing, keening sound, more terror than threat. Omar shouted back, standing to shield his brother. Ali, now emboldened, yelled too, waving one of the fallen cuffs like a weapon.

The tall figure staggered back, startled. For several tense moments, all three of them shouted over one another in confusion and fear, until finally the being slumped into a corner, breathing heavily, his long fingers pressed against the floor for support.

Then, silence.

The man raised his face again and locked eyes with Omar. Without moving his lips, a clear voice echoed in Omar's head: "Who are you? What are you doing here? *What*... are you?"

Omar instinctively responded aloud, "I'm Omar. This is my brother, Ali. We don't know where we are, but—"

The man responded with guttural sounds, words that carried no meaning to the boys' ears. He tilted his head, brow furrowed, and then once again spoke directly into Omar's mind. "Use your mind, not your mouth."

Omar blinked. "How?"

The man's tattoo-like markings—complex, fluid symbols winding up his arms—began to glow faintly. "Focus. Not with words. Feel your thoughts. Find the frequency. Shape them like water in your skull. Push... gently."

Omar shut his eyes and tried.

He imagined his name floating in his head and pushed it outward—nothing. He tried again, squeezing his fists, gritting his teeth, but all that came was a dull ache in his temples.

"No," came the voice again. "Not force. Feel. Not muscle... mind."

Frustrated, Omar opened his eyes. "This is impossible."

The man remained still, watching him with unsettling calm. "Try again."

Omar closed his eyes a second time, slowed his breathing, and let the silence seep into him. He pictured his thoughts not as a message, but as light—soft, flickering light—moving through fog. He let go of tension and simply felt his presence, then pictured the word: Omar.

A flicker.

Faint, weak, but there.

Encouraged, he tried again. His head pulsed with strain, but he relaxed into it. The thought grew stronger, more defined.

Omar... and Ali. The thought echoed forward, raw and clumsy—but clear.

The man's obsidian eyes sparkled. He smiled—not warmly, but not coldly either. The symbols on his arms pulsed with approval.

Ali clutched Omar's arm. "What happened?"

Omar grinned, breathless. "He understood me. I think... I think we're learning to talk like him."

With the man's mental guidance, Omar coached Ali to do the same. It took longer, but eventually, Ali projected his name into the stranger's mind. The man smiled again, nodding once.

Telepathy, he explained, was not limited to this planet—but here, it was far easier. The electromagnetic makeup of the atmosphere and subtle neural harmonics made the mind's signal stronger, more direct. Elsewhere, only a few species knew how to do it. Here, nearly all could. You only needed to unlock the rhythm.

Only after several more mental exchanges—slow, halting, but increasingly coherent—did the man reveal his name. It was long and resonant in their minds: **Xa'rekthul-Yenu-Vaahn.**

The boys blinked at one another. Omar tried to repeat it, then gave up. "Is it okay if we call you... Vaan?"

The man nodded once.

From the folds of his cloak, Vaan pulled out a handful of small, round fruits—dull purple with mottled green skin, slick with an odd sheen. They smelled sharp, earthy, and utterly unfamiliar. The boys hesitated.

"Safe," Vaan said in their minds, taking a bite himself. Juice dribbled from his thin lips.

Omar bit one. The taste was bitter at first, then gave way to something juicy, like spiced plum and sea salt. Ali followed, still uncertain, but hunger got the better of him.

The boys sat down again, this time in a triangle with their strange new cellmate. There were no more threats. Just fatigue, the buzz of the red barrier, and the strange, lingering taste of alien fruit on their tongues.

And then—merciful sleep. No dreams. No fear. Just stillness.

CHAPTER 6
THE TALISMAN'S TRUTH.

Omar awoke to the sound of soft whispers—no, not whispers, more like a gentle hum resonating in the silence. His eyes blinked open slowly, and the first thing he saw was Vaan, the tall alien with glowing tattoos, in a deep state of prostration. His forehead touched the ground and his arms were stretched forward—almost the same way Omar had seen his father pray five times a day back home. Something about Vaan's posture—solemn, reverent, and full of purpose—triggered an avalanche of memories. Images of his father quietly laying out the prayer mat, his mother gently waking him for Fajr, the peaceful hum of Qur'an recitations filling their home—all of it washed over him at once.

A lump formed in Omar's throat. He missed them so much, it physically hurt. He missed the smell of his mom's cooking, the way his dad ruffled his hair after prayers, the teasing between him and Ali during dinner, and even the old creaky stairs of their house in Old Bridge, New Jersey. Even though it felt like days, something inside him told Omar that time here didn't move the same way. But everything suddenly felt more real—and more terrifying. The fear, which had been dulled by adrenaline until now, hit him full force. He was just a kid, lost in a strange world with no idea how to get back. But then he looked at Ali, still sleeping peacefully beside him. Omar wiped his eyes quickly. He had to be strong. He was the older brother. He had to get them both home.

A few minutes later, Ali stirred and rubbed his eyes. As he sat up, Vaan lifted himself from his prostration and returned to a seated position. The tattoos along his neck and forearms began to glow faintly as his thoughts reached theirs.

"The guards brought food earlier. It is not much, but it will nourish us."

From a dark corner, Vaan retrieved a small bundle of what looked like long, cylindrical objects—smooth, slightly glossy, and beige in color. Omar picked one up hesitantly. It was soft and chewy, with a texture somewhere between bread dough and boiled mushroom, but with none of the taste. There was no way to tell if it came from a plant, an animal, or something entirely alien.

"It's healthy," Vaan reassured them, seeing the uncertainty on their faces. "It will energize you. You need energy."

The boys chewed slowly, their expressions tight as they forced it down. It was food, at least.

Once they had eaten, they all sat cross-legged on the floor of their stone cell. Despite the strangeness of the situation, there was a kind of peace in just sitting and talking.

"Who are you really?" Vaan asked, his symbols glowing as he communicated telepathically. "And what are you? You are not from this world. How did you get here?"

Omar nodded. "We're from a planet called Earth. It's... far. We live in a town called Old Bridge, in New Jersey. It's in a country called the United States. It's an awesome place!"

Ali added, "We miss our parents. A lot. Our mom makes the best tagine, and our dad always takes us out for pizza and halal fried chicken."

Vaan watched them quietly, then leaned over and gently wiped a tear from Ali's cheek. His eyes held a warm, understanding sadness. At that moment, both boys felt it—not just kindness, but a deep humility. Vaan wasn't just helping them. He cared.

"How did you get here?" Vaan asked.

Omar explained the events in New Jersey—the mysterious triangular talisman, the way it had started glowing, the portal it opened.

"Do you have it still?" Vaan asked, his glowing marks pulsing with interest.

"No," Omar replied. "It's still back on Earth—"

But Ali reached into his backpack, untouched and somehow overlooked by the guards, and pulled out the triangular talisman. Omar was a bit startled and pleasantly surprised—he hadn't known Ali had brought it with him.

Vaan's eyes widened, and he took it with gentle reverence. The edges shimmered faintly, and symbols along the side glowed as he turned it in his hands.

"This is a sacred artifact," he said slowly. "It originates from this world. Our planet is called Orulenthia. This talisman should be inside the Vault of Elders with its rightful keeper—Voraal Zenthir Kael. According to this writing, it was forged in his domain, on the faraway continent of Tzuraan'dhel-Monkaar. I fear it might have been lost long ago. I do not know how it reached your world."

The boys leaned in, fascinated and overwhelmed. Vaan traced the edges of the artifact as he spoke.

"You might have opened a gateway between different realms. I am uncertain. I didn't know that was even possible. I'm really as lost as you are about this artifact."

The entire day passed with the three of them learning about each other. Omar and Ali told Vaan about their school, their favorite shows, their friends back home. Vaan told them more about Orulenthia—its floating continents, red-tinged skies, and cities carved into mountain spires.

"Why are you here?" Omar asked with his mind. "In prison, I mean."

Vaan's tattoos dimmed for a moment. He looked down before speaking telepathically again.

"I was once a leader among the scholars of Veltharuun, this city. But I spoke out against its ruler—Xar'Vulek Thaarn. He spreads lies, manipulates councils, and extorts people to control the city. I stood with the rebels from Dhaelorun Viis and the distant city of Vael'Sythrin Reach. We formed a small resistance. I was captured during a secret meeting. That's how I ended up here."

The boys were silent for a while, trying to absorb the scope of Vaan's story. It felt like they had stepped into the middle of a giant, ancient conflict.

As they sat talking, the boys realized something strange—they hadn't seen a sunrise or sunset. Just a constant red through a tiny hole in the wall near the ceiling.

"Does your red sun not set?" Ali asked. "On Earth, we wake up and sleep when the sun rises and sets," he added, explaining to Vaan that they follow the rhythm of sunlight for daily life.

The idea puzzled Vaan, who blinked slowly. "Fascinating," he said. "That is unusual. Here, we have no such cycle. The red giant remains constant in our skies. We rest when we need."

Omar glanced at his Casio G-Shock. The display read just 12 minutes since they had entered the portal. He showed it to Ali, and both boys stared in disbelief. It felt like they had been gone for days. Omar looked closer and noticed the seconds ticking by at an excruciatingly slow pace—time itself was stretching here. Earth time and this planet's time didn't match at all.

Vaan leaned in with interest. "What is that device?" he asked.

Omar hesitated. "It's a watch. It tells time. There's a power source inside—a battery—that keeps it running."

Vaan's eyes lit up with fascination. "A compact power cell... extraordinary."

"We have to get back," Omar whispered to Ali. "Mom and Dad must be freaking out."

But there was nothing they could do yet. The stone walls surrounded them. The portal was gone. And the talisman's secrets were only just beginning to unfold.

That night, they curled up in the corner of their cell. Vaan sat close by, a quiet guardian. The boys' hearts were heavy with longing, but a tiny flicker of hope remained.

They were not alone. Their newly found friend and protector, Vaan, was with them.

And somehow, that made all the difference.

CHAPTER 7
THE FIRST ALLIANCE.

It felt like three days—maybe more—since Omar and Ali had first woken up inside this strange, obsidian cell. Time didn't pass normally here. They had no windows, no sunrises or sunsets—only a low ambient red glow leaking through the shimmering forcefield that sealed them in. Over those days, they had grown more familiar with Vaan, who slowly began to open up about his past, his people, and the planet's cruel ruler. Despite their fear and confusion, the long hours of doing nothing but talking, guessing, and waiting gave them an odd sense of rhythm.

Strangely, they didn't feel very thirsty. They had expected dehydration, especially in such a sterile, alien environment, but their need for water was infrequent. Still, Ali's backpack had miraculously survived their journey—likely thanks to the talisman—and inside it was a water bottle they both sipped from now and then. The liquid had a slightly metallic taste now, but it quenched their thirst. They hadn't seen a single guard open their door, but food kept appearing—always neatly arranged in glowing ceramic trays, sometimes while they slept or during moments when no one was paying attention. It was as if the guards knew exactly when to avoid being seen—appearing and disappearing at precise moments, like ghosts behind the scenes.

Frustration finally snapped. Omar stood, his fists clenched, and roared, "Let us out! We're not your prisoners! Show yourselves!"

Ali joined in, his voice raw and cracking. "We know you're out there! Enough of this!"

Their shouts bounced uselessly off the smooth black walls. There was no reply, no reaction. Vaan remained sitting, calm and unmoved. "Your voices won't reach anyone," he said telepathically. "There's a sonic barrier in place. You could scream for hours and still hear only yourselves. Save your strength."

The silence that followed was heavier than any wall.

To pass the time, the boys tried everything—from games they remembered from back home to imaginary escape plans. Omar carved lines into the cell floor using a sharp edge of a broken food tray to keep track of what he assumed were days. Ali did push-ups until his arms trembled and forced Omar into shadowboxing rounds for distraction. They told stories from school, cracked jokes about how they'd rather be doing homework than this, and imagined what their parents were doing back in New Jersey. Sometimes, they just sat in total silence, listening to the strange hum of the forcefield. Vaan spoke often in slow, cryptic sentences—explaining the fundamentals of telepathic communication, the lore of his people, and how the tyrant Xar'Vulek Thaarn ruled with fear and illusion. Every word deepened the boys' awe of where they were and how impossibly far from Earth they had come.

Their routine shattered one cycle when a low humming sound pulsed through the air like a vibration in their bones. The forcefield shimmered and then parted. Two towering figures stepped inside. They wore long crimson cloaks that brushed the ground, with tall black hats perched atop jet-black helmets that covered their entire faces. A glowing black insignia—a jagged V-shape—rested on their chests. In their gloved hands, each held a massive dark staff crowned with a crackling sphere of violet lightning that hissed and spat arcs of electrical energy into the air. Omar and Ali instinctively took a step back.

The two guards shouted in a language that sounded like electric saws cutting through stone:

"Zkrell voth'nakk thol'rakk grazum vel'tirra! Skarnoth jelk'vrel danorokh viir'zek karull'an!"

Then louder, more aggressive:

"Zkrell voth'nakk thol'rakk grazum vel'tirra! Skarnoth jelk'vrel danorokh viir'zek karull'an!"

Ali covered his ears. Omar's legs stiffened. The language was terrifying—not just the sound, but the vibration it sent into their chests.

"They're telling you to stand straight and don't move," Vaan translated telepathically. "We're being transferred."

Omar and Ali exchanged a fearful glance. Transferred where?

With heavy footsteps echoing behind them, the two guards herded the boys forward, their staffs held high, sparking arcs of electrical energy into the air as a warning. Vaan walked beside them. The hallway outside their cell was long and dark, the walls a shimmering obsidian black like melted glass. Every few steps, they passed more cells—identical glowing red forcefields sealing off whatever was within. But they couldn't see or hear anything from them, as if each was isolated in complete sensory lockdown. Ali stared at the ground, afraid of making eye contact with the floating surveillance nodes mounted along the corridor. Omar kept clenching and unclenching his fists, trying to steady his breathing. The air smelled faintly metallic, and the shadows seemed to stretch unnaturally long, adding to the sense of being swallowed by something ancient and merciless.

Eventually, they were steered into a massive chamber with a floor of smooth black metal and an open forcefield. At the opposite end stood a thick metallic door, clearly sealed. A third guard, identically dressed, stood inside, facing them with his staff raised. The boys were motioned into the room and told again—through more guttural shouting—to remain still. The forcefield behind them closed with a low thrum, locking them in. The silence was thick again.

Then something surreal happened. One by one, the guards removed their helmets. As their faces were revealed, Vaan stepped forward with a smile and hugged each of them in turn. The stiff, dangerous aura vanished instantly as laughter and low murmurs of their alien tongue filled the air. Omar and Ali stood frozen, their mouths open.

"They are my friends," Vaan spoke with his mind, turning to the boys. "Trusted members of The First Alliance—a resistance against the dictator of this city, Lord Xar'Vulek Thaarn."

Omar blinked. "Wait... you know them?"

"They've been waiting for this moment."

The three guards spoke quickly and warmly in their strange language, their voices soft and urgent. Then Vaan turned again. "They will now remove their uniforms. You must wear them—on top of your clothes. Quickly. We don't have much time."

The boys didn't waste a second. Excitement exploded inside them like fireworks. Their hands shook as they pulled the tall boots, crimson robes, and black helmets over their own outfits. Their small frames made the uniforms slightly loose, but with the helmets and cloaks on, they looked the part. Omar turned to Ali, eyes wide with adrenaline, and whispered, "Alhamdulillah."

Ali whispered back, "Alhamdulillah, finally!"

"What will your friends do now?" Omar asked Vaan as he adjusted the helmet's visor.

"They'll hide behind that metallic door in the back of this room. It's a storage area. Don't worry—they are escape artists. They'll find another opening."

Vaan led them forward and whispered telepathically, "Don't speak out loud at all. Follow my steps. Eyes forward. Walk straight. No hesitation."

They stepped into a wide corridor—a colossal artery running through the prison complex. Crimson lighting pulsed above like veins of lava. Their boots clicked against polished black floors that reflected their every move. High above, floating surveillance drones hovered silently—black, orb-like machines with a single glowing red eye. They moved like predators.

Vaan's voice returned in their minds: "Do not make sudden movements in front of the Krell-Syth Orbs. They will scan and alert the sentries. Keep walking."

The fear was suffocating, but the boys followed—one step at a time. The silence was absolute. They passed rows of walls and unmarked doors. The red laser-eyes of the Krell-Syth Orbs followed them but didn't react. They were halfway across the longest stretch when a second wave of fear struck. Ali's knees felt weak. Omar's heart pounded. But Vaan remained composed, transmitting a soothing sense of calm through his presence alone.

At the corridor's end, they reached a towering open archway. There was no forcefield here, only a long metallic ramp sloping downward. They descended slowly, boots echoing against the incline. At the bottom stood a final massive door—sealed behind a humming red forcefield.

Floating beside it was a white orb, bright and levitating at Vaan's chest height. Nothing supported it. As he stepped forward, the glowing insignia on his borrowed uniform pulsed. The orb flared brighter, recognizing the signal. With a deep chime, the red forcefield vanished.

They stepped out into the world.

The air was dry and still. A deep crimson light bathed everything—cast by the red giant sun looming in the sky above. Towering, jagged black mountains surrounded them, their edges so sharp they looked carved by blades. Floating far above were massive pyramid-shaped landmasses, suspended like silent gods in the bleeding sky. A ringed planet hovered in the far distance, filling the heavens with eerie majesty.

In front of them stood a vehicle—nothing like anything from Earth. It resembled a stretched teardrop of molten black glass hovering just inches off the ground, pulsing with soft violet energy underneath. Spines and fins curled along its back like some armored insect. It had no wheels, no doors—only a smooth sloped platform that shimmered like liquid metal.

Vaan removed his helmet. His facial tattoos glowed faintly as he raised one hand. The vehicle responded to his command, floating forward silently, a low hum vibrating the ground.

"There are no guards out here," Vaan said telepathically, "because no one ever escapes the cells. That's the flaw. No one plans for what is impossible."

He smirked and motioned them in.

Omar and Ali climbed aboard, speechless. As they stepped onto the sleek, humming surface, it felt like climbing into a dream—or falling into one. The moment their feet settled on the strange platform, the vehicle glided forward as though reading their intent. The prison faded behind them, shrinking into the horizon like a dark memory being erased. For a long moment, they didn't speak. There was too much to take in. Jagged cliffs sliced across the land like obsidian daggers, and the sky burned with surreal, bloody light. It was like riding through a painting come to life—except they were inside it, real and fragile.

They didn't know where they were going or what would happen next—but they knew they were free. And that word—*free*—meant more in that moment than it ever had back home. Every breath they took felt sacred. The air, thin and sharp as it was, carried a weight of meaning. The road ahead might be filled with dangers and unknowns, but it was their road now. Their escape. Their first real step toward something greater.

They smiled wide under their helmets—grins of disbelief and wonder—as the alien wind whipped past them. Awe shimmered in their eyes. Adrenaline still surged through their veins. Gratitude pressed tightly against their hearts. They were still just two brothers from New Jersey, but now they were part of something bigger, riding through a world no human had ever seen—warriors in disguise, fugitives of fate.

The red world flew by.

CHAPTER 8

THE IRON WILL OF VELTHARUUN.

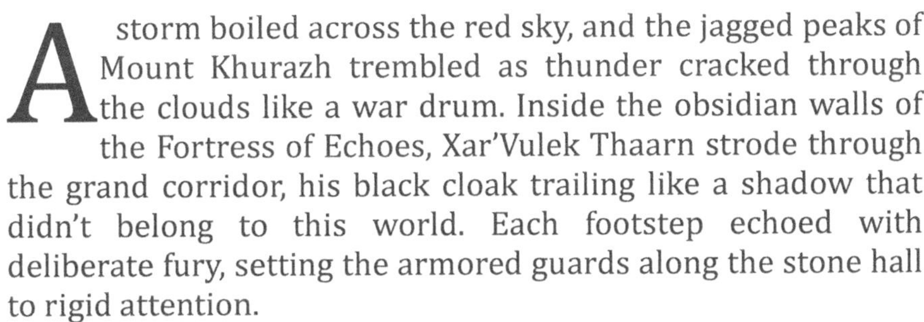

Astorm boiled across the red sky, and the jagged peaks of Mount Khurazh trembled as thunder cracked through the clouds like a war drum. Inside the obsidian walls of the Fortress of Echoes, Xar'Vulek Thaarn strode through the grand corridor, his black cloak trailing like a shadow that didn't belong to this world. Each footstep echoed with deliberate fury, setting the armored guards along the stone hall to rigid attention.

Nine feet tall and carved like a living monument to war, Thaarn wore black from throat to heel—clothes woven with threads of rare obsidian silk, and a cloak that fluttered like smoke around his mountainous frame. His bald head gleamed in the cold firelight of the sconces, and his face—square-jawed, brutal, and permanently scowling—looked as if it had been sculpted from wrath itself. He was a man who seemed to snarl even when silent.

Thaarn was easily offended, and his temper flared like wildfire. He trusted few and punished betrayal—or even the suspicion of it—with pitiless creativity. He enjoyed the suffering of others, not for sadism alone, but as a means of control. To him, fear was loyalty's sharpest twin. Every interrogation chamber beneath his fortress echoed with screams, and every public execution served as a hymn to his iron will. Veltharuun did not thrive. It obeyed.

He was not heading to his private chamber—no. Today, the court of Veltharuun demanded blood.

The Hall of Verdicts yawned ahead—vast, windowless, and reverberating with dread. Blackstone columns rose like ancient tree trunks into shadows that no torch dared reach. Along the walls, masked ministers and half-metallic inquisitors stood in grim formation. Suspended above them, the Kryth-Orbal Sentinels hovered—mechanized orbs glinting with surgical instruments, toxin needles, and neural flayers, twitching in silent anticipation.

On the central dais, bound in grav-chains, knelt a battered prisoner. His name was Arukha-Selven-Dorr'jaal, but none would remember it by sunset. His bloodied robes clung to him like soaked rags, and his eye—swollen shut—dripped slowly onto the tribunal floor.

Thaarn took his seat upon the high throne, carved from ancient metals and cooled lava. The silence thickened like smoke.

Councilor Drevvos Varn stepped forward. Gaunt and incredibly shrewd, he was Thaarn's most loyal inquisitor—an artist of agony with a mind full of malice and a taste for spectacle.

"You spoke the name in the lower districts," Drevvos snarled, his voice carrying across the court. "Xa'rekthul-Yenu-Vaahn. The freak. The mind-infected filth. What were you planning? Answer, or bleed."

The prisoner raised his chin, defiant even through the pain. "We weren't planning anything," he rasped. "But you're terrified of him. You locked him away because you know—deep down—you can't kill what you don't understand. Ahahaha!" He made a mocking laugh, then coughed up blood.

Drevvos's expression twisted in rage. "You dare suggest fear in the heart of our Lord Xar'Vulek Thaarn?"

He stepped aside and motioned toward the Sentinels. "Strip him."

A Sentinel dove down in a blink, latching onto the prisoner's back with metallic claws. A thin probe snaked into his spine, delivering a pulse of electric agony. The man's scream echoed through the fortress, high and raw.

"Let the truth find its way through fire," Drevvos muttered, pacing.

After minutes of searing interrogation, Thaarn raised a single gloved hand. Silence fell instantly.

"He's useless," Thaarn said, voice like crushed stone. "Burn him in the lower furnaces."
"As you command," Drevvos bowed, already signaling the guards.
The prisoner was dragged away, twitching and barely conscious. Blood marked the floor behind him like a trail of guilt.

Thaarn sat still, breathing slow but heavy. He hated that name—Xa'rekthul-Yenu-Vaahn. He had tried to erase it from every corridor, every mind, every whisper in Veltharuun. But names were like embers in dry fields. They waited for air.

Why now?

The lower city had been restless. The First Alliance—rebels, saboteurs, cowards—were striking bolder targets. Last week, a weapons factory in the Iron Scar was reduced to rubble. A transport ship loaded with phase rifles never arrived. And Thaarn's intelligence officers were beginning to report impossible readings coming from the Searrveuune Rift.

He did not trust anyone. Not his generals. Not his advisors. Not even the walls of his own fortress, which he often had stripped and re-examined for secret etchings.

Fear was rising—but not among his people. Among them, it was mutiny.

Thaarn's jaw clenched as stormlight flickered across the throne room. The clouds outside pulsed red with fury. Something was shifting in the world—and he could feel it in his bones like a blade sliding between the ribs of fate. There was an ache deep within his spine, like ancient armor remembering battle. The temperature in the throne room seemed to drop, though no wind stirred. Candles guttered. The shadows along the walls twitched as though watching. He had known wars. He had conquered species. But this... this was not a threat born of ambition or politics. This was something older. Deeper. The kind of shift that unsettled history itself. The kind that rewrote destinies without asking. It was the threat of an idea. Freedom.

There were no words spoken—yet he felt the whisper of a presence pushing at the edges of his perception. He stood slowly, moving toward the massive window that overlooked the fortress gates, and beyond them, the splintered expanse of the wastelands. Thunder cracked again, but this time it sounded different. Less like sound. More like a warning.

He did not yet know that a breach had occurred on the other side of the Rift—and that Xa'rekthul-Yenu-Vaahn had escaped with two strangers found wandering the charred outer rim of Veltharuun, in a forbidden zone where even his patrols feared to go. An irradiated wasteland of black glass and sulfuric fog.

He did not know yet... But he would find out soon enough.

CHAPTER 9
EMBERS OF THE
FORGOTTEN CITY.

I held the control threads of the skimmer tightly in my mind, steering it westward through the jagged Blackspine Hills that ringed Veltharuun like the teeth of some ancient buried beast. The vehicle bucked against the scorched winds, but on Orulenthia, telekinesis flowed like breath—effortless and natural. The boys—Omar and Ali—sat behind me in the humming cabin, wide-eyed and silent. I didn't blame them. They were alien here, more alien than I could possibly imagine. And that made them vulnerable. If even one of Thaarn's bloodhounds caught wind of their presence—of how they arrived here, of what they carried—there would be no mercy. Someone would rip the truth from them shard by shard. That talisman hidden in their bag... even I could feel its pull. Something ancient. Something dangerous. In the wrong hands, it could unmake entire cities.

I glanced at them through the reflection on the skimmer's obsidian dash. They were frightened, confused—but brave. Too brave for their age. I felt something stir in me. Paternal. Fierce. I thought of my own children—Rellan-Vaahn and Maeia-Vaahn—back when their laughter still filled the halls of our home. Before the purges. Before Thaarn's drones vaporized half the Resistance families in one orbital strike. I had failed them once. I could not fail these boys.

Veltharuun had once been beautiful. I remember the crimson dawns lighting up the sky like molten rivers, and the smell of spicebread curling out of alley ovens as the red sun light kissed the rooftops. I was born in the shadow of the southern spires, where roof leaks were patched with prayer flags and the air always smelled faintly of rust. My mother, Qleiya-Daaq-Yenu, was a gentle woman—a seamstress who never quite got over the death of my father. She was often too sick to work, and I became her limbs, her eyes, her legs. I walked two kilometers to fetch water, and another three to barter cloth for medicine. Even as a child, I knew love through sacrifice.

I studied by the dim crimson glow that passed for night here while my mother slept, piecing together scraps of old tech manuals and philosopher treatises. Eventually, my scores earned me a rare spot at the Trinxyyaeth Citadel of Cognitive Arts—a sprawling ivory compound suspended on grav-columns above the Bay of Shifting Glass. There, I learned how to bend the world to thought. How force and motion were merely obedient cousins of the will. I mastered telekinesis before my twentieth name-day and graduated with high honor, then returned to Veltharuun to serve. I built energy grids in the gutter districts. Repaired hover rails with my bare hands. Advocated for the mute, the broken, the discarded.

People began to follow me—not out of obligation, but belief. I never sought power. I sought balance. But when Xar'Vulek Thaarn came to power nearly three Orulenthian solar cycles ago, balance was outlawed. Mercy became treason. And so I spoke—at first quietly, then boldly. I told the crowds what they already knew in their hearts: that Thaarn was a disease wrapped in iron robes, that we were being hollowed out from the inside. It made me a target, but it also gave others the courage to rise.

We called ourselves the First Alliance. Old scholars. Rogue engineers. Smugglers. Survivors. Our first strike was on the Helix Drone Field, where we hacked and short-circuited nearly a thousand of Thaarn's patrol units in a coordinated blast. Next, we hit the Mindgate Barracks—where hundreds of suspected dissidents were held in neural stasis. We freed dozens. Some couldn't even remember their own names. Then came the raid on the Skyforge Refineries, where Thaarn's grav-fuel was purified. We poured sand into turbines, burned maps, and escaped with blueprints that could destabilize half his aerial fleet.

The thrill of rebellion coursed through our veins, but it came with cost. We lost Dainar to the sonic mines. Vara disappeared on a mission to the Verdant Array—likely flayed for secrets. And my brother, Ezel-Yenu-Vaahn... he died shielding a child from a drone's plasma burst. That child lived. Sometimes that's all we fought for: one more child, one more breath of hope.

Now, as I drove through the fractured twilight with these two boys behind me, I felt the weight of new choices forming like stone around my shoulders. What was I to do with them? I couldn't keep them with me—not with Thaarn's tendrils probing every alley, every tunnel. But I couldn't abandon them either. They didn't belong here, but they couldn't go back—not without answers. And that talisman... even I didn't know how it worked. Only that the wrong mind could awaken devastation.

I felt torn—more than I've ever been. Part of me wanted to protect them like I would my own, to shield them from this world's cruelty, to find some far-off place and hide them under false names and simple lives. But the other part—the cold strategist in me—knew that any mistake could cost them their lives, and maybe ours too. I didn't know if I was being wise, or just afraid of letting them go.

I needed help. And fast. My allies would know more—especially the ones with access to deep-tech sanctuaries or hidden portals. But bringing them into the fold meant risking more lives. I closed my eyes briefly, listening to the wind howl over the skimmer's fins. I could feel something shifting, like the planet itself was waiting for a choice to be made.

Then, the answer arrived—not as certainty, but instinct. I veered the skimmer off the main veinway and cut toward the outer ridgelands. We would not stay in Veltharuun. We would head north, beyond the firefields, toward Vael'Sythrin Reach. There lived my trusted friend—Ytelthuun Blaamorr Wam'Kesh—a reclusive scholar and former soldier who owed me more than just old loyalty. If anyone could help me find truth—or safety—for the boys, it was him.

Vael'Sythrin Reach was an ancient city, with towering spires of obsidian and crumbling arches that predated even the earliest star charts, clinging to the cliffs of the Stone Crescent—far from Thaarn's scanners and paranoia. Its infrastructure was a living memory—part decaying marvel, part forgotten riddle—where echoes of lost technologies whispered through the catacombs beneath its glowing streets. But the journey would take days, maybe more, and we would have to cross unstable tectonic bands and abandoned warfronts. I didn't care. If it gave these boys a chance, I would cross burning oceans. And Ytelthuun... he would sacrifice himself to save a city block. Maybe he could bend fate for us now.

Everything was unraveling. The lines I had drawn in the sand were now smeared with wind and ash. My purpose, once so clear, had become clouded by the chaos of love, of guilt, of duty. I felt like a man caught between stars—no ground beneath, only echoes.

But I held on. I gritted my teeth and steered toward that final hope, praying to gods I no longer believed in that this road was the right one.

Somewhere beyond the ridges, the storm was waiting. And behind us, Thaarn's fury was catching fire.

Ahead of us lay a journey long and perilous, through treacherous lands that bore the scars of forgotten wars and unstable riftfields where even shadows whispered lies. We would be far from safety, and farther still from certainty—but each mile forward felt like defiance carved into the bones of a dying world.

CHAPTER 10
ACROSS THE BURNT HORIZON.

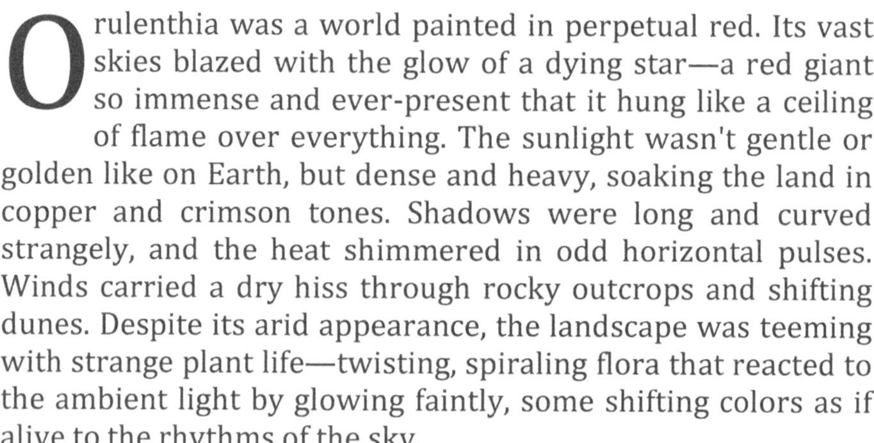

Orulenthia was a world painted in perpetual red. Its vast skies blazed with the glow of a dying star—a red giant so immense and ever-present that it hung like a ceiling of flame over everything. The sunlight wasn't gentle or golden like on Earth, but dense and heavy, soaking the land in copper and crimson tones. Shadows were long and curved strangely, and the heat shimmered in odd horizontal pulses. Winds carried a dry hiss through rocky outcrops and shifting dunes. Despite its arid appearance, the landscape was teeming with strange plant life—twisting, spiraling flora that reacted to the ambient light by glowing faintly, some shifting colors as if alive to the rhythms of the sky.

Dominating the heavens like a second sun was a massive ringed planet, visible day and night. It loomed like a sentinel—its golden rings clearly visible even in daylight, shimmering like rivers of fire around its body. This celestial body wasn't just a natural marvel—it was militarized. High-orbit fortresses circled it, belonging to Lord Xar'Vulek Thaarn. Vaan had once told the boys in a hushed moment that Thaarn's most powerful sky-armories were stationed on that planet, serving both as deterrents and as iron chains against rebellion. Sometimes, the boys could faintly see movement along its orbiting stations—tiny glints that might've been ships or weapon platforms.

The air on Orulenthia felt light, but there was a gravity to the place. The silence between gusts of wind wasn't empty—it was ancient. Every horizon seemed to cradle some forgotten history, as if time here moved sideways, curling back upon itself. The boys felt it too. Omar could sense it in the way the rocks seemed to remember footsteps, and Ali in the way the light refracted off surfaces just a fraction too late.

Veltharuun was the iron jewel of the red wastelands—a city of impossible size and sorrow. Its architecture pierced the sky—pyramidal towers, yawning causeways, and radiant glass fortresses pulsed with energy harvested directly from the red giant. Lord Xar'Vulek Thaarn ruled it with a vice grip, his military caste patrolling every inch. Citizens lived under constant surveillance. Dissenters were silenced. And yet, beneath the dread and order, there was an undercurrent of longing. The people of Veltharuun hungered for freedom. The Resistance, whispered of in alleys and behind sealed doors, was more than myth—it was a lifeline. A billion voices waited for something to change.

But the boys weren't heading to Veltharuun. Vaan was taking them far from that shadow—deep into the west, to the forgotten city of Vael'Sythrin Reach. Once a beacon of pre-Empire civilization, it now lay at the edge of mountains and memory. It was there they would meet Ytelthuun Blaamorr Wam'Kesh, regional leader of the First Alliance.

Inside the smooth-gliding vehicle—a pod-like skimmer made of light black alloy with translucent windows—the boys sat without their helmets. The vehicle didn't seem to have a steering wheel or an engine. Vaan navigated it through telepathic nodes embedded in the console. Curious, Ali leaned forward and asked via thought: "Why don't you just call your friend with your mind?"

Vaan's reaction was sudden—a bizarre laugh, like dry hiccups mixed with chirps, completely alien in tone. He tilted his head with amusement. "Ah! No, young sprig. We do not speak across endless space with thoughts. Telepathy has limits.

You shout with your voice—you only reach as far as the air lets you. Thought is similar. It rides frequencies that do not cross the world. Just as a whisper fades into the wind, so too does the mind's call."

Omar nodded, intrigued. "So... it's not like Wi-Fi or phones."

Vaan blinked. "I do not know your 'Waii-Fai,' but no. Thought has distance. Emotion strengthens it, sometimes. Desperation, love, rage—but still, it is a short-range weapon."

The terrain sped past them as the skimmer sliced through valleys and plains. The boys had earlier compared it to their father's car. *"It's kinda like Baba's Mazda,"* Ali said telepathically.

Vaan tried to imitate the word. *"Maa... Zuh... Daa,"* he muttered, struggling. Then came that odd laugh again. "Strange human noises." He grinned through his spiraling tattoos. "This runs on the red giant's luminescence. No fuel. Just the power of falling firelight."

There were no restaurants or kiosks along the path. When they stopped briefly to eat, Vaan plucked rough, spiky fruit from a spiraled tree. The boys bit into it—and instantly regretted it. Omar tasted it first and recoiled in horror, yelling, *"Astagfirullah!"* as he nearly gagged and spit it out. His face twisted like he'd swallowed a rotten fish. Ali burst into uncontrollable laughter, falling over himself in his seat.

"Dude! You look like you just saw Shaytaan!" he cackled.

Embarrassed, Omar shoved the fruit at his younger brother. "Oh, you have to try it now. C'mon, be brave, big man."

Ali took a reluctant bite—and immediately let out a strangled wheeze. "BRO, WHY DOES IT TASTE LIKE SWEATY SOCK JUICE?!" he screamed, eyes watering.

Both brothers howled with laughter, doubled over in the heat, fruit forgotten in their hands. It was disgusting—but it was their shared moment of joy. And in that instant, in the middle of an alien world, they didn't feel so far from home.

Curiously, neither Omar nor Ali had felt thirst since their arrival. Even in the dry, hot landscape, their mouths never dried. Omar licked his lips, still puzzled by this.

They passed floating mountains—massive rocks suspended by invisible forces, with cities carved into them like nesting hives. Roads twisted around their curves, and skimmers zipped between them. The sight transfixed the boys. It was like seeing the future and ancient myth collide. Some floating peaks even had cascading lights pouring downward, like vertical rivers of color.

The journey was long. Sometimes the road stretched endlessly across dead plains. The boys nodded off, helmets resting on their laps. Other times, they woke up restless, bored. Ali kicked the floor lightly. *"I wish we had music,"* he whispered. They played hand games, made up stories, and watched the skies for movement. Once, they saw something like a manta ray glide silently across the clouds—its belly lined with lights.

Hours later, Orulenthia's red glow continued flaring as the sun dipped behind the Stone Crescent. Towering silhouettes emerged—the jagged, crumbling walls of Vael'Sythrin Reach. The city loomed ahead like a forgotten god's monument. As they neared, the boys saw black spires like obsidian fangs, arched bridges wrapped in glowing tendrils of moss, and strange aerial devices that pulsed like jellyfish suspended in air. Vaan motioned them to put their helmets back on.

"Eyes like yours don't go unnoticed," he said with urgency.

As they entered, the streets unfolded like a dream. Buildings glowed from within with bioluminescent veins. The tech here was unlike Veltharuun. Floating data-orbs hovered beside doors. Creatures moved inside tubes of liquid that arced above the road. Some citizens wore robes made of metal-thread that changed color with their emotions. Others had mechanical wings or floating shoulder-plates. Vael'Sythrin was a clash of the ancient and the future.

The boys gaped. Ali saw a creature like a giant centipede with the face of an ugly dog. It grinned at him, clearly friendly, and somehow communicated in Urdii—Vaan explained it was the dominant language of Orulenthia. Other creatures resembled tall frogs with wings, some shaped like trees with eyes on their branches. Despite appearances, they coexisted peacefully with the human-like citizens.

The vehicle finally slowed before a low, gray structure tucked between giant towers. It was unimpressive—exactly the point. As the doors slid open, they were met by a figure approaching the vehicle—Ytelthuun. He was tall, draped in his signature cloak, and bore the glowing tattoos that shimmered like circuitry beneath his skin. His expression, however, was curiously neutral—almost cold. There was no outburst of joy, no warmth in his gaze. His eyes briefly glanced over Vaan, then to the boys, and back again. With a brief nod, he turned and led them wordlessly indoors.

It wasn't until the floor opened and the group descended far below, into the depths of the rebel stronghold, that the facade cracked. As they stepped away from the surface and into the flickering light of the underground base, Ytelthuun suddenly turned and embraced Vaan fiercely, his tattoos flaring with emotion. They pressed foreheads, their connection sparking visibly in the air. The moment was raw and real—two comrades reuniting after risk and time.

The base was vast—filled with crystal screens, artifact racks, armor plating, and hoverboards. Plants grew sideways across the walls in geometric patterns. A mural of old battles wrapped around the chamber like a timeline. Ytelthuun Blaamorr Wam'Kesh stood near a console—tall, cloaked, and tattooed like Vaan, though older, with glowing scars.

Only when they were far underground did the tension ease. The boys stayed back, quiet.

Then Vaan turned to them. "Remove your helmets."

Omar hesitated. They obeyed. As the helmets hissed off and their faces were revealed, Ytelthuun gasped. He stepped back, his mouth open in horror.

"They are not of this world!" he shouted, nearly falling.

Vaan quickly steadied him. "Calm! They are friends. More than that—they are vital."

Ytelthuun's eyes widened. He looked from Omar to Ali and back again, visibly shaken.

The boys didn't feel welcome. Not yet. The base was cold. The walls unfamiliar. The fear in Ytelthuun's eyes matched their own. As they stood there—two Earth boys in a rebel hideout beneath an alien city—they felt more alone than ever. The weight of this strange world settled on their shoulders, heavy and red and unrelenting.

And for the first time, Omar quietly asked himself—*"What if we can't ever go back?"*

CHAPTER 11
YTELTHUUN'S RESOLVE.

The shouting echoed through the underground stone walls—harsh and furious. Omar and Ali sat on a low bench in the next room, listening to the rage of an argument in the alien language of Urdii. The voices belonged to Vaan and Ytelthuun—and they weren't holding back. Ytelthuun's voice boomed like thunder, full of disbelief and something else... fear?

Vaan—or rather, Xa'rekthul-Yenu-Vaahn, as Ytelthuun called him—responded with that calm but firm edge the boys had come to recognize. The guttural syllables bounced off the metallic walls, creating a surreal chorus that made Omar's stomach twist.

On the floor before them sat a tray of alien produce—some fruits, maybe vegetables, or perhaps something in between. Ali hesitated, poking a blue, gelatinous cube with his finger. It jiggled like jellyfish meat. Omar braved the first bite of something that looked like a prickly crimson pod. To his surprise, the inside was soft, filled with golden strands that tasted like cinnamon and mango wrapped in cool mint.

"Hey," he muttered, surprised. "This one's actually good."

Ali smiled and picked up another oddity—a lumpy black vegetable with green veins. He bit it and gagged instantly.

"Yuck! It tastes like burnt battery acid!" he groaned, wiping his tongue with his sleeve.

Omar laughed, grateful for the distraction. He took another bite of the minty fruit and leaned back.

Done eating, Omar got up and wandered around the small chamber. The room was lit by what looked like floating stones that pulsed softly with inner light. On the walls were metallic panels etched with shifting geometric patterns. One device looked like a small box that hummed when he passed near it, and another seemed to be a set of discs that hovered in midair, rotating slowly and adjusting their altitude when he moved his hands beneath them.

There was a transparent tube on the side wall, filled with a swirling silvery mist that changed color as he walked past. There was also a hologram of a tactical map, which would move and shift if a hand passed above it. Everything felt ancient, yet alive—as if the technology wasn't just smart, it was aware.

Back in the adjoining chamber, Ytelthuun's voice cracked with barely contained emotion.
"Xa'rekthul-Yenu-Vaahn... how dare you bring them here! You know what Thaarn would do if he even sensed such beings existed on Orulenthia!"

Vaan's response was calm but resolute.
"You think I don't know the risk? I've fought beside you for ages, Ytelthuun. I wouldn't have brought them here if I didn't believe with all my essence that they pose no threat."

"They're aliens!" Ytelthuun shouted. "From another world! This has never happened before. Not once in the history of Vael'Sythrin Reach or any of our cities. This... this changes everything."

"And they're children," Vaan said simply. "Terrified, lost, and entirely dependent on us. You looked into their eyes—tell me you didn't see innocence."

Ytelthuun was pacing, fists clenched, his normally composed demeanor cracked. The legendary rebel who had destroyed Thaarn's facilities and led uprisings without fear now looked shaken.

"I've buried too many innocents, Xa'rekthul-Yenu-Vaahn. I can't lose more. Having them here... what if we're seen? What if they're tracked?"

Vaan stepped closer and placed a hand gently on Ytelthuun's shoulder.
"I'll take responsibility. They trust me. And I trust you. These boys—Omar and Ali—they didn't choose this. They were brought here by a relic older than even our oldest archives."

Ytelthuun's posture softened. His lip quivered, and his eyes glossed with memory.
"I lost my son to Thaarn's purges," he whispered. "He was very young. A poet. Not a fighter. Thaarn's skyburners leveled the district to root out one rebel. My son was turned to ash."

"I remember," Vaan said gently. "And I remember how you rose from the ruins and led the charge at Cereluunyc Basin. You survived that fire not with hate, but with purpose."

Ytelthuun inhaled slowly, composing himself. At last, he gave a small nod.
"Fine. For you, Xa'rekthul-Yenu-Vaahn. And for them. I'll help them however I can."

Moments later, the stone door to the boys' chamber slid open with a soft hiss. Vaan and Ytelthuun entered, both wearing small, tight-lipped smiles. Vaan's voice rang in Omar and Ali's minds like warm sunlight. "Do not fear. Ytelthuun is my closest friend. He will aid us."

Ytelthuun's black eyes widened slightly. "They can hear me?" he asked telepathically.

"Yes", Vaan replied. "They are not like us, but somehow, their minds are open. Adaptive. Intuitive. Go ahead and try."

Ytelthuun stepped forward and looked at them closely.
"Then let me tell you who I am," he said, his voice calm now.

His mind reached into theirs. "I was born in the city of Vael'Sythrin Reach—its towers carved into living crystal, suspended above the azure chasm of Seruun-Khal. My parents were lost in the Stormfallen Cataclysm when my age was only half of a solar cycle. The skies broke apart that day with acid rain and terrifying lightning, and the winds tore entire districts from the cliffs. I survived... just barely.

I was raised by engineers and stone-scribes, taught the old ways, the lost ways. I learned to wield tools before weapons, to heal before harm. But when Thaarn came... when he imposed his Dominion over our lands, over our freedom... I could not stand aside. I became a fighter—not for blood, but for dignity. For choice.

Every life matters to me. Every person has value, no matter their strength. That is why I defy Thaarn. I do not seek power. I seek peace. But peace must be protected... even if it costs everything."

Ytelthuun knelt before the boys.
"I reacted in fear. I saw you as threats. But I see now... you are just boys. Young, far from home, and burdened with something far older than you should carry. I am deeply sorry."

The boys felt the sincerity of his mind. It was like standing in a river of sorrow and honor. Omar looked at Ali, who nodded silently. They both smiled back.

Together, Omar and Ali reached out with their minds—not just to Ytelthuun, but to Vaan as well. Telepathy, they had realized, didn't have to be one-on-one. It was like radio waves—they could speak and include others.

"We're from Earth," Omar said. "New Jersey. We were born there. Our parents... they're amazing. We love them so much."

"We miss our home," Ali added. "We used to ride bikes in the park near our school. I had a pet turtle named Laser."

Vaan chuckled then spoke out loud.
"Turr Tull? Ley Zurr?"

Ali replied, "Yeah, he didn't do much. But he looked cool!"

"Tell him about the artifact," Vaan prompted gently.

Ali reached into his bag and pulled out the triangular talisman. Its ruby-like stone pulsed faintly. He handed it to Ytelthuun.

The old warrior took it carefully, examining its surface. His fingers traced the glowing inscriptions carved along its edge. His eyes widened.

"This is ancient beyond reckoning," he whispered. "It reads: ***Voraal Zenthir Kael is the rightful keeper. Let this be returned to the Vault of Elders in the sanctuary of Tzuraan'dhel-Monkaar.***"

"That's where it belongs?" Omar asked.

Ytelthuun nodded.
"A continent away. Across the Broken Expanse. And possibly guarded."

He turned to Vaan, and the two began speaking again in Urdii, their tones hushed but intense. They debated routes, dangers, factions that may try to intercept them, and the risk of exposing the rebellion.

Finally, Ytelthuun turned to the boys.
"A plan has been made. But you must be ready for anything. We cannot keep you here. This base sees many travelers—some loyal, some... uncertain. If even one of them speaks of you, Thaarn's enforcers will descend upon us like locusts. We leave for *Tzuraan'dhel-Monkaar* soon. It is very far from here."

He walked to a small cabinet and returned with two folded garments. They looked like rugged workers' cloaks—grayish, hooded, stitched with thread that shimmered faintly.

"These will help you blend in," he said. "No one will see soldiers. Just two helpers from the outer sectors. And here..."
He handed them small, sleek helmets that looked nothing like weapons—more like the gear of miners or engineers.

"Prepare yourselves, my new friends," Ytelthuun said telepathically. "The road ahead is uncertain. But you are not alone. We will get you back home somehow!"

CHAPTER 12
THE MAKER OF DOORWAYS.

Long before the rise of Lord Thaarn or the founding of the city of Veltharuun, on the rugged continent of Tzuraan'dhel-Monkaar, high atop a jagged peak where destructive lightning danced with clouds, lived a solitary hermit. His name, lost to all but the oldest myths, was Veluun-Trass'Zorith. He was a recluse by every definition, a being who had severed all ties to his people and their politics. Veluun-Trass'Zorith was obsessed not with war or wealth, but with knowledge—particularly the hidden laws of the universe.

His mountain tower, sculpted from obsidian and humming quartz, overlooked no city or road. Birds avoided it. The wind whispered strange things as it coiled around its spires. He had no neighbors. No visitors. Only the stars kept him company.

Veluun was not mad, though many believed he must be. He was a tinkerer, a scholar of impossible things. His inventions included whisper-orbs that stored thought and crystal plates that bent sound into color. His hands were scarred from heat-metal and soulglass; his eyes glowed faintly with telepathic residue. But it was time itself that truly fascinated him—not the hours of a day, but the structure of time and space as an interwoven cloth.

He believed it could be folded. Bent. Torn. He spent his days forging circuits that responded to thought alone and built generators powered by emotion. This was over 80,000 solar cycles ago—approximately 26 million Earth years in the past.

His solitude grew deeper with time, until he spoke no words aloud for centuries. He communicated only with machines and, sometimes, with the mountain itself, whispering ideas into its stones as if they could listen. His mind moved beyond language, beyond emotion. He wasn't lonely—he had become something else. Something apart.

One solar cycle, while testing a new device that combined focused gravimetric fields with energy-laced thought-matter using telepathy, he stumbled into something he hadn't predicted.

He had built what he called a graviton-pike lens—a dense, cube-like machine of obsidian plates and glowing nerve-fibers. Alongside it, he had connected a device he named the Vorthan Coil, which generated mental harmonics that mimicked thought-waves. When he activated them together for the first time, space itself seemed to ripple.

Right in front of him, the air shimmered, bent inward, and cracked—like glass touched by fire. A slit of darkness hovered in his tower laboratory. Then it closed.

It had lasted less than a second. But Veluun-Trass'Zorith had seen it. A fold. A tear in the veil of space-time. He hadn't meant to do it. The entire event was an accident. That fact shook him more than anything else. For all his brilliance, all his control, the thing he had chased for millennia had simply... happened.

This both terrified and thrilled him. He didn't sleep properly for years after that day.

From that moment, Veluun dedicated every breath to replicating the phenomenon. He constructed more advanced graviton-pike lenses, refined his Vorthan Coil, and experimented with newer alloys that could withstand the strain of localized warping.

But for decades, every attempt yielded only fragments—brief flashes, flickers of distortion, echoes of half-opened doors. Sometimes he saw nothing. Sometimes he saw stars. Distant galaxies. Fragments of reality so remote they could never be reached. These folds opened to places he could not identify, and they never lasted long enough to study.

His obsession deepened. He forgot to eat, forgot to log his work, and stopped recording dates. His life became a stream of trials. He succeeded only in creating small tears that drifted into the void, unanchored and wild. He learned to shape them better but could never choose their destination.

Until one day, in the silence of his mountain tower, he forged a device unlike any other. A triangle of memory-steel, wound with thin filaments of pulsed platinum and set with an exceedingly rare ruby-like gem from deep within the ice caverns beneath Seruun-Khal. It was shaped to echo the sacred geometry of the Elder Lexicons.

He called this final artifact **Kha'Len**—the **Key**. In the ancient Urdii tongue, it implied a meaning of *The Key to Doorways*, to be precise. It responded only to an intense and focused beam of light at the center of its red crystal. And it worked.

When activated, the Kha'Len tore open a doorway not into chaos, but to somewhere else—another world. For the first time, Veluun controlled where the tear would land. He had done it. He had created a portal key. Not just a tool—but a legacy.

Kha'Len was no simple machine. It was alive in its own way—aware of its purpose. Veluun tested it again and again, stepping through its red-lit doorways and arriving in alien landscapes of fire and fog, oceans of crystal, forests that breathed, and stars so close they filled half the sky. He never lingered long. He always returned, cataloging what he found.

From each world, he took a stone, a leaf, a shard of something strange. He preserved them in stasis bubbles, arranging them in silent reverence on shelves that circled the great dome of his tower.

He visited dozens of worlds. Some were barren. Some teemed with insectoid cities. Others were flooded with sound, where air itself shimmered with color. He recorded each journey in his mind, knowing no one would read it but himself.

The Kha'Len pulsed with new energy after every use, almost as if it remembered the places it had touched. Veluun began to sense that the talisman itself was learning, adapting to new coordinates, improving with each traversal. The talisman would open a new world, and the next portal it opened would return him to Orulenthia.

Each return grew harder. His body aged, even as his mind sharpened. Time moved differently between worlds. Eventually, he realized he was dying.

With great sorrow, he returned to Tzuraan'dhel-Monkaar and chose a successor. A friend—an artisan who had helped design the triangular ruby-gem housing of Kha'Len. Veluun passed the Key into his care with final instructions:

"Guard it. Do not use it. The worlds are not ready."

And then, Veluun-Trass'Zorith vanished into his tower and was never seen again.

The friend, true to his promise, kept the artifact sealed. Decades passed. Then centuries. Then several millenia. Eventually, the talisman was entrusted to Voraal Zenthir Kael, the noble Keeper of the Vault of Elders.

Voraal was the one who engraved the inscription onto the back of the device:

"Voraal Zenthir Kael is the rightful keeper. Let this be returned to the Vault of Elders in the sanctuary of Tzuraan'dhel-Monkaar."

It was then hidden away beneath the sanctuary's deepest chamber, behind eleven concentric vaults of stone and crystal. There it lay for countless more millenia.

But a thousand solar cycles ago, it was stolen.

The thief was a petty outlaw whose name even time has forgotten—desperate, reckless, and completely unaware of what he was taking. He slipped into the Vault with help from a corrupted warden, stole what he thought was a priceless gem, and fled into the night. His plan was to sell it.

But as he escaped through the desert ridges of Ashwe'Voleen, he dropped the talisman. The morning sun hit the ruby triangle dead center. A sharp, focused ray of light struck it just right.

And it activated.

The petty thief vanished from his world, dragged through a screaming fold in time and space. He landed violently in an alien wilderness. Thick jungles. Massive primordial beasts. No civilization.

It was Earth—but Earth millions of years ago. He wandered for weeks, surviving on fruit and sheer luck. But the portal had closed. The Kha'Len required precise light to trigger, and he had no idea how it worked. Eventually, wounded and exhausted, he died in a cave. The artifact lay beside his bones.

That cave, over the course of eons, became a hollow in what we now call Morocco in North Africa. The smooth and unbreakable metal structure of the Kha'Len kept it preserved. Shifting sands buried it. Mountain rains swept over it. Oceans turned into deserts.

Millennia passed. Civilizations rose and fell. Dust covered secrets. But the Talisman endured—silent, patient, and unchanged.

It passed through hands unknowingly—merchants, collectors—lost to obscurity, until it found itself resting in an antiques shop in Tangier.

There, at last, it was purchased by Omar and Ali Jamali, who mistook it for a curious souvenir. The Kha'Len, the Key to the Doorways, had returned to waiting.

Its heart still beat red. It continued waiting for reactivation.

CHAPTER 13
BEYOND THE BORDER GATE.

Vaan tightened the last strap on the utility satchel and tossed it into the supply crate, exhaling sharply. "That should be it," he said, his voice laced with urgency. His old friend Ytelthuun, tall and sinewy with pale skin that shimmered faintly in the torchlight, was scribbling coordinates onto a fiber-plasm scroll. He glanced over and smirked.

"Still feels odd calling you just 'Vaan,' you know," Ytelthuun chuckled, his mind brushing lightly against Vaan's with amusement. "Nicknames are such a strange Earth custom. Shortening Xa'rekthul-Yenu-Vaahn into something that sounds like a sneeze. Hilarious."

Vaan allowed himself a rare laugh. "You get used to it. Humans don't like mouthfuls. Besides, it's easier when you're trying to stay off every registry Thaarn ever hacked."

"Fair," Ytelthuun said, his smile fading as he scanned the cluttered table. "This is going to be long, Vaan. You know that, right? We're not just dodging patrols. We're crossing nearly half of Orulenthia. Tzuraan'dhel-Monkaar isn't a casual stroll through the fields."

"I know," Vaan said softly. "But the boys need to get home. Kha'Len belongs there only as a conduit. It was never meant to stay. And if anyone can help us find the right frequency and anchor point back to their Earth, it's Voraal Zenthir Kael." Ytelthuun nodded grimly. "The rightful Keeper."

Inside the stone dwelling, Omar and Ali sat on the cushioned floor, giggling as they bit into slices of the soft, mango-minty fruit. The flesh was juicy and sweet with a cold aftertaste like peppermint tea, melting instantly in their mouths. Omar chewed slowly, savoring the flavor, while Ali licked his fingers and reached for more.

"Wow," Omar spoke telepathically, "this stuff should be illegal. It's like candy and Gatorade had a baby. It's too good!"

Ytelthuun, sitting cross-legged across from them, gave a small laugh. "You might be closer to the truth than you think. That fruit comes from the hydrabloom trees of the lower marshes. Its molecular lattice is structured to retain hyper-aquatic vesicles. Your Earth physiology interprets a single bite as the hydration equivalent of several days' water."

Ali blinked. "So that's why we're not dying of thirst?" "Exactly," Ytelthuun replied. "Most fruits here are designed by the biosphere to overcompensate. It's a harsh planet. Evolution learned to prepare."

But while Omar seemed settled, Ali had spent most of the past hour sniffling, eyes red. He clutched a patch of blanket as if it were his mother's hand. His small face trembled.

"I want to go home," he whispered. "I want Mama and Baba. I miss them so much."

Omar shifted closer and put an arm around his brother's shoulders. His own heart was aching, but he knew he had to be stronger.

"I know, Ali. I miss them too," he said softly. "But just have stronger faith in Allah. Inshallah, everything will be alright. We just have to be patient, okay? We're gonna get back. I promise." Ali nodded slowly, tears streaking his dusty cheeks. Ytelthuun watched quietly, absorbing the strength of the bond between the two.

The time to move came just after firstlight, under the never-setting glow of the red giant star. Vaan led them outside to the military skimmer he had originally used to flee the prison citadel, but they could no longer risk using it. Its registration signature was embedded with Thaarn's networked tracking glyphs.

Together, they pushed it beneath a crumbled archway where vines hung like curtains, draping the skimmer in shadow. Ytelthuun pulled a dark velvet tarp from storage and covered the vehicle completely.

"That should keep it hidden for now," he muttered. "Not perfect, but good enough to fool a surface drone scan."

They gathered their gear, bags slung across their backs. Omar adjusted the strap on Ali's shoulder, and Vaan double-checked the containment pouch carrying Kha'Len.

The front gate to Ytelthuun's yard creaked open with a mechanical whir, and everyone turned their heads in unison. They had just finished throwing the tarp over the skimmer, crouched among the drooping vines and broken stone. From the outer path stepped a cloaked figure, her silhouette framed by the faint shimmer of heat and dust. She moved with silent authority, each step deliberate as she entered the courtyard.

She was tall and striking, her dark brown traveling cloak hanging from her shoulders like a cascade of weathered silk. The lower half of her face was veiled, and atop her head sat an oversized pair of dust goggles, their twin lenses catching the sunlight like tiny moons. As she stepped fully into view, she removed the veil slowly, revealing sculpted features—high cheekbones, a narrow, regal nose, and lips curved in a soft, knowing smile. Her skin held a subtle rose-gold undertone that shimmered faintly beneath the daylight. Her eyes were vast and completely black, reflecting the light like pools of polished obsidian, framed by long, elegant lashes. Her thick dark brows arched with natural poise, and strands of rich auburn hair peeked from beneath her hood, windswept and tangled with flecks of dust. There was something fierce yet calm in her posture—a strength that didn't need to be announced.

She smiled as she removed her veil. "So these are the visitors from beyond the Rift."

The boys stared, captivated. Omar, in particular, felt his chest flutter. There was something comforting, powerful, and beautiful about her presence all at once.

She knelt before them and spoke directly into their minds: "My name is Nyshira-Valis-Kae."

Ali grinned immediately. "Hi, Nyshira-Valis-Kae," he said, doing his best to pronounce it correctly. "But if it's okay with you, I'd love to call you Nysha instead," he said telepathically.

Nysha chuckled, her eyes glinting with amusement.

She smiled and touched his shoulder gently. "You two are brave. Don't let fear shrink your hearts. I'll be with you now."

Vaan clapped a hand on her shoulder. "Glad you could make it." He gave her a big smile.

"Ytelthuun called me last cycle," she said. "I wouldn't let you leave without me. Besides, it's about time we kicked this journey off."

The new vehicle was Nysha's—a copper-toned skimmer with a sleek, low-profile design and a hull that shimmered with age, caked in dust and desert grime. It hovered a few feet above the ground, humming gently with the resonance of embedded telekinetic conduits woven into its core. There were no wheels, no visible engines—just smooth, seamless metal curved like a sand-worn shell, gliding effortlessly over the terrain. The interior, in contrast to its weathered exterior, was spotless and meticulously arranged. Nysha, ever the clean freak, had maintained the cabin in near-sterile condition. The air inside carried the faint scent of dried mint and polished alloy.

They all climbed aboard. Inside, there were two long rows of seats and a rear cargo hold. Nysha took the driver's seat. Omar and Ali, now dressed in coarse brown-and-grey workmen's outfits with helmets and visors, nestled into the back.

Even Vaan and Ytelthuun had donned dull-toned garb, blending in with the population. A team of wandering salvagers. Nothing out of place. Nothing suspicious.

They headed southward. Past the great stone pillars of Vael'Sythrin Reach, through cracked fields and forests of coral-bark trees. The land grew drier. Thornbrush replaced moss. The red sky pulsed overhead like a giant slow-beating heart.

Eventually, the towering walls of the southern border gate came into view. Enormous, jagged structures of black stone and electrified mesh, they loomed like the jaws of a fossilized beast. A network of cables and pylons crackled faintly along the top.

The rover came to a halt. Vaan, Ytelthuun, and Nysha stepped out. A trio of border guards, clad in deep bronze armor, approached. Their faces lit up in recognition.

"Heading out again so soon?" one of them called with a grin, nodding toward the group. "Hope you're not planning to leave the rest of us to the boring scraps."

"Something like that," Vaan said smoothly. They shared a few laughs and quiet murmurs about weather and watch rotations.

Once the small-talk ended, the three travelers returned to the rover. The great border gates groaned, gears grinding as they slowly swung outward. Light from the red star spilled onto the road ahead, which turned into a dusty, thorny path leading into a vast and silent desert.

They drove forward, the gates closing behind them with a seismic clang.

But from high on the tower wall, half-hidden in a crow's nest lookout, a silent figure watched. He wore the insignia of a standard border guard, but there was a rigid precision to his stance, like a coiled wire waiting to spring. His eyes, narrow and predatory, scanned the landscape with cold efficiency. In his gloved hand, he held a thin silver disc no larger than a coin—its edges beveled with intricate notches like a gear. As he clicked the edge with his thumb, a soft whir emitted from within. The surface of the disc shimmered, opening like the iris of a mechanical eye. A fine red lens emerged from the center, casting a pinpoint beam that began to sweep and record silently. It was a high-fidelity surveillance device—a relic from the pre-collapse Velthari military, now outlawed across most of Orulenthia. Compact, nearly undetectable, and capable of storing weeks of encrypted footage, it was a tool meant only for covert operations.

The man whispered to himself, "Councilor Drevvos will want to see this."

He slid the disc into a small metal socket embedded in his palm. The device glowed faintly blue.

Data recording: transferred to memory crystal.

The spy melted back into shadow.

And so, the first subtle move of a deadly game had been made. Unseen and silent, the moment the recording was captured, a threshold was crossed. Without knowing it, Vaan, the boys, and everyone connected to them had stepped into the crosshairs of forces far more dangerous than they could imagine. Councilor Drevvos would see, and others would follow. And because none of them were aware of this intrusion—because they still moved with the illusion of safety—the danger became even more acute. The shadows had eyes now, and the air itself seemed to shift in anticipation. A slow, silent descent into peril had begun, and it would not be easily reversed.

The boys' safety was now under serious threat.

CHAPTER 14
WHEN THE CALL GOES UNANSWERED.

The golden hour painted the neighborhood in shades of honey and amber, casting long shadows across the neatly trimmed lawns of Old Bridge, New Jersey. Birds chirped softly in the trees, and a warm breeze rustled the sheer curtains in the Jamali household. Inside the modest two-story home, Hassan Jamali sat at his desk near the front window, hunched slightly as he squinted at the screen. He was putting the finishing touches on a quarterly project report for the township office, sipping from a heavy ceramic mug that read *"#1 Baba"* in bold green letters. The coffee had gone cold, but he barely noticed.

From the kitchen came the familiar shuffle of slippers against linoleum, followed by the soft thump of cabinet doors closing. Khadija Jamali appeared in the doorway, wiping her hands on a dish towel. Her brow was furrowed, lips pressed into a tight line.

"Hassan," she said, her voice tinged with worry. "It's five twelve. The boys aren't home yet."

Hassan glanced at the digital clock in the bottom corner of his screen and then looked up, unconcerned. "They probably stopped somewhere. You know how Omar gets when he's with Ali—time just disappears."

"But I've called them. Both of them. Several times." Her voice rose slightly. "My messages aren't going through, and the calls go straight to voicemail. Hassan, both their phones! Not just one—both! Doesn't that sound strange to you?"

He sighed and turned to face her. "Khadija, you worry too much. Maybe they forgot to charge their phones. Maybe they're with friends, maybe there's no signal—"

"—Or maybe something happened! You know I wouldn't be worried if it was just one of them. But both? And neither have responded to any of my texts since right after school. Hassan, I have this terrible feeling. I don't like this. Please!"

He stood and walked over, placing a reassuring hand on her shoulder. "Inshallah, they're fine. Don't jump to the worst-case scenario. I'll go ask around, alright? Maybe they're at Sohail and Shoaib's place. I'll check there first."

Just minutes later, Hassan was walking down the block toward the Aziz household. Sohail and Shoaib Aziz lived within walking distance and were best friends with Omar and Ali. The early evening light reflected off parked cars, and the air smelled faintly of backyard barbecues and fresh-cut grass. He carried himself with a steady gait, though a growing knot of unease had begun to tighten in his chest.

The Aziz home was a cozy brick colonial with green shutters and a blue mailbox shaped like a minaret. As he approached the door, it opened before he could knock.

"As-salāmu ʿalaykum, Hassan Bhai!" said Nadeem Aziz with a wide grin, stepping forward and pulling him into a warm hug. He was a tall Pakistani man with graying hair at the temples and laugh lines that gave him a fatherly charm.

"Wa-ʿalaykumu s-salām, Nadeem brother," Hassan replied, stepping into the familiar home that always smelled like spices and musk. The worn rug in the hallway bore the footprints of decades of guests. Pictures of Makkah and Madinah hung beside family photos and Quranic calligraphy.

"Come, come. Sit. The boys are out at the basketball courts. They'll be back soon. I'll have Faiza bring us some chai."

Hassan smiled politely and took a seat in the living room. Minutes later, Faiza arrived with her Salams and a polished tray bearing two cups of steaming milk chai, thick with cardamom, and a small plate of pastel-colored Pakistani burfi topped with edible silver foil.

"JazakAllah, sister," Hassan said gratefully.

"You're welcome as always," she replied kindly before returning to the kitchen.

The two men sat in silence for a moment, sipping tea and enjoying the sweets. The chai was hot, creamy, and just the right amount of sweet—comfort in a cup.

Finally, the front door swung open with the clamor of sneakers.

"As-salāmu ʿalaykum, Uncle Hassan!" chorused Sohail and Shoaib, their faces bright and flushed from a game of basketball. Both boys were lanky, wearing gym shorts and sports hoodies, their Air Jordan sneakers squeaking slightly on the floor.

"Wa-ʿalaykumu s-salām, boys," Hassan replied warmly. "I was actually hoping Omar and Ali were here with you."

The two brothers exchanged glances.

"We haven't seen them since school," Sohail said. "I saw them near the side exit of the building. They were running. I thought maybe they forgot something."

"Yeah," Shoaib added. "Ali looked kind of freaked out. I thought it was just another one of their weird after-school plans."

Hassan's brows knit together. "You're sure you haven't seen them since?"

"No, Uncle. Not at all."

Nadeem patted his friend's shoulder and smiled. "Inshallah, they're fine. Boys wander. They'll pop up somewhere soon, you'll see. There's no need for worry."

Hassan didn't linger. After exchanging a few more pleasantries, he thanked the Aziz family and made his way back home, this time walking faster. The light in the sky had dimmed, turning a warm orange-pink, but there was nothing calming about it now.

A neighbor, Jim Meyers, waved from his driveway. "Hey Hassan! How's the family? Weather's perfect today, huh?"

Hassan barely nodded, offering a distracted "Yeah, right," before continuing down the street.

He pushed open the front door with more force than necessary.

"They're not at Nadeem's," he said before Khadija could even ask.

Her face paled and eyes widened. "Ya Allah! What's happening? Now what do we do?"

Hassan rubbed his temples and sat down heavily at the kitchen table. He pulled out his phone and began dialing every number he could think of—family friends, neighbors, classmates' parents. No one had seen Omar or Ali since school. One mother remembered them walking toward the woods by the parking lot but hadn't paid it much mind.

With a deep breath, Hassan finally called the local police department. His voice cracked as he explained the situation.

The officer on the line sounded sympathetic but firm. "I understand, sir, but unless they've been missing for 24 hours, we can't file an official missing person's report. They're teenagers. They could've just gone somewhere. Please try to stay calm and give it a little more time."

Hassan didn't bother to argue. He hung up, placed the phone on the table, and stood silently for a moment.

He opened the cabinet, pulled out his Marlboro pack—usually reserved for high-stress days—and stepped outside. The breeze had cooled slightly, brushing against his skin like the whisper of something ominous. With shaky hands, he lit a cigarette, then another one minutes later. The smoke curled upward into the fading light.

He made a strong black coffee and stood under the porch light, sipping it in silence. His mind ran in endless loops, caught between disbelief and dread. More Marlboros were lit.

Little did Hassan Jamali know, his sons were already far beyond his reach—swept into a world light-years away, where floating mountains drifted under crimson skies and ancient beings walked the sands of forgotten cities. The search had only just begun.

CHAPTER 15
BEYOND THE REACH: INTO THE WILDS.

The rover hummed low and fast as it skimmed just feet above the rugged terrain beyond the southern border of Vael'Sythrin Reach. Red rock plains stretched endlessly in every direction, broken only by eerie, brittle trees with twisted limbs. Though seemingly lifeless, their slow, deliberate swaying hinted at some kind of strange awareness — as if the land itself were watching.

Nyshira-Valis-Kae sat poised at the helm, her hands resting gently on her knees, unmoving. The vehicle responded entirely to her mind, guided by her telekinetic power. Glowing symbols tattooed across her forearms pulsed faintly with golden-blue light every time she manipulated the rover's speed or adjusted its course. Behind her, Omar and Ali sat wide-eyed, pressed against the window panels, their gazes fixed on the alien world streaking past in a blur.

"It feels like we're flying," Omar projected in awe. His thoughts, like all conversation on this world, passed telepathically.

"We kinda are," Ali replied, grinning. "This is better than that dune buggy ride in Tangier. Remember that?"

Nysha smiled brightly without turning around. Her thoughts entered their minds with a warmth that felt like sunlight. "You haven't seen anything yet. This is just the quiet edge of Orulenthia."

"You're seriously the coolest driver we've ever met," Ali beamed. "This thing feels like it's gliding on air."

Nysha laughed softly in their minds. "I've spent more time in this rover than in my own room. I've raced across valleys chased by Kholari dust-beasts. Once outran a collapse tremor from the Deighran Scar. This? This is relaxing."

Omar watched her with admiration. Her kindness was magnetic, her confidence effortless. Every time her tattoos lit up, he felt something stir in his chest — a strange mix of curiosity and admiration that he wasn't quite ready to name.

"Nysha," he asked telepathically, "who are you? I mean... you're amazing."

Nysha's glowing tattoos dimmed as she let the rover coast for a stretch. Her tone turned more reflective, though still light. "I was born in Vael'Sythrin Reach. My father, Vwarun-Kae, was a trader of starleaf resin and luminous stones. He traveled often — across half the continent sometimes — and always brought home little gifts and bigger stories. My mother, Talaan-Ollquis, was a healer. She treated the sick for free whenever she could. There was so much love in my house that even the walls felt warm. My childhood was great."

Ali smiled. "That explains why you're so kind. And brave."

"I try to be," she answered. "When I was less than three solar cycles old, I joined a volunteer guild called the Protectors of the Weak Flame. We help the ones who can't fight back — the displaced, the lost, the scared. That's how I met Vaan and Ytelthuun. And that's how I got captured."

Her expression didn't falter, though her thoughts grew heavier. "Thaarn's spies intercepted us during an intelligence run near the Korravine Ridge. They dragged me to one of their black sites — no name, no windows, just cold. They beat me, starved me. Wanted names, locations, secrets. I gave them nothing."

Omar's eyes widened. "You didn't tell them anything?"

"Not a word," Nysha projected calmly. "On the fifth night, Ytelthuun and a strike team from the First Alliance stormed the prison. They tore through Thaarn's outer guards like paper. When they found me, I was barely breathing. They brought me back. My family wept when I came home."

Ali was quiet, overwhelmed by the thought. "You're seriously incredible."

Nysha laughed again — not boastfully, but with a kind of deflecting humility. "You'd do the same if it was your people. I just hope I'm strong enough when it really counts."

A few minutes later, she asked Omar to retrieve her small backpack from the rear cargo bay. When he handed it over, she unzipped it and revealed a tiny creature curled in a nest of silky fibers. It had the floppy ears of a rabbit, the nose of a shrew, and the soft, pudgy body of a hamster. Its fur shimmered like polished pearl and its eyes glistened like diamonds.

"This is Luma," Nysha announced proudly into their minds. "He sleeps a lot, but he has his uses. He's my little companion."

Luma yawned and stretched his little paws, blinking at the boys with sleepy friendliness before burrowing deeper into his nest.

The rover gradually decelerated as they approached a formidable mountain range that looked as if it had been carved by ancient fire. Its peaks were jagged and angular, composed of obsidian-black stone with razor edges that jutted like the shattered teeth of a long-dead titan. The air grew heavier, tinged with mineral heat and ozone, as if the earth still remembered the violence that had birthed these peaks. But then, as they turned around a bend between two craggy outcrops, the land opened to reveal a startling contrast — a hidden sanctuary cradled in the heart of this volcanic fortress.

There, like a secret painted in sapphire, lay a radiant lake — its waters an otherworldly hue, not blue from any sky above, but alive with a deep, mineral luminescence born of the planet's unique elements. The glow shimmered in soft pulses, as if the lake itself breathed with some ancient memory. A thunderous waterfall tumbled from an unseen source high above, veiling the cliffs in mist that shimmered like powdered crystal and carried the scent of metal and wildflowers. The water surged into the basin below with a force both deafening and hypnotic, carving smooth terraces into the volcanic stone over countless millennia. Lush, alien vegetation clung to the stone in defiant bloom — flowers with translucent petals like living stained glass, and leaves that shifted color subtly as they responded to changes in air pressure and temperature. Strange insects glided silently between them, their wings refracting light like shards of broken prisms. No roads touched this place. No settlement intruded. It was a world within a world — sacred, remote, and untouched by war or time, as though sealed in a moment beyond decay or memory. An oasis.

They stepped out of the rover, greeted by warm, mist-filled air. Omar and Ali stared at the lake.

"Is this water safe?" Ali asked Vaan telepathically.

"Absolutely," Vaan replied. "This region lacks microbial life due to the mineral-heavy strata below. You'll be perfectly fine."

The boys each took a sip and found it fresh, clear, and surprisingly familiar. They looked at each other — it had been days since they'd last washed.

Blushing slightly, they asked the adults to turn around as they stripped down to their boxer briefs. With a running leap, they dove in, surfacing with joyous yells.

Unable to resist, Nysha removed her tunic and boots, revealing a sleek, form-fitting black bodysuit that hugged her like a second skin. The material shimmered slightly in the light, accentuating the elegant curvature of her figure — long, powerful limbs shaped by a lifetime of movement and discipline, a narrow waist, and a sculpted back that spoke of strength as much as grace. Her presence was that of a dancer and a warrior combined, both fluid and precise. With effortless poise, she dove in, her lithe form cutting through the air before she vanished beneath the glowing waters in a smooth arc. The splash that followed was playful and light, sending droplets like tiny pearls across the boys' faces as they laughed with surprise. Even Vaan, usually so reserved, was moved to join them. He set aside his outer robe and waded into the warm water, his expression softening for the first time in days. Ytelthuun, ever watchful, remained stationed near the rover, his eyes scanning the horizon, his hand resting near the hilt of a concealed weapon — a silent sentinel in this paradise.

For the first time since arriving on this world, Omar and Ali felt carefree. The water, the laughter, the mountains — it all reminded them of their summer trip to Tangier and the Mediterranean Sea.

Eventually, they emerged, shivering slightly despite the warmth. Ytelthuun handed each of them a square device no larger than a deck of cards.

"Press the center," he instructed.

They did — and within seconds, their bodies were dry, the moisture pulled into the device and evaporated harmlessly.

"On Earth, we usually shower once or even twice a day," Omar explained.

Nysha and the others stared at them. "You must have oceans of water," she thought aloud.

"We kinda do," Ali grinned.

Once everyone had freshened up, their spirits noticeably lighter, they climbed back into the rover, their skin still tingling from the warmth of the mineral-rich waters. The scent of wildflowers clung faintly to their clothes as they settled into their seats. Nysha activated the engine with a pulse of her mind, and the hum of the vehicle resumed like a low song beneath their feet. They began to eat preserved food cubes that, once activated with a drop of water, expanded into savory, steaming meals — aromatic spiced rice of sorts with crystalline vegetables, and chewy strips of some kind of bio-protein. The boys exchanged impressed looks, marveling at how good the food tasted despite its appearance. More conversation followed as they traveled: light-hearted teasing, cultural comparisons, and a growing number of curious questions between Omar, Ali, and Nysha. Their laughter echoed softly within the rover, blending with the subtle thrumming of the engine as the landscape rolled by in shifting hues of crimson and gold.

But Omar grew curious. "What's the plan now?"

"We're headed to a liftport — a hub for flying craft — deep in the hinterlands," Nysha replied. "From there, we'll board a Skyraleon-class glider. They are huge crafts that fly in the sky — very large, organic-powered, and fast."

Vaan added, "The Kha'Len — the Key — was forged in the continent of Tzuraan'dhel-Monkaar. That's where we must go."

Nysha's tone darkened. "The rover could never make that distance. We need gliders to cross almost half the planet."

She explained how Orulenthia was unfathomably vast. Some regions were flooded forests where it rained constantly; others were jagged wastelands of volcanic glass where no life could survive.

"There are trillions of beings here," she said. "In some cities, we have more than ten billion residents."

"Planet Earth has only around eight billion total," Omar offered.

Even Ytelthuun looked surprised. "How curious. Your world is efficient with its limits."

"But the gravity?" Omar asked. "Shouldn't we be, like, squashed since this planet is so huge?"

Ytelthuun answered, "Orulenthia's planetary core is vast but porous. It lacks density due to inert crystal fields and non-reactive mineral seams. The result is lower mass than you'd expect for our size."

As they sped forward, a colossal pyramid-shaped mountain loomed into view, defying gravity as it hovered in the crimson sky like a divine relic of a forgotten age. Its structure was vast beyond comprehension — the base alone could have swallowed entire cities on Earth. The sheer faces of its polished obsidian sides were etched with luminous lines that pulsed in complex sequences, forming what looked like ancient runes or circuit-like glyphs glowing softly in hues of violet, emerald, and gold. Suspended bridges arced between distant points on the pyramid's multi-tiered levels, like cobwebs spun from light, and sleek vessels glided between them in graceful silence. Whole districts clung to its sides, some carved into the stone, others built outward on platforms that shimmered with anti-gravitational support. Towering spires rose from the apex, radiating with ethereal halos that flickered with energy from sources far beyond human understanding. The moving shadows of beings and machines were barely perceptible — as if the mountain itself breathed with life, eternally active and watching from above. The boys sat frozen in silent awe, their hearts pounding. The scale, the mystery, the haunting beauty — it all eclipsed anything they had ever dreamed of.

"Welcome to Zarkhaal-Teth," Nysha said, her voice rich with pride and reverence. "One of the ancient Skyholds — still alive, still remembering."

The boys gasped, stunned.

Soon after, they passed glowing trees shaped like spirals, their tops crowned with clusters of light-emitting pods. Herds of translucent, antlered beasts galloped in the distance, their hooves never touching the ground. Trails of light followed.

Omar and Ali kept snapping photos with their iPhones until the batteries nearly gave out, drained from the relentless documenting of their surreal journey. They shut down their devices to preserve the last bit of battery life, leaving the boys with only memories and a handful of images captured in time. The others marveled at the tiny Earth tools, intrigued by their shape and blinking lights, but couldn't quite grasp why anyone would need to trap a moment inside a machine when they could just remember it in perfect detail.

Nysha's tattoos began to glow again as she veered the rover toward a greener expanse. "This is my family's farm," she projected. "We grow shilvara root — its fibers are refined into conduit threads for our tech."

They passed a small stone dwelling surrounded by symmetrical rows of pale blue plants. Nysha parked beside the house and entered, connecting immediately to a crystalline grid to communicate with her friend at the glider port.

Meanwhile, the boys lay on the cool, bare floor of the house and passed out almost instantly, using their backpacks as pillows. Their bodies were still not used to so much movement and wonder. Nysha returned quietly, carrying soft blankets made from the fur of a gentle nocturnal creature called a traelyynew. She covered them gently, then stood back and watched them sleep.

Her heart tightened.

"They're just children," she thought. "Lost, brave, and so far from home."

She knelt beside them and kissed each of their cheeks.

"I will protect you," she vowed silently. "No matter what happens. Even if it costs me my life."

Omar stirred faintly, feeling her warmth. He kept his eyes closed — but his heart, somehow, opened wider and fluttered. He smiled, not on his face, but inside his heart.

And for a brief, impossible moment, all felt right again.

CHAPTER 16
OF GEYSERS, GLIDERS, AND GHOST WINDS.

Omar awoke to a strange kind of silence—a silence not born from absence, but from stillness. The kind of silence you might hear on a planet that never truly sleeps. As he stirred from the bare floor, shifting slightly against the backpack he'd used as a pillow, he stretched his arms out wide and felt an odd sense of renewal in his limbs. His mind, still foggy from dreams of home, slowly acclimated to the alien ceiling above—a swirling metallic architecture shaped like coiled leaves, glowing faintly with the reflections of the ever-bleeding red sky. Though he missed his family, especially his mother's gentle humming in the kitchen back in New Jersey, Omar felt surprisingly refreshed. Maybe it was something about the air here, or maybe it was the adrenaline of their otherworldly journey—but either way, his mood was light. He rose slowly, noting that the room glowed in a constant crimson hue. Here, it was neither day nor night. Just red. Always red. Like a setting sun frozen in the sky forever. It was a strange comfort—but a reminder that this place was not Earth, and he was far from everything he knew.

He wandered to the edge of their chamber, drawn by a voice—not just any voice, but *her* voice. Nysha stood framed in the archway of an adjoining room, her tall form haloed by the warm lighting and curved crystal walls. She was speaking rapidly in Urdii, the local language, to what sounded like multiple individuals at once through a thin crystalline shard she held between her fingers. The shard pulsed in rhythm with each voice on the line, giving the illusion that it was alive. Her tone was commanding, elegant, and fluid. Omar leaned silently against the curved arch and simply watched, completely enchanted. There was a kind of grace in the way she moved, the way her lips formed the alien syllables. It wasn't just that she was beautiful—though, to Omar's eyes, she was easily the most breathtaking person he'd ever seen—it was the way she existed. She seemed to glow with confidence and purpose. His heart thudded unexpectedly hard in his chest. The crush he had on Lyndsey back home now seemed like a clumsy child's fascination. This—whatever this was—felt even deeper.

Ali's voice broke the spell. "Yo. Loverboy," he mumbled from his mat, rubbing his eyes and smirking as he caught sight of his brother gawking like a puppy. "You planning to propose, or should I give you two some alone time?"

Omar spun around, red-faced. "Shut up, dork," he said, grabbing an empty, lightweight bowl from beside his backpack and tossing it at Ali. Ali laughed, snatching it out of the air with ease.

"No, seriously. You were staring so hard I thought your eyeballs were gonna fall out. Man's in love on another planet!"

"Dude. She's like... twenty-something... Probably."

"So? Age is just a lightyear when you're an intergalactic heartthrob," Ali teased, flashing a grin. "Next thing you know, you'll be marrying her and having little alien babies with antennae. Admit it—you're in love, Romeo!" He burst out laughing, clutching his stomach.

Despite himself, Omar laughed. The kind of laugh only brothers can pull out of each other, even in alien worlds with skies dipped in blood. For a moment, the weirdness of the universe didn't matter. They were just kids. Just brothers.

A low, graceful tone resonated in the hallway, and in stepped Ytelthuun, cloaked in his usual flowing robe that shimmered like graphite. In his long-fingered hands, he held a shallow dish filled with odd, lumpy vegetables. They looked more like sea creatures than food.

"You must replenish your bio-energy reserves," he said telepathically. "This species"—he pointed to something yellow and lumpy—"looks vile. Tastes tolerable. Please eat."

Ali poked at it with suspicion. "Eww! Smells like boiled eggs that've gone rotten!"

Omar took a bite. "Honestly, it's really not bad. Doesn't have much of a flavor. Try some, Ali."

They ate while Ytelthuun watched quietly. Afterward, the boys got dressed in their strange but snug gear—tight-fitting suits that flexed like second skin and offered protection from the elements. Their boots hummed slightly as they sealed around their ankles. Outside their room, the others were already prepared. The mission ahead awaited.

As the boys zipped up their final straps, Nysha stepped into the room. She lightly tapped the glowing shard in her palm, and the voices within it faded with a series of blinking pulses until silence reclaimed the space. The way she ended the communication reminded Omar that here, nothing worked like on Earth—no "clicks" or "beeps," just the shimmer of alien light and resonance.

Nysha beamed at them. "Ready yourselves. Time here flows differently—we must leave before the winds shift."

Ali blinked. "Wait... You guys never say 'good morning' or 'good night.' Why is that? No greetings at all?"

Nysha tilted her head, thoughtful. "Our sun does not set. There is no morning or night—only cycles and rest."

"That's... weirdly awesome," Ali responded telepathically.

The five of them gathered their belongings. Nysha hoisted her bag over one shoulder, scooping up her furry, half-awake companion, Luma, who squeaked once and burrowed deeper into the satchel.

They exited into a shimmering corridor and stepped into Nysha's sleek rover, the vehicle humming as they each found their places. Omar and Ali took their usual spots at the rear, near the side ports that gave them wide, panoramic views of the scarlet-hued landscape. Ytelthuun sat with his limbs crossed like a statue, and Vaan adjusted the rear storage units, making sure the supplies were secured. The rover hissed as its anti-grav system engaged, and then, without a sound, they glided forward.

Hours passed—or what felt like hours—as the rover sailed over barren wilderness and the occasional rise of tall, jagged hills. The boys passed the time in chatter, pointing out strange flora and debating whether some crawling, purple critter had six legs or eight. The world here stretched endlessly. Everything felt open, raw, and ancient.

Suddenly, Nysha cursed under her breath. "I knew I forgot something." She glanced back at them. "Ali, reach into the rear cargo bay. Look for a black case—rectangular, with a red glowing symbol," she said with her mind.

Ali found it quickly and handed it forward. Nysha pushed the red symbol. With an immediate mechanical whir, the sides of the box slid open like petals, revealing a smaller box lined with ultra-thin black wires, almost like strands of hair.

Vaan's voice entered their minds clearly, without sound. "These are translation fibers. They sit just within your auditory channel and translate Urdii into your mental language, and vice versa. You will hear us speak as if in English. When you speak, it will be understood in Urdii. Come closer to me."

He placed a threadlike device into each of their ears, then turned to Nysha and spoke in Urdii.

Nothing happened.

Vaan blinked. "It is still calibrating to your neural and genetic profiles. Be patient."

Moments later, Ali's eyes lit up. "Hey—do you understand my words now?" he said, in clear guttural Urdii.

Omar gasped. "Bro! That's... whoa. You sound like one of them. Mine is working too!"

Everyone cheered. Nysha clapped, and even Luma made a celebratory squeak before crawling back into the bag for a nap.

The boys could now communicate with everyone without the need of telepathy. They were ecstatic.

The rover crested a ridge, and the boys' breath caught in their throats. Below stretched a vast geothermal valley, alive with chaos and beauty. Steam erupted from the earth in violent bursts—not in dozens, but in hundreds, maybe thousands—of geysers, each one roaring upward like a dragon's exhale. Towering columns of boiling water shot into the blood-colored sky, some spiraling and twisting as if alive, others blasting straight up like natural cannons. They reached staggering heights, many of them easily a kilometer tall, their scalding spray catching the scarlet sunlight and refracting it into fiery prisms. The air was thick with mist, glowing crimson and gold, like a battlefield lit by fire and glass. The rover's windshield fogged briefly before auto-clearing, revealing the full surreal panorama: a seething plain of volcanic breath, as if the planet itself were sighing in slow, steaming pulses. It was at once majestic and terrifying—a place where nature declared its supremacy in every blistering spout. Omar leaned closer to the window, wide-eyed. He felt tiny. Insignificant. And yet, deeply alive.

"Wow," Omar whispered. "This place doesn't stop being insane."

As they continued past the geysers, the sky dimmed to a deeper crimson, the air thickening with warm mist that shimmered like molten glass. Then, from above, a breathtaking phenomenon unfolded: an enormous migration of winged creatures filled the sky—millions of them, sweeping in majestic unison. They moved like a living river across the heavens, each one resembling a manta ray sculpted from faintly glowing crystal, their wings transparent and speckled with glimmering dots like constellations. Long, ribbon-like fins trailed behind them, creating slow, fluid spirals in the air. Some flew in tight spirals, others drifted with lazy grace, but all of them exuded a calm, ancient intelligence—as if they had been doing this for millennia. The sky itself seemed alive, pulsing with the hypnotic ballet of their movement. Omar pressed his face to the glass, unable to speak, his chest rising and falling with awe. Beside him, Ali simply whispered, "They're like ghosts in the sky..."

"Those are *Khyzraal Skharnuun,*" said Ytelthuun. "Egg-laying season. They head to the glassfields—no predators dare follow. Highly intelligent animals. Harmless to us. Also considered a culinary delicacy in some regions."

The boys stared, speechless, as the sky filled with gliding shapes. It was like watching a dream come to life.

With the translators now fully functional, the boys enjoyed chatting with Nysha and Vaan aloud. Their excitement was palpable. Eventually, the rover crested another rise—and the boys saw it.

The Liftport.

It was like a vast alien airfield stretching from horizon to horizon, bigger than anything they had ever seen or imagined. The surface below was a dark, polished metal etched with glowing lines, and parked atop it were hundreds of thousands of gargantuan gliders—each one a towering behemoth of brushed alloy and crystal canopies. They stood in precise, almost military formations, their enormous wings swept back like the fins of prehistoric leviathans. Each glider dwarfed a Boeing 747 many times over, their hulls humming faintly with dormant energy. Giant exhaust ports glistened beneath them, hinting at propulsion systems unlike anything on Earth.

Walkways and light-bridges crisscrossed the complex, bustling with figures in flight suits moving between the mechanical titans. The whole area pulsed with purpose, like a spaceport readying for a mass exodus—or an invasion. It was a metropolis of aircrafts. It was a kingdom of machines, anchored to the ground but humming with the promise of flight.

The rover wove through the towering giants until they pulled up beside a facility that resembled an alien warehouse, all hexagonal domes and dark matte plating.

Nysha turned to the boys. "Right! Helmets on. No one sees your faces. Not even my contacts. We cannot risk it."

Inside the warehouse, her contact greeted them. He gave a name, though the boys couldn't quite repeat it. He was tall, wore dark robes. He bowed deeply and spoke with reverence.

They were told their Skyraleon-class glider would be prepped shortly—a marvel of advanced engineering and aerodynamic precision that dwarfed any aircraft the boys had ever seen. While waiting, they wandered to a nearby observation platform, a vantage point designed for visitors to gaze up in awe at the colossal gliders lined up like sleeping giants on a cosmic runway. From below, the immense scale of the Skyraleon-class vessels was overwhelming—sleek, polished wings stretching wider than a football field, their surfaces shimmering faintly under the alien sun's crimson glow. The air was thick with the hum of hidden engines and the faint buzz of anti-gravity systems waiting to spring to life. As they stood entranced by the sheer power and beauty of these gigantic flying machines, their minds raced with anticipation for the journey ahead. After some time, the contact returned, breaking the spell of silence.

"It is ready. This way, please."

They stepped onto a transport platform—a white, smooth flat board with no visible controls, joints, or seams. As their feet touched its surface, it gave off a faint hum, as if acknowledging their presence. The contact's tattoos shimmered with radiant pulses, and with a mere flick of telekinetic will, the board lifted a few inches above the ground and began to glide forward, soundless and steady. As it moved through the Liftport, the boys passed beneath an astonishing parade of aircraft—some slender and needle-like, others so massive they cast city-sized shadows. Towering landing struts, glowing exhaust rings, and iridescent hulls loomed above them, each design alien yet purposeful. The air buzzed with faint magnetic energy and the deep thrum of idle engines. Omar and Ali stood wide-eyed, their earlier tension fading into wide-mouthed wonder. They drifted beneath bridges of glowing latticework, past vessels with strange rotating fins and spiraling antenna arrays, utterly dwarfed by the immensity around them. It was a cathedral of machinery, and they were ants passing beneath titans.

At last, they reached *their* glider. A ramp jutted out to the ground. It was immense.

The pilot was waiting. Taller than others, but stockier. Almost chubby. His deep voice boomed warmly. "I am Pwaa'Shukree Gheltraxxa and I will be flying us into the sky," he said.

"He is a friend," Nysha whispered and winked. "First Alliance."

They climbed the ramp slowly, their hearts pounding not just from the dizzying height but from the overwhelming sense of awe and anticipation. Inside, they found themselves in a vast, cavernous space that was surprisingly plain and stark compared to the complexity outside. The interior was devoid of the usual cockpit controls — no buttons, levers, screens, or steering devices cluttered the smooth walls. Instead, the surfaces were sleek and seamless, finished in soft matte colors that diffused the ambient light from hidden panels above. Rows of wide, spacious seats stretched in neat lines, each upholstered in a simple, muted fabric that promised comfort but no unnecessary luxury. The lighting was calm and even, bathing the cabin in a gentle glow that made the space feel almost serene, as if the glider itself operated on silent, unseen forces rather than human intervention. The emptiness of the cabin was almost reverential, a quiet testament to advanced technology far beyond what Omar and Ali had ever seen. Nysha moved with quiet assurance among them, guiding each brother to their seats with a gentle but purposeful touch, the only living presence amid the vast, silent expanse.

Suddenly, without any warning or the gradual rumble of engines that they had expected from Earthly planes, the glider surged forward and then upwards with a terrifying swiftness. There was no build-up, no comforting roar of a motor, only an instantaneous, jarring lurch that threw the boys against their seats. Omar and Ali's hearts hammered wildly in their chests, their breath caught in their throats as the world outside blurred into streaks of crimson and shadow. The speed was unlike anything they had ever experienced—no earthly airplane had ever rocketed upward so abruptly, bypassing the slow, grinding acceleration of takeoff, instead ripping through the atmosphere with a force that was both exhilarating and deeply frightening. The glider shot upward, piercing the scarlet sky with a velocity that made their stomachs lurch as if they had been catapulted into the stratosphere. Over 100,000 feet above the planet's surface, the air grew thin and the fiery hues of the horizon deepened into endless shades of crimson and black. Both boys screamed in shock and awe, gripping their seats with white-knuckled hands, as the glider climbed higher and higher into a silent, alien sky.

"WHAT IS HAPPENING?!" Ali shouted, gripping his seat.

Omar had his eyes shut and his heart pounded as they

soared into the sky, the ground dropping away at terrifying speed.

Moments later, the violent ascent eased, and the glider leveled out into a smooth, steady glide. The vast red sky stretched endlessly in every direction, a boundless canvas painted with shades of crimson and burnt orange. Below, the alien landscape faded into a distant mosaic of glowing geysers and jagged mountains, while far off on the horizon, blood-red storm clouds churned ominously, their violent lightning flickering like silent warnings. Slowly, the tension gripping Omar and Ali's chests began to loosen. Their pounding hearts settled into a steadier rhythm, and the tight grip on their seats relaxed as the initial shock of the sudden, impossible speed faded. Breaths, once shallow and quick, deepened, and a calm awe replaced their earlier fear. Omar exchanged a glance with Ali, both silently acknowledging the surreal beauty of the scene around them—a terrifying, breathtaking moment of stillness high above an alien world.

"Alhamdulillah we're not flying into *that*," Omar pointed towards the violent storms in the distance.

Nysha laughed and pulled Luma from her bag. The boys pet the lazy creature, grateful for something soft and non-threatening.

At the front, Pwaa'Shukree Gheltraxxa stood calmly, arms behind his back, his glowing tattoos controlling the ship.

He spoke. "This glider uses T'zahrion Jetwinds—planet-wide currents. We intake the wind from any direction and then expel it at propulsion speeds from the rear or sides. We can travel very fast on this thing!"

The boys' jaws dropped. They must have been flying at an altitude well beyond 120,000 feet.

With a deep rumble, the glider cut across the heavens, heading for the distant land of Tzuraan'dhel-Monkaar.

And in the silence between their excitement and fear, a question lingered in the air:

What awaited them there?

CHAPTER 17
THE JOY OF BURNING FLESH.

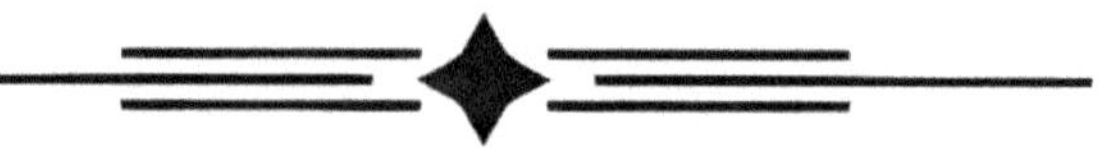

The chamber was always cold. Despite the rivers of molten rock pulsing far below the obsidian floor, despite the boiling geysers that breathed sulfur through the mouths of distant mountains, and despite the constant heat bleeding into the air from the red giant that loomed beyond the jagged skylights above, the Grand Convocation Hall remained unnervingly still. Cold. Quiet. Like a tomb waiting for its next inhabitant.

I sat alone beneath the towering spires of the Hall of Echoes, the vaulted inner sanctum of the Fortress of Echoes. The room was vast—a cathedral to dominion carved into the heart of Mount Khurazh. Its walls were obsidian, etched with glyphs that murmured when no one spoke. Ancient tongues. Forgotten gods. Power bound in stone.

I liked the way the silence coiled around me like a lover.

My fingers brushed over the curved armrest of the throne—not Lord Thaarn's throne, of course. His seat was higher, centered, wreathed in shadow and smoke. Mine stood to the side. Slightly lower. Slightly lesser. But not without its weight. Not without its fire. I sat and thought of the siege of Rhex'Yfalmaaz.

Oh, how they screamed.

The memory spilled into me like wine from a freshly cracked urn. It had been dusk—though on this cursed planet, dusk was merely the deepening red of that ever-watching star.

I'd stood atop a volcanic ridge with the Gozzpru-Null, my personal legion of aerial incineration drones. Thirty thousand obsidian-shell beasts, each the size of a scythe-talon skimmer, hovering with wingless poise. Their underbellies glowed like caged suns, energy cores churning with molten plasma. They weren't just machines. They were symphonies of precision and pain, each programmed to hunt warmth, to seek cries, to feast on motion.

I'd commanded them to descend like the wrath of a forgotten deity. The rebel stronghold below—mere huts and bunkers laced with children and broken soldiers—never stood a chance. Flame cascaded across that valley like a living veil. Buildings melted. Screams were cut short. Men tore their own armor off in a panic to escape the heat chewing through their veins. I watched through visors that translated their agony into soundscapes—*orchestral in their misery*. I closed my eyes to remember the devastation more clearly. Pure bliss.

That was artistry. That was meaning. It was my pleasure.

A hiss like slicing silk tore me from the beautiful memory. One of the side doors opened.

A lesser drone—a floating sentry orb with one glowing blue slit of a lens and spindly shadow limbs—hovered forward. Behind it walked the spy. Thin, tired, wrapped in a border guard's uniform stained with ash from the southern roads. He held something the size of a heartstone in both trembling hands.

"Councilor Drevvos Varn," he said, lowering his head. "I bring urgent intelligence."

I motioned lazily for him to step forward. "Speak."

He placed the orb on the pedestal before me. A flick of my nail activated it. The Cryspectra Node hummed, projecting a blurred field of blue light. Within the swirling haze, a scene emerged: the large southern gate, marked with the iron sigil of Vael'Sythrin Reach. Just beyond the barrier, a sleek desert rover stood idle, its flanks scarred with dust and half-draped in trade banners. Three figures were visible—Xa'rekthul-Yenu-Vaahn unmistakably among them—standing just outside the vehicle in quiet exchange with the border guards. The image sharpened for a brief moment: lean and tattooed, he gestured as if confirming passage, while the other two remained less distinct in the shimmering dusk. Then, they all reentered the rover, and the vehicle surged forward, rolling into the crimson horizon and disappearing past the checkpoint.

"This footage is from two solar cycles ago," the spy whispered, his voice already shaking. "They... they passed through the checkpoint disguised as workers. I only recognized him after comparing to our archived images."

I rose.

"So," I said slowly, each word sharpened, "the traitor escaped his cell in the Depths of Silence, and no one thought to tell me until he wandered free past my borders with companions I do not recognize."

"My Lord, please—I came straight here. I'm simply a messenger. The prison commander claims he—"

"Enough."

I turned to a weapon mounted beside my throne—a Shaal'traven Disruptor Pike, taller than a man, its shaft etched with whorls of null-metal and coiled memory-threads. With a flick of my wrist, it activated. The air shimmered. The spy took a step back.

"Councilor, I did what I was told," he begged. "I was your eyes at the gate, Your Excellency. I came directly—"

I lunged forward. The pike thrummed and shot a bright orb of red light straight into his heart. His chest ruptured in a burst of sizzling energy, his scream cut off before it could even echo. The scent of cooked marrow filled the hall.

Two retrieval orbs drifted down slowly from shadowed alcoves, their tentacle-limbs extending to collect the spasming corpse. With a mechanical chirp, they carried him away to the Lower Pyrelith Vault, where the dead became ash in the incinerator.

I watched them go, then exhaled.

What now?

Xa'rekthul's escape changed everything. Lord Thaarn had planned to burn him publicly—an example to the other tribes and turncoats. Now that symbol had vanished into the wild, and worse, he was not alone. Who were the two with him? Outsiders? Accomplices? Were there more inside the rover? I needed answers.

I moved down the Hall of Echoes, boots clicking softly on onyx tile. The columns loomed like giants, and tall windows of glass revealed the dying light of the red sun casting its glow across the twisted crags of Mount Khurazh. Lava rivers pulsed below like arteries. In the silence of this place, every thought echoed.

Would Thaarn kill me too, when I informed him of the escape? Perhaps. I had delivered bad news before—each time, I survived by burying someone else beneath it. But today, I had no one left to burn.

I turned a corner, my silhouette stretching across the obsidian wall like a specter. The corridor narrowed. At its end stood two massive doors: *The Sanctum of Sovereign Flame*, Thaarn's private chambers.

I paused.

No.

Not yet. Not just yet.

I veered right instead, stalking toward the tower's third spire: the Neural Command Atrium. A domed vault of living systems and ghostlight circuitry, its ceiling shimmered with slow-pulsing nerve-fibers, each strand glowing with a sickly emerald luminescence. Thick comm-vines hung down like a tangle of biomechanical entrails, swaying in response to unspoken queries, their surfaces slick with crystalline nodes that hummed faintly with raw data. The floor was a spongy lattice of synth-root and hardened glass, warm beneath my boots, pulsing in sync with the rhythm of distant command pulses traveling from deep below the fortress.

This was no mere control room—it was a thinking, dreaming appendage of the Fortress, as alert as any sentient sentinel.

In the Atrium's heart rose the Veyl'Shaqr Communicon—a towering, gnarled column of obsidian crystal that spiraled upward like a petrified scream. It pulsed when I approached, responding to the touch of my aura.

"Initiate high-clearance channels. Prison Command. Guard Command. Tactical Overseer Grid."

Streams of static resolved into three hovering visages.

"Explain," I growled. "Explain why Xa'rekthul-Yenu-Vaahn is not in his prison chamber."

The prison commander's hologram blinked in confusion, then realization, then horror.

"Councilor—I—he was there earlier this cycle, I swear—"

"Lies! The footage is verified. He was seen exiting Vael'Sythrin Reach two cycles ago. That means he escaped prison many days before that, because the journey is long from Veltharuun to Vael'Sythrin Reach."

"No one informed me, I—"

"Silence. You will be placed in Concussive Stasis until Thaarn himself decides your fate. Your failure is absolute, and you will not be forgiven."

The man broke, sobbing into the glowing mist.

"Mercy... please... my family—"

"Let them know their bloodline ends with you."

The line went dead.

I issued a series of slicing commands, my voice like fire through snow. Guards, commanders, checkpoints—every contact point was now aflame with fear and warning. Every checkpoint alert. Every spy, every soldier, every commander on the highest alert. Death threats had been issued, and failure would not be accepted.

Then I severed the channels.

The Hall of Echoes waited.

I made my way back, the long corridors swallowing me whole. Red light poured through the tall arches like blood in a chalice. Every step brought me closer to that door, to the throne of the tyrant who ruled above all.

This time, I did not knock.

I stepped into the chamber with the scent of burning still clinging to me.

"My Lord Thaarn," I said, voice smooth as broken glass. "We have a serious complication."

And the shadows stirred.

CHAPTER 18
THE SANCTUM SHATTERED AND THE FEAR THAT FOLLOWED.

The Sanctum of Sovereign Flame shook with the sound of fury. Towering nine feet tall and thick as a siege engine, **Lord Xar'Vulek Thaarn** was a living hurricane of wrath. His black silk cloak snapped behind him like a banner of war as he brought a crystal table crashing into a jagged wall, where it exploded into a blossom of shards. With a roar that made the plasma sconces flicker, he turned and slammed his colossal fist into the curved stone column beside his throne. The impact reverberated like a quake through the chamber. Cracks spiderwebbed outward from the crater his hand had left, distorting the alien glyphs etched into the stone like warped bone.

Thaarn paced the room, his shadow towering and twitching against the windowed walls. The Sanctum itself was immense—an elliptical cathedral of polished black stone and crimson glass, nestled within the hollowed crown of Mount Khurazh. Its ceiling stretched high, nearly lost to darkness, though pale light pulsed from veins of alien circuitry webbed through the rock—silver-blue threads that crawled like insects, flickering with indecipherable data. The western wall was entirely made of transdimensional panes: floor-to-ceiling windows that stared out over a nightmare of jagged black peaks and flowing lava rivers, all dyed crimson by the relentless gaze of the red giant sun that loomed forever in the sky. The light bled in like the memory of a wound.

Councilor Drevvos Varn stood frozen just inside the chamber, each crash from Thaarn's destruction making him flinch like a beaten dog. A floating sculpture of quantum-glass—once a prized artifact gifted by the fallen emperor of Varnyx-Theta—was shattered beneath Thaarn's boot. Carbon-fiber pillars snapped like brittle bones as Thaarn swept his arm across a shelf of scroll-tablets and datacores, sending them crashing to the floor. The councilor dared not speak.

"You dare come to me," Thaarn snarled at last, his voice like iron tearing silk, "with news that the prisoner is gone? That Vaahn—the traitor I was to burn before the eyes of a hundred million—is now free?"

He kicked a chair into the wall. It embedded itself halfway through before dropping to the obsidian tiles with a clang. "Do you know what that means?"

"My Lord..." Varn tried, voice barely more than breath.

"Silence!" Thaarn howled. "This was to be one of the greatest spectacles of my rule—a purge to silence the tribal insurrections, a ritual to unify the fractured governors of Orulenthia through fear—and now? Now I must explain why his bones are not hung from the gates of Veltharuun City!"

Another punch. Another dent. The councilor's knees trembled. He had seen Thaarn eviscerate officers for far less. Drevvos knew this could be his end. But then—as quickly as the fire rose—it abated. Thaarn's fists dropped to his sides. He breathed, deep and animalistic, like a forge cooling after a storm of flame.

The fifth moment passed in eerie stillness. The ruined chamber moaned with settling debris.

Thaarn turned to face Varn fully, his gaze molten. "Speak. And do not waste what mercy remains."

Varn swallowed and stepped forward with a stuttering breath. "My Lord... the escape from imprisonment occurred several solar cycles ago. And then, two solar cycles ago, he passed through the southern border checkpoint of Vael'Sythrin Reach dressed as a simple worker or merchant. Our border sentinel failed to recognize him until it was too late. He had already fled through the border, and only then was he identified."

"Others were with him," Thaarn muttered, his voice low but dangerous. "Strangers. Outsiders?"

Varn nodded quickly. "Unidentified. They wore local garb. I will find out who they are, I swear it. I've already begun implementing countermeasures. Spies are being dispatched. We'll begin with Vael'Sythrin Reach City, of course. I will expand our net to Xon-Rheel Docks, Dalkhorre Plains, and the merchant sectors of Kwezraav-Nulvai."

Thaarn paced in a slow circle, a panther in thought. "Expand the scope. Include the hinterlands. The Myrrhak Dune Groves. The Shattered Ring of Phovakhal. If he vanished beyond our lines, he's either buried in filth or hidden by those who still whisper his name with reverence."

"Yes, my Lord. I will speak with Director Yovarith of the *Eyes Beneath Agency*. He will comb the archives, review all exit points, and track supply chains moving through the south."

Thaarn paused before the largest window. The red sun painted his already monstrous form in a sheen of dread. "And when you find him?"

"I will bring his head to you, my Lord. With or without his body."

Thaarn gave a single, cold nod. "See that you do. Have this mess cleaned before I return. I want no trace of weakness in this sanctum."

The councilor bowed so deeply his shoulder cracked. "At once, Sovereign Flame."

He turned, nearly sprinting from the chamber.

Drevvos Varn's boots clicked furiously across the obsidian floors as he rushed down the corridor toward the Neural Command Atrium. He nearly collided with a maintenance droid and cursed it into submission. When he entered the atrium, his sweat steamed off his scalp in the dry heat.

The chamber was a living core of the fortress—pulsing green neural roots coiled through walls of crystalline conduits, throbbing with data. In its center, the Veyl'Shaqr Communicon glowed like a fossilized tree of alien thought. He slammed his hand onto the interface.

"Priority one link to Commander Varran-Kreith of the Pyrelance Legion," Varn barked.

The face that appeared was all scars and wounds.

"We deploy tonight," Varn ordered. "Sweep all trade caravans along the southern belt. Interrogate merchants. Burn non-compliant outposts. Use tether-drones to scan for encoded trail beacons. If he's anywhere within five leagues of that gate, I want him."

"Understood. I have already started the search since your last call. And what if we find civilians assisting?"

Varn sneered. "Torch them. Let the smell be a warning."

He ended the transmission and called the Eyes Beneath Agency. Director Yovarith's pale, expressionless visage flickered into view.

"Director," Varn hissed. "Begin archival deep-trace on all caravan activity two solar cycles ago. Start from the southern border gate of Vael'Sythrin Reach. I want every route, manifest, and travel signature compared against pre-cleared identities. Hunt for anomalies. Prioritize Vael'Sythrin Reach, but don't stop there. I'm transferring you the archived images of

Xa'rekthul-Yenu-Vaahn and his possible accomplices, as well as the rover they used to cross the border."

"I will begin immediately," the director intoned. "I will update you within two cycles."

"You have one."

Panic spread through the Fortress of Echoes like blood seeping into cloth. Alarms buzzed behind closed doors. Elite squads scrambled across gantries. Informants whispered. Drones hummed overhead. The air was full of tension, of sweat and consequence. One name hung heavy in the halls: **Xa'rekthul-Yenu-Vaahn**. The traitor. The rebel. First Alliance scum and filth.

Everyone feared the wrath that would come if he was not found. And more than Thaarn's fury, they feared becoming the next example.

Councilor Varn returned to his seat in the Hall of Echoes, hunched in the low throne beside the smoking scar where the spy had died just hours before. His fingers trembled. His thoughts whirled.

What if they never found him? What if this escape shattered the illusion of control? What if Thaarn's eyes turned next on him?

He rested his head in his hands and whispered into the silence:

"I am already dead."

CHAPTER 19
HELMETS ON, HEARTS AWAKE.

The Skyraleon-class glider soared like a blade of light through the upper stratosphere of Orulenthia, slicing between curtains of crimson haze and metallic-silver clouds. Inside its sleek, humming interior, silence reigned—broken only by the gentle thrum of unseen engines. Far ahead in the cockpit dome, the pilot—Pwaa'Shukree Gheltraxxa—stood like a statue, his muscled arms calmly clasped behind his back. Bioluminescent tattoos pulsed faintly in geometric patterns across his shoulders and spine, interfacing with the glider's controls through an invisible neural link. The ship responded to his will like an extension of his body and mind.

In the lounge chamber near the rear of the vessel, Omar and Ali sat around a curved obsidian table with Nysha, Ytelthuun, Vaan, and the sleepy creature Luma curled up beside them. Helmets still on—per Nysha's strict request—the boys' faces were partially obscured behind thin, translucent visors.

"Not even our allies should see you just yet," she had said.

The faint filters in the helmets made their voices sound slightly distant, dreamlike. Still, the mood inside was intensely focused.

The object of their attention lay in the center of the table: the **Kha'Len** artifact. A triangular talisman, forged from iridescent metal and ruby crystal, it shimmered faintly under the glider's ambient lights. Lines of inscription crawled along its sides and back, swirling in curves and sharp angles, vanishing and reappearing like ink sinking into water. Omar gently rotated it, watching how the red jewel in the center caught the light and refracted it into patterns that seemed almost alive.

"It's more than just old," Ytelthuun murmured, his elongated fingers tracing the glyphs. "There are layers of meaning here. Some of these lines read like poetry. Others... like directives. Instructions, perhaps."

He narrowed his eyes.

"Look here. This one says: *'Voraal Zenthir Kael is the rightful keeper. Let this be returned to the Vault of Elders in the sanctuary of Tzuraan'dhel-Monkaar.'*"

Nysha leaned in closer.

"That's where we're headed. *Tzuraan'dhel-Monkaar.* Maybe this 'Vault of Elders' is the destination this talisman was always meant to reach."

"And here," Ytelthuun said, pointing again. "*Return to previous location. Select random destination. Choose destination.* They're etched like menu options—mechanisms for control."

Nysha's brow furrowed.

"So this thing might not just open portals... It might let you steer them. But how does it operate?"

A soft hum rose from the talisman as they examined it, almost like a sleeping creature reacting to their interest. Then Vaan read aloud from another section, his voice tentative:

"When redlight fades to hearth-born flame / and crystal drinks the blaze again / the way shall open to names unknown / where stars remember and stones have flown."

They were silent.

"That... sounds like a poem," Ali said slowly. "But I have no idea what it means."

"It refers to light," Nysha said. "And the ruby crystal. But it's phrased in an ancient dialect—designed to obscure meaning unless you already know what you're looking for. I'm not really sure."

Omar leaned forward.

"Do you think it's hinting at something with light? Like... maybe the red gem needs to react to something?"

His voice faltered, uncertain. The others glanced at each other, clearly just as lost. The cryptic message remained stubbornly unreadable, and the artifact's secrets still cloaked in confusion.

"Possibly," said Ytelthuun, thoughtful. "But what kind of light? From what source? And how do we avoid triggering something dangerous?"

They went quiet again, pondering the artifact and swapping possibilities. Hypotheses rose and fell like waves. Still, no one dared to tamper recklessly with the relic. There was too much they didn't know.

Eventually, the boys' attention drifted to the curved window panels lining the ship's starboard side. Omar rose first, stepping close, and Ali followed. Their jaws dropped.

Outside, the skies were alive with terrifying beauty. Silver-rimmed clouds stretched like serpents across a blood-red sky, flickering with immense, slow-motion lightning that crackled in branching veins miles long. The lightning didn't flash—it moved, glowing steadily, like liquid electricity poured across the heavens. The spectacle made Earth's storms feel like candle flickers.

The red giant sun loomed larger now, a searing disk of molten amber suspended beyond the stormline. Its massive, swirling corona cast haunting shadows across the high-altitude cloud sea. Floating between these storms were city-mountains—levitating pyramidal peaks suspended impossibly in midair by ancient tech or unknown physics. Each bore terraces and glowing structures, their edges limned with golden lights like distant temples.

"SubhanAllah," Omar breathed.

"Yeah…" Ali murmured. "It's like seeing… floating countries. Are those cities? On mountains?"

"Looks like it," Omar said. "Maybe even civilizations. Look at the towers… the bridges… the lights. There's people living up there."

Suddenly, a chirping alert snatched away the boys' attention for a few seconds. It sounded almost like an incoming phone call from the console where Captain Pwaa'Shukree Gheltraxxa stood. The pilot looked at the blinking console and, between the chirping sounds, connected with the transmission privately.

The boys turned back to the fantastic view outside the window. And then, farther in the sky, they saw it: the other planet. Vast and ringed like Saturn, it hovered with impossible grace on the horizon, now clearer than ever. Its gaseous swirls glinted in hues of green and silver. The rings wrapped around its girth like glittering trails, catching the sun's fire.

Ali put a hand on his brother's shoulder.

"That's the most beautiful thing I've ever seen."

"Same," Omar whispered. "It makes me feel tiny… but also lucky. Alhamdulillah."

Ali nodded, his eyes still locked on the cosmic marvel.

"Remember our trip to Turkey?"

Omar chuckled.

"Istanbul. Galata Tower. That hotel we stayed in near Karaköy? With the cat that always slept by the lobby door?"

"Bro!" Ali grinned. "And we ate like fifty doner kebabs. With that salty cold ayran?"

"Uff, I still dream about that."

"And remember Adana?" Ali added. "Man, that city lives for its kebabs. We sat in that open-air restaurant with the sizzling grills and smoke in the air. They brought out like a mountain of meat. Uff, what a treat!"

"My mouth's watering just thinking about it," Omar laughed. "Those Adana kebabs were next-level, dude! May Allah bless those chefs."

Ali leaned his head back.

"Alhamdulillah, we've been so lucky. Mom and Dad took us everywhere. America, Morocco, Türkiye, Japan, England, France, Dubai. Now, even this place..."

"MashAllah," Omar added. "Even here, on Orulenthia, in this crazy sky... it's still something to be grateful for. Even though it's incredibly scary!"

Ali looked at him, eyes full of warmth.

"Inshallah, we'll get back. Allah is the best of planners. Don't forget those words."

The brothers fell into a peaceful silence, side by side in wonder.

Then, suddenly—the soft patter of paws.

Luma, the cuddly and furry creature, came scampering toward them. With a yawning squeak, it hopped right into Ali's lap and curled up into a warm, vibrating ball. The boys laughed quietly, petting its fluffy head.

They walked back toward the cushioned walls, still in their helmets, next to Nysha, who had already closed her eyes, her body slowly rising and falling with sleep. Ytelthuun and Vaan had also slumped into stillness, their breathing deep and steady.

Ali was the last to drift off. His eyelids sagged, thoughts swirling. But as sleep pulled him under, he glimpsed movement—Pwaa'Shukree Gheltraxxa, the silent pilot, stepping away from the front of the glider. The alien's broad silhouette moved quietly toward the sleeping passengers.

Ali blinked once as the pilot approached.
Then again. The silhouette was even closer.
And then... darkness. Sleep.

CHAPTER 20
SKIMMER GHOSTS AND GLIDER LIES.

Beneath the cold spires of Veltharuun, buried within a monolithic complex called the Citadel of Precision, the nerve center of the Eyes Beneath Agency hummed with unseen activity. It was here, in the Sanctum of Strategic Whisperflow and Clandestine Analytics, that Director Yovarith labored without pause. His face—ashen, lean, unnervingly still—reflected no signs of fatigue, though he had not consumed food or water in over thirty hours. Neither sleep nor slouch had dared touch him. His movements, exacting and silent, resembled that of an automaton sculpted for surveillance—an instrument honed by necessity and bound by terror to serve one master above all: Lord Thaarn.
Failure, for Yovarith, was not an option. It was a myth he refused to acknowledge.

His long, skinny-fingered hands danced across a curved obsidian console, its surface pulsing with soft teal lights that shifted beneath his touch like liquid intelligence. That morning, he had spoken with his agents at the Arux'Tel cargobay—an enormous seaport—then later with field handlers in the storm-buried ruins of Merikhaal Null, and briefly with an operative embedded within the mind-market auctions of Orokhel Synne. Through each encrypted holo-call, he dispensed orders and received slivers of intel, each piece slotted perfectly into a growing latticework of speculation.

But one thread obsessed him more than any other: the last known movements of Xa'rekthul-Yenu-Vaahn. That aberration, that volatile memory from the past, had reemerged in the city of Vael'Sythrin Reach. Drevvos Varn had sent him visual footage—Xa'rekthul-Yenu-Vaahn, cloaked, fleeing through the Southern Border Gate alongside others, boarding a weathered, copper-hulled rover with a low-hovering chassis. Yovarith knew without doubt: the rover was the key.

He summoned his regional team stationed deep in the outskirts of Vael'Sythrin Reach—Unit Dryryaal-Seven, specialists in ground-level urban pursuit and drone augmentation. Their feed flickered to life on the panoramic panel at the edge of his chamber. A cluster of shadow-draped figures responded, voices low and crackling.

"You've deployed the Qen'tari Seekers?" Yovarith asked. These were no ordinary spy drones; the Qen'tari Seekers were orb-like constructs with scanning veils that fluttered like gossamer wings, their obsidian cores embedded with auric trace-matrixes designed to detect low-gravity disturbances in hovercraft paths, even hours after departure.

"Yes, Director," came the reply from a gruff agent called Rulth Varaz. "We've released four units into the sub-ravine routes south of the gate. Their scanners have picked up a fluctuating ion wake—possibly a masking signature. It matches the trail of the skimmer you described."

Yovarith's voice was calm, deliberate. "Continue trailing it. Split into silent cover pairs. Do not engage. I want location confirmation, not bloodshed—yet."

"Understood."
"Report again within two cycles."

With a gesture, Yovarith terminated the call and leaned back in his chair for the first time in hours. Slowly, he rose. The long folds of his translucent black robe whispered as he walked, departing the sanctum through a silent, sliding archway. He entered the adjoining quarters—his Recalibration Cell. Sparse, lit by a singular beam of green luminescence from a sunwell tube in the ceiling, the room held only a long obsidian sideboard and a recliner shaped like a twisted spine.

From the sideboard, he retrieved a small black dish and picked up a fruit—a smooth, scale-skinned orb called a keluunisz. Its scent, musky and spicy, stung his senses awake. He sat down and began to peel it with long, precise fingers. Beneath the skin lay a vibrant, gel-like pulp that shimmered with threads of pale blue. He chewed in silence, letting the tart, effervescent tang tickle his throat. Still, his mind roamed.

Who else could hold clues? What weak link had been overlooked? Even while chewing, even as he sank into the recliner and let his eyelids close for a precious few minutes, the mental engine inside him churned.

But peace was a stranger, and it did not stay long.

A sharp three-tone chime burst from the room's audio lattice: the wall-mounted, wave-respondent channeler had been activated. It was no common communicator; it responded only to signals coded with director-level clearance.

He sat up immediately.

"Director," a female voice crackled through. "This is Agent Virell-Qaa at Watchpost Three. I have something you'll want to see."

He was already halfway back to the Sanctum before she finished speaking. The channel reconnected in his chamber as Virell's face, sharp-eyed and windblown, appeared.

"We were sifting Liftport activity logs across the Southern Quadrant, per your standing directives. We found an incident report—small complaint from a hinterland technician."

Yovarith stared, unmoving. "Explain."

"The technician logged an obstruction report," she continued, tapping a datapanel beside her. "Someone parked an unauthorized skimmer outside warehouse control station Kilo-7-Delta. The complaint states that the skimmer blocked access to the heatflux conduit relays and the pressure gauge manifolds. Basic stuff—but the skimmer matches your description. Rust-cast hull, angular driftwing supports, forward thrust ports embedded low on the stern. No registration beacon."

Yovarith's lips pulled into something that might, by some definitions, be called a smile.

"Where?"

"Liftport 1122-XAV, eastern fringe of the Sandgrove Belt."

"Deploy our assets. I want full access to their outbound flight records. Now."

"Already done, sir. Three embedded operatives are on comms."

"Connect them."

The screen split into three, revealing the weathered faces of Agents Korin, Thael, and Jassiva—all Liftport staffers under deep cover.

"You are to search for unregistered or irregular launch data from Liftport 1122-XAV within the past three cycles. I need anything anomalous. Begin."

A minute of silence passed as fingers danced across consoles and holo-grids flickered to life. Alien characters scrolled in rapid columns.

Suddenly, Korin spoke.
"There is one anomaly, sir."

"Report." Yovarith leaned forward.

"Captain Pwaa'Shukree Gheltraxxa," Korin said. "He took off twelve hours ago. Manifested no passengers. No cargo. But he launched in a full Skyraleon-class glider. We triple-checked. That ship could carry a hundred thousand tons or four thousand passengers. Yet... nothing logged."

Yovarith stood up with an intensity that vibrated through the walls. "There. That's them!"

"Shall I initiate contact, Director?"

"Immediately. Threaten the pilot if you must!"

Moments later, Agent Korin's voice boomed through the secured frequency, directed at the glider's encrypted signal relay.

"Captain Pwaa'Shukree Gheltraxxa. My name is Agent Korin of the Eyes Beneath Agency. By order of Lord Thaarn, you are ordered to respond. We know you have fugitives aboard. This is your final chance. Your silence is betrayal. If you do not respond or comply, your family—wife, children, kin—will be taken. They will be made examples. First imprisoned, then broken, then displayed before the city and decapitated in front of screaming crowds.

You will not only die. You will watch them die in your mind until your last breath.

Unless... you comply. Immobilize the passengers. Detain them. Kill Xa'rekthul-Yenu-Vaahn if you must. Bring us his body. And you will be forgiven. Rewarded. Elevated.

Your failure means the death of your family.

This is not a threat... This is a guarantee."

The line clicked off. Silence.

Agent Korin's image disappeared.

Director Yovarith stood frozen for a moment, a hand hovering above his private signal line to Councilor Drevvos. His finger nearly tapped it—then withdrew.

No. Not yet.

Yovarith almost called the Councilor to give him great news. But he would deliver results, not theories.

Only certainty could shield him from the wrath of Veltharuun's true master.

The room dimmed slightly as he turned away, mind already racing.

What if the pilot didn't comply?

Then... alternate contingencies would need to be activated. He would prepare them all. Now was the time for action.

CHAPTER 21
BETRAYER IN THE SHADOWS OF THAARN.

Nysha's eyes snapped open. Something was wrong. Her breath caught as she blinked in the dim ambient glow of the glider's internal lights. A sharp noise. A struggle. Then she saw it—Captain Pwaa'Shukree Gheltraxxa, the pilot, crouched behind Xa'rekthul-Yenu-Vaahn, a wire pulled tight around Vaan's neck. Vaan thrashed wildly, his legs kicking against the metallic floor, his hands clawing uselessly at the garrote biting into his flesh.

"GET OFF HIM!" Nysha screamed, her voice piercing the air like a blade.

She launched herself forward, fists flying. Her knuckles cracked against the captain's cheekbone, then his ribs. Blood sprayed. The pilot grunted, trying to maintain pressure on the wire, but Nysha's onslaught was relentless. The commotion woke everyone—Ytelthuun leapt up with a gasp, Omar and Ali stumbled to their feet, blinking through the chaos. Ytelthuun surged forward and grabbed the pilot's shoulders, prying him back just as Vaan collapsed to his knees, gagging, coughing, and retching on the glider's floor.

"Hold him!" Nysha yelled as she wrestled with the flailing captain. Ytelthuun seized the assassin's arms. Omar and Ali rushed over, still dazed, and joined the struggle, throwing punches under Nysha's direction. The captain growled, twisting, but couldn't free himself. Ytelthuun, eyes burning with fury, grabbed a metal plate from the nearby table and slammed it against the captain's head. He collapsed, unconscious.

Over an hour dragged on in suffocating silence, the Skyraleon-class glider drifting on auto-pilot like a ghost through the sky, save for the low, almost haunting hum of its engines. The stale air inside felt thick with tension and dread. The captain lay slumped, now forced upright and tightly bound with heavy, unforgiving cables pulled from a grim auxiliary storage panel. His head lolled dangerously for a moment, weighed down by exhaustion and defeat, before a sudden spark of fury ignited within him. He snapped to consciousness with a guttural roar that shattered the stillness—"LET ME GO!" he howled, black eyes blazing with wild desperation and rage, his entire body trembling and straining violently against the restraints that held him captive.

Nysha was on him in seconds. "Why did you try to kill Xa'rekthul-Yenu-Vaahn? WHO sent you?" she shouted. He sneered, silent. She smashed her fist into his face. Blood gushed from his mouth.

"I said—WHO SENT YOU?" she repeated.

Again, silence.

Another brutal punch. More blood. A tooth hit the floor.

"ANSWER ME!"

The pilot glared at her with bloodshot, swollen eyes, defiant.

Ytelthuun stepped forward, placing a hand on Nysha's shoulder. "Let me try."

She stepped aside. Ytelthuun knelt, seized the captain's finger, and snapped it backward with a sickening crunch.

The pilot screamed in agony, eyes rolling. "HWWAAAAAA!!! WAAAA!! Alright! ALRIGHT, I'LL TALK!"

Still writhing, he gasped, "I got a message. From Lord Xar'Vulek Thaarn's agents. They said they'd kill my family if I didn't... eliminate Xa'rekthul-Yenu-Vaahn and whoever was with him. Said they'd find my family, decapitate them, make an example out of them. I wasn't ready... I didn't know what to do. I thought... while you all slept, I could do it fast. I'm sorry! I was trying to protect my family! I was forced into this!"

Tears mixed with blood. His face was a mess of bruises, cuts, and snot. He looked broken.

Nysha punched him again, not as hard. "You betrayed us. You betrayed me! You were my friend! How could you?!"

"I had no choice," he sobbed. "I'm sorry. Nysha, I'm sorry! I didn't want to... please believe me. It was for my family. Please—just tell Xa'rekthul-Yenu-Vaahn... I'm sorry."

She grabbed his chin, forcing his eyes up. "Apologize to him. Apologize yourself"

"Please," the captain cried, turning his battered face towards Vaan. "I'm sorry! I didn't want to! They threatened my wife, my children, my family! I didn't know what to do. I'm sorry. Please forgive me. This was never planned. Please!"

Nysha's voice was colder. "You could've told me. We could've found a way. Instead, you chose betrayal. You'll stay tied. But... answer our questions, and maybe—just maybe—I'll help your family."

Ytelthuun stepped forward. "First—are we still heading to Tzuraan'dhel-Monkaar?"

The captain nodded, wiping his nose with his shoulder. "Yes... auto-pilot engaged. We're not far. I kept us fast, nonstop. We should be over the continent very soon if not already."

They moved to the pilot's control console. The curved interface shimmered with alien glyphs, reacting subtly to motion. The telekinetic controls pulsed faintly, but the auto-pilot was active and correct.

The five huddled, speaking in hushed tones.

"We can't let him go," Nysha whispered.

"But we need him," Ytelthuun replied.

Omar's voice cracked. "Does... does Thaarn know about us? About me and Ali?"

"We don't know for sure. I doubt it," Nysha said. "But he knows about Vaan. That's clear. Vaan is the probable target."

"What do we do with the pilot?" Ali asked. "He could still betray us again. I mean, his family is in danger."

Ytelthuun stared at him. "Let her handle this."

They returned to the back. The pilot was still crying. "Please... just warn them. Please! My family! If Thaarn sends someone— It will be all over. Please just help my family."

Ytelthuun stepped forward. "We'll try. Where are they?"

"Dhaelorun Viis," the captain said quickly. "My brother—he works at the Garazhul Spire, the city's air-control nexus. Call there. Tell him—tell him to get my wife and kids, and our mother, and run. Please. I'll do whatever you want."

Ytelthuun nodded slowly, activating the communication equipment at the pilot's console. Nysha untied the pilot, who winced but stayed still. She stepped back.

"Go," Ytelthuun ordered, pointing to the control console. "Call your brother and save your family."

The captain stumbled forward, blood dripping from his mouth, and took the communicator in his hand. His voice cracked through sobs. "Ghurak... it's me. Don't ask. Just listen. Take Irah'Flo-Tepp, the children, and Mother—go now. Leave Dhaelorun Viis. Don't pack. Just go. Anywhere far. Please. They're coming. It's real. Go! Go NOW!"

The transmission ended. He turned to them, straighter now but still weeping. "Okay. I'll help. I swear it. But Thaarn's forces will call again soon. I don't know how much time we have. I doubt they will give up so easily."

Fear returned. No one knew what to do.

"We can't stay on this glider," Nysha said. "He was ordered to kill us. They probably tracked the glider's signature and know its location."

The captain raised his trembling hand, still stained with blood and grime, and spoke in a low, hoarse voice that carried the weight of desperation. "There's... there's a solution," he began, his eyes flickering with urgency as they swept across the frightened group. "Cargo pods. Massive ones. Military-grade. Designed for high-altitude, high-speed sky-drop deployments into hostile territory. Each is shock-resistant, insulated against extreme temperatures, and equipped with automatic stabilization systems and pre-packaged food. They were built for warzones—tested to survive orbital falls without killing what's inside. One of them... could easily hold all six of us. That is the only chance."

He paused, inhaling shakily. "It won't be pleasant. It'll be tight and violent. But it'll keep us alive. I'll set the trajectory, calibrate the descent, and launch it with everyone inside. No signal trace. No heat trail. You should be undetected."

The captain looked around the cabin as if memorizing it for the last time. His eyes met Nysha's for a long, aching moment—then drifted to Vaan, shadowed with remorse. "I'll do it now," he whispered, turning away with a heavy breath, and began entering the emergency override sequence with trembling hands.

They ran, following him. The pod bay was massive. Huge metallic crates lined the walls, each the size of a truck, glowing faint blue from stabilization fields. The captain took a few minutes and quickly explained the controls to Nysha and the others—release clamps, target input, rear hatch launch protocol.

"I'll program it for the Yhraan Valley just outside the Tzuraan'dhel-Monkaar perimeter," he said. "It'll drop us there without detection." He clicked some buttons; lights activated and the pod beeped. "There! It's done."

Everyone walked back to the front of the craft by the controls. The captain wiped his mouth and activated his communicator. "I'm contacting Agent Korin of the Eyes Beneath... I'll tell him I succeeded in terminating all of you. Then we can leave in the pod."

But just before he could finish speaking, a massive boom rocked the glider. Alarms blared. The vessel shook violently. Everyone lost their balance instantly and fell over.

"INCOMING!" Nysha screamed.

The Sky Reavers of Thaarn had found them.

Another missile hit. The nose dipped. The glider went into a sickening dive. Everyone was thrown to the ground.

"GO! GO! INTO THE POD!" the captain yelled. He shoved himself upright, tattoos blazing, connecting to the controls via telekinesis.

"I'll crash this ship into the mountains. They'll think you're dead! Move! Now! Let me do this for you."

"Just come to the pods with us!" Nysha yelled.

"Just go! I need to fly closer to the pod's target location—otherwise nobody will survive! Now go!!" the pilot yelled.

Vaan lunged and snatched the boys, his arms locking around their shoulders like iron. Nysha and Ytelthuun yanked them to their feet as the glider convulsed underfoot, groaning like a dying beast. The deck split in places, spitting sparks and fire as the vessel shuddered violently. Wind howled through the ruptured air ducts, slicing past them with razor force. Ceiling panels blew apart, slamming against walls or spiraling through the cabin like shrapnel. A deafening explosion erupted from the rear—flames roared out of the engine room, hot enough to blister skin at a distance. Pipes burst overhead, releasing clouds of steam, and the scent of scorched circuitry and melting alloy filled their nostrils. The entire structure tilted at a brutal angle. Alarms shrieked. Gravity dragged them sideways. They didn't stop running.

The pod bay doors were ahead. Debris flew everywhere. Omar tripped. Ali caught him. They dove into the cargo pod. Ytelthuun and Vaan were already inside. Nysha sealed the doors behind them.

The glider's back hatch opened—and the pod was shot out with a roar so intense it knocked everyone over.

They were falling. Fast.

Screaming. Holding on to handles for their dear lives.

The world became a dizzying blur, a chaotic whirl of colors and shapes that smashed against their panicked minds. Gravity crushed their ribs with merciless force, making every breath a desperate struggle, their chests aching as if a giant's fist squeezed relentlessly. Their ears popped violently, the sudden pressure causing sharp, piercing pain. The pod hurtled through layers of the atmosphere at terrifying speed, spinning wildly at first—an uncontrollable tumble that sent their stomachs lurching—before it finally twisted into a steadier spin. Panic clawed at their throats as the deafening roar of rushing air filled their ears, drowning out every thought except primal fear. Then, with a brutal, earth-shaking impact that jarred every bone and muscle, they crashed hard into the alien ground, the violent collision sending shockwaves through their battered bodies.

All went still.

Silence.

Ytelthuun moved first, shaking Omar and Ali. "You alright?"

Groans. "Yeah... I think so," Omar whispered, lifting open his helmet visor.

Everyone slowly got up. Battered. Alive.

Ali had a bad bruise on his arm, but they were all intact.

Ytelthuun triggered the pod door. It hissed and slid open.

They stepped into a red forest.

The forest was alien, a graveyard of tall trees—towering trunks blackened like charred bone, gnarled and crooked, each one twisted as if screaming toward the blood-red sky. No leaves hung from the branches, only brittle spines that jutted out like claws, rattling softly in the dry breeze. The ground was a thick carpet of crimson ash, cracked and shifting beneath their feet with every cautious step. In the heavens above, the red giant sun loomed like a monstrous eye, glaring down with oppressive heat, casting warped shadows that writhed across the scarlet terrain like phantoms.

Suddenly, far in the distance, a mountain erupted in a deafening explosion. A column of fire and black smoke speared into the sky, visible even from miles away. The boom arrived seconds later, rumbling through the valley like the roar of some ancient god. Nysha's eyes widened. "That... that was the glider," she whispered, her voice shaking. "He crashed it into the mountain. The captain... he did it. He stayed behind to make sure they thought we died. He could've come with us—but he chose to burn with the ship to protect us. I didn't like what he did to hurt Vaan, but... he gave up his life so we could keep ours."

None spoke. Horror twisted in their hearts. Pwaa'Shukree Gheltraxxa was very surely dead. The explosion tore the sky.

"Inna lillahi wa inna ilayhi raji'un," said Omar in Arabic. "Indeed, to Allah we belong, and to Him we shall return," he translated for the others.

They were all shaken and shocked. But safe—for now.

The boys whispered a quiet *Alhamdulillah*, thankful for still being alive.

But what awaited them next?

The silence had no answer. There were only questions. Questions that went around in circles with no answers. Horror crept under their skin as they continued watching the exploding aircraft against the huge mountainside.

CHAPTER 22
THE SOVEREIGN WHO SMILES AT FEAR.

They gathered in the Sanctum of Sovereign Flame, but to Lord Xar'Vulek Thaarn, it was a den of stammering fools and quivering cowards. The obsidian chamber—lit mostly by veins of molten fire running beneath the translucent floor—throbbed with oppressive heat and quiet menace. Thaarn sat upon his crescent-shaped throne, carved from a single slab of emberstone, silent, unmoving, regal. But behind his burning crimson eyes, rage coiled like a serpent.

He listened to their meaningless words, their shallow plots, their self-important theories about Xa'rekthul-Yenu-Vaahn, and imagined, with vivid pleasure, slicing their throats one by one while they begged for mercy they did not deserve. Especially Drevvos Varn, his once-esteemed Councilor, now steadily decaying into utter mediocrity.

Varn stood closest, gesturing with eager precision as if proximity might earn him redemption. The others—military attachés, spylords, the head of planetary logistics—spoke in turns, offering pathetic little stratagems as if they possessed vision. But Thaarn trusted none. Not one. To him, they were all liars—rats in cloaks, smiling only to hide the knives behind their backs.

He toyed with the idea of ordering all their executions in that moment—not as a warning, but as entertainment. Only the thought of wasting good blood on such insects restrained him.

They were deep in discussion about Xa'rekthul-Yenu-Vaahn: what to do when the traitor was found, how to break him in public, how to turn his fall into a spectacle that would choke the resistance's morale. Thaarn raised a single finger. The room froze.

His voice was a blade drawn in silence.

"If he is not found soon, each of you will be torn limb from limb, your screams echoing through the citadel plaza as children watch your entrails spill. That is my mercy. Test me, and learn the alternative."

Faces blanched. Sweat rolled. No one met his eyes. Their fear was delicious.

He did not smile—but inside, the Sovereign Flame smoldered in dark delight.

A sudden beep broke the tension. A hologram shimmered into existence above the center of the table. The transmission bore the seal of the *Eyes Beneath Agency*.

"Director Yovarith," Varn muttered, tapping commands into the control rune.

The hologram resolved into a pale, thin figure cloaked in shadow, his voice smooth but urgent.

"My lord. We good bring news. You will be pleased, my liege!"

Thaarn tilted his head, watching. "Speak."

Yovarith gave a curt nod. "Our Sky Reaver squadron tracked and struck the Skyraleon-class glider believed to be carrying Xa'rekthul-Yenu-Vaahn. The target was destroyed near the outer mountain ranges beyond the Tzuraan'dhel-Monkaar borderlands. We have recorded video footage."

"Show it," Thaarn commanded.

The chamber dimmed as the video began to play. A grainy camera angle from a Reaver drone showed the sleek, alien glider soaring across jagged peaks. Then, with blinding force, two missiles struck it mid-flight. The ship exploded in a thunderous bloom of fire and ash, pieces of its hull cartwheeling into the distant cliff faces. The mountains shook. Black smoke rose into the blood-colored sky.

Cheers erupted around the chamber. Varn clapped. So did the others. Fools. Blind fools.

But Thaarn said nothing, simply watching with eyes that missed nothing.

The others celebrated what they believed was the death of Xa'rekthul-Yenu-Vaahn. But Lord Thaarn… questioned.

As the footage ended and the hologram faded, Thaarn's thoughts turned inward once again.

Why had the glider been so far from expected paths? Tzuraan'dhel-Monkaar was remote, underdeveloped, largely unmonitored. Why go there? If Xa'rekthul-Yenu-Vaahn had intended to disappear, he could've chosen a hundred other cities—less guarded, less wild.

The journey to that region was long, perilous, and seemingly purposeless.

He narrowed his eyes.

"Director," Thaarn said slowly. "Is it possible they survived?"

Director Yovarith's tone hardened. "My lord, the detonation was immense. The glider was vaporized. No living being could have endured it. I believe it's impossible."

Varn exhaled in obvious relief. "Then we've won. The traitor is gone."

Thaarn said nothing, only stared. He watched the sweat bead at Varn's temples. The subtle shudder in the Councilor's hand as he wiped it away. So fragile. So weak. Thaarn's disappointment twisted into something colder.

"Acceptable," he finally said. "Leave me."

They bowed and obeyed, backs stiff, eager to escape. The towering ironwood doors of the Sanctum groaned closed behind them. Thaarn remained still for a long time.

Even in the silence, his mind boiled. The glider's presence near Tzuraan'dhel-Monkaar still clawed at his logic. Was it coincidence? Or misdirection?

Had Xa'rekthul-Yenu-Vaahn truly died in the fire? Or had his cursed cunning paved a path out before the flames took hold? Thaarn had lived too long and seen too many lies to believe in neat conclusions.

A low whistle escaped his lips, sharp and commanding.

From the shadowed rear alcove of the Sanctum, a beast emerged.

It padded forward on clawed feet the size of dinner plates. Its fur was thick, black as pitch, almost metallic in sheen. Its face was angular, lizard-like, with glistening eyes of glowing orange. A snake-like tongue flicked from between rows of jagged teeth, tasting the scorched air.
The creature's long tail, barbed at the end and slick with venom, swayed like a pendulum of death. This was Vorrak, Thaarn's pet—and perhaps the only thing in the universe that he loved. An creature as deadly as Thaarn himself.

The beast growled softly and rubbed its head against his thigh. Anyone else would have been torn apart in seconds. But not Thaarn. He stroked the creature's neck with one gauntleted hand, admiring the way its muscles rippled beneath the fur. Vorrak purred—a guttural, monstrous sound—and curled at his master's feet, nuzzling closer.

"You understand, don't you?" Thaarn whispered. "They lie. All of them. But you... you never lie. You hate them like I do."

Time passed in slow stillness. The rage ebbed, a tide pulled back by a moon of venom and silence.
Thaarn sat with Vorrak curled against him, the beast's warmth grounding him like nothing else ever could.

Finally, he reached for his communicator and called the Councilor.

The line clicked. "M-My Lord?" Varn stammered.
Thaarn leaned back, smiling for the first time that day.
"You came very close to death, Drevvos. Very, very close. Do

you know how easy it would have been to kill you?"
Silence.
"I could have let Vorrak rip your spine out while your men watched. But... I didn't. I hope, for your sake, that you and your agencies have completed the job."
Varn's voice trembled. "Th-thank you, my Lord. I am... forever in your debt. I'm very happy my team eliminated the traitor. I can assure you the job is done, sire."
Thaarn closed his eyes, savoring the fear. "Good. Hold on to that feeling. Sleep with it. Let it remind you who keeps you alive."

He ended the call.

Vorrak stirred and hissed softly, content.

Thaarn reclined deeper into his throne, the heat of the Sanctum enveloping him like a womb of fire and blood.
For the first time in days... he smiled.
Sleep came easy that night.

CHAPTER 23
FOLLOWING THE PRONG OF FATE.

A smoky twilight lingered above the forest, its crimson sky dimming beneath the reach of gnarled, towering trees whose limbs creaked and twisted with unnatural grace. Their branches moved slowly, sensuously—not with the sway of wind, but as though testing the air for scent or sound. The blackened bark of their trunks was covered in vein-like grooves that pulsed faintly with silver-blue light. Omar, Ali, Nysha, Vaan, and Ytelthuun had taken refuge inside the compact escape pod that had crash-landed hours earlier, now nestled between the sprawling roots of these whispering giants.

Inside the pod, its curved walls shimmered faintly with internal lights. Compact supply cabinets had been unlatched, revealing nutritional rations, collapsible tools like mini-hammers and knives, beacons, and a medical field kit. Several torches had been found, and one now sat between Omar and Vaan, casting a flickering glow on the exhausted faces around it. Nysha leaned back against the wall, arms wrapped tightly around her knees, her mind weighed down with grief for the heroic pilot who had sacrificed his life for their escape. The small furry creature, Luma, had emerged from Ali's backpack—where the triangular talisman was still safely hidden—and had curled up against the boy's chest. Nysha smiled gently as she saw Ali and Omar resting close together, Luma nestled between them, their breathing finally slowing into the rhythm of sleep.

"Sleep well, little warriors," she whispered.

Ytelthuun, ever vigilant, had volunteered to keep guard, his sidearm in hand and his angular eyes never leaving the shifting shadows beyond the pod's door.

A silence fell across the clearing beyond the pod, but inside, sleep brought no peace—especially not to the boys. In their dreams, Omar and Ali were being called. Their bodies rested, but their minds were pulled into currents far older and deeper than they could comprehend. The air inside the pod felt thick with something unseen, as though the talisman itself were breathing in rhythm with their dreams, ushering them into realms that defied the waking world.

"Omar. Ali."

The voice echoed—not as a sound, but as a presence that filled their minds. The boys floated together in a world unlike any they had seen—an unspace of glistening prisms and skyless vaults. Below them, molten rivers flowed in labyrinthine coils, casting a burning orange light that refracted across their suspended bodies. The triangular talisman hovered before them, its red crystal pulsating with blinding intensity.

They turned to one another but could not speak—only feel. They floated and hovered. Then came the riddles.

"When the road forks like the tongue of a serpent, follow the tooth that bites the deepest."

It meant little to them in the moment, spoken in tones that vibrated the very marrow of their bones. The voice sent chills down their spines, yet at the same time, they were at peace.

"Let those who carry stars upon their wings lift you through the breathless pass."

The vision began to blur. The crystal dimmed. Lava bled into sky. Prisms shattered. And they fell upward, pulled into darkness and void.

Omar gasped awake, heart hammering. Ali stirred a second later, sitting up so quickly that Luma leapt from his lap. Their eyes met, wide and knowing.

"You—" Omar began.

"You had it too?" Ali interrupted.

They whispered together, recounting every word, every image, every fire-lit sky and fractured realm. Nysha, rubbing sleep from her eyes, listened in awe. Vaan sat up, expression unreadable, while Ytelthuun slowly stepped back into the pod.

"This isn't the first time," Omar said, his voice low and thoughtful. "Back in Morocco... the night we visited that strange shop in Tangier and saw the artifact for the first time, we had a dream—just like this. We were in some weird place full of colors that didn't make sense, and there was this... pressure in the air, like something trying to speak without words."

Ali nodded slowly, eyes wide with memory. "It felt like our bones were vibrating, like the message wasn't just in our heads—it was in our bodies. The talisman—it was glowing even though we weren't touching it. Just being near it was enough."

Omar leaned forward, the torchlight catching the sharp angles of his face. "It's doing something to us—or through us. Like... it's tuning us to a frequency we weren't meant to hear before. Like it's more than just a relic—it's a transmitter. A beacon. And every time we sleep, we tune in deeper. Maybe? I dunno."

"Or... someone through it is trying to reach you," Ytelthuun said slowly, voice laced with wonder and caution. "Such connections aren't unheard of—though rare. The talisman could be a channel—one bound to your thoughts, your choices."

Vaan frowned. "Then it's speaking only to them?"

"Not speaking," Ytelthuun replied. "Calling."

The group sat on flat stones just outside the pod, sharing ration packs. Ali chomped on a dense, tasteless protein cake, eyes still sleepy. The mood was quiet—uncertain—but momentarily light. Nysha encouraged everyone to eat well; they had no idea when the next chance would come.

Then Ali froze.

His eyes widened, and his half-eaten ration fell from his mouth.

"Ali, that's disgusting," Omar muttered, shaking his head. "Chew before you—"

"Omar, look!" Ali whispered urgently, grabbing his brother's arm and swiveling him around.

High above, scattered between streaks of red cloud, floated a trident-shaped formation—one fork pointing straight ahead through a narrow mountain valley. The middle prong glowed faintly as the red sun's light struck it just right.

"The fork..." Omar breathed. "It's the fork from the dream. Those clouds look just like a fork! The message from the dream! This is it!"

Nysha and Ytelthuun exchanged skeptical glances. "Clouds are not maps," Nysha said gently.

"Maybe not," Vaan cut in, his voice firm. "But dreams shared in perfect synchronicity are no accident. I trust the boys. This has to be a sign. We follow that prong."

They packed quickly. Backpacks filled with torches, tools, food, and medical kits. The talisman hidden. Luma tucked back into Ali's pack.

"I'll grab these two combat binoculars," Ytelthuun called from inside the pod. "These are the last items from the supply cabinets." He tossed one to Vaan.

With their supplies neatly packed, the five heroes set off toward the valley. An air of hope and worry surrounded them all.

The forest groaned—not loudly, but with a sentience that made every step feel watched. Tree limbs bent ever so slightly toward them as they passed, like the slow movements of blind serpents. No branch touched them, but the feeling of being measured—tasted—was inescapable.

Terrifying shrieks rose in the distance. Far too guttural to be wind.

Ytelthuun kept his sidearm ready and whispered, "Eyes forward, ears back. Anything moves that shouldn't—we don't hesitate."

Ali flinched at every sound. Omar, though terrified, gritted his teeth. His hand brushed Nysha's accidentally, and she smiled warmly.

"You boys give me strength," she whispered, pinching Omar's cheek playfully. "I'm always amazed at you both!"

Omar flushed deep red. Ali snickered and nudged him for blushing.

"Shut up," Omar muttered, as they continued trekking through the alien wilderness.

Hours passed. The trees thinned, and a jagged clearing opened into a glass-shard field. The earth glittered with razor-thin crystal shards, jutting from the ground like frozen lightning. Each shard refracted the red sunlight into dozens of hues, painting the clearing in a kaleidoscope of living color. A breathtaking sight awaited them—an alien mosaic of gleaming splinters, as though the world had shattered and decided to remain broken in the most beautiful way possible. Even the wind moved more cautiously here, whistling through the glass with a mournful, melodic hum that sounded eerily like distant singing. The group stood in silence, awestruck and wary, unsure whether they had stepped into a sanctuary or a graveyard of forgotten light.

Above them, darkening the sky, flew the **Khyzraal Skharnuun**—enormous flying creatures whose wings resembled Earth's manta rays.

Massive and elegant, they glided in intricate formations—like living constellations. Their wings shimmered translucent, dotted with glows that twinkled faintly with every movement. Long streaming filaments trailed behind them in slow spirals. Hundreds of thousands drifted across the sky, and below in the valley were many more, gliding low over the crystalline fields.

Ali and Omar both shouted, pointing upward.

"The winged beasts! From the dream!" Ali cried. "This is from the dream! *Let those who carry stars on their wings lift you!* This is it! Look at their wings! They have glowing dots on them, like stars! Whoa! Un-freakin'-real!"

"They'll bring us—whoever spoke said so!" Omar added.

Nysha's face darkened. "Or lure you to a trap. We don't know who or what gave that message. We don't know if the voice you heard is friend or foe."

"It's a risk we have to take," Vaan said. "We follow. This cannot be coincidence." He was astounded by the revelations.

Near the valley's edge, they found several Khyzraal Skharnuun resting on the ground. One was larger than the rest, wings gently folded, eyes like silver pearls half-lidded as she lay near a cluster of glowing eggs. Her scales shimmered with hues of sapphire and lilac, and the ground around her seemed unnaturally warm, infused with the heat of her protective presence. The eggs pulsed with a gentle inner light, casting shifting shadows on her sleek form. A faint, melodic hum vibrated in the air around her, like a lullaby meant only for the unborn. She exhaled slowly, a mist of glittering vapor curling from her nostrils, her massive tail wrapped protectively around the clutch. Even in stillness, she radiated an aura of fierce, maternal power—serene but ready to defend with elemental wrath if needed.

Ytelthuun knelt and closed his eyes. The symbols on his neck and hands glowed faintly. He reached out telepathically.

We seek help. Will you carry us across the shards? Can you understand me?

To his astonishment, a reply came.

I am Kshalriya. You are safe. I will call others. We will help. We are friends.

Vaan's jaw dropped. "She spoke to you?"

"She's intelligent. Very. Not all creatures can be reached, but she opened her mind. Lesser-minded creatures cannot connect telepathically."

Kshalriya lifted her head and emitted a low trill. Three others in the field raised their wings and drifted over.

Two riders each, she said. *One rides alone. It is done. We are friends. We will help.*

Ytelthuun bowed. "I will go alone."

Vaan looked at Omar. "You with me."

Nysha placed a hand on Ali's shoulder. "Let's fly, little guy."

Their assigned Skharnuun bent low, wings unfurling in elegant arcs that shimmered with refracted red light, allowing them to climb atop with reverence and awe. Each person grasped long, ribbon-like filaments near the creature's head—tough but soft, pulsing with bio-light that danced between their fingers like strands of living silk. Omar's heart pounded so fiercely he thought it might burst, a strange blend of terror and exhilaration flooding through him. Ali was grinning uncontrollably, but his fingers trembled as he clutched the filament, his excitement barely masking his fear.

The Skharnuun stirred beneath them. Their vast wings began flapping in rhythm with the low, rising hum of crystal wind. The vibration passed through the filaments into their bones, as if the creatures were singing to the skies before lifting off. The ground fell away in a dizzying swoop. The boys gasped, eyes wide as the crimson sky opened around them like a blooming, endless dream.

Omar turned and caught his brother's eye. They grinned at each other.

The creatures rose higher. The forest shrank. The crimson sky yawned wide.

Then the Khyzraal Skharnuun turned west, flying over the jagged obsidian mountains, their wings cutting through the blood-red light like celestial blades. Below, the peaks jutted up like broken teeth, each glistening with volcanic sheen, as if the earth itself bore wounds too ancient to heal. Shadows pooled in the range's crevices, deep and impenetrable, while molten streaks of lava snaked between ridgelines like glowing veins. Above, the sky deepened into a darker crimson, and the winds thickened with a strange electric charge that made their hair stand on end. The air shimmered with latent energy, humming faintly, as though the sky itself whispered secrets in a forgotten tongue.

Toward that glowing horizon they soared, the fangs of fate waiting in silence beyond the darkened range—unseen but palpably real.

The wind carried them now—on wings whispered into dreams.

CHAPTER 24
VELTHARUUN IN CHAINS THE TRIUMPH OF TYRANNY.

Councilor **Drevvos Varn** stood atop the obsidian balcony of the Spire of Ashes, his breath visible in the acrid morning haze that loomed over Veltharuun. From this vantage point, he could see the avenue where the military parade would soon thunder—a serrated path of black crystal that cut through the heart of the city like a fresh wound. His hands were gloved in polished bone-leather, his ceremonial robes fastened with dark clasps carved in the image of Lord Thaarn's flaming sigil.
The victory was complete. The traitor Xa'rekthul-Yenu-Vaahn was dead—or so every report claimed. Drevvos had personally watched the security footage: the flaming descent of the Skyraleon-class glider, struck by the precision fire of the Sky Reaver squadron, plummeting beyond the Tzuraan'dhel-Monkaar borderlands and erupting in explosive flames against the jagged maws of the Varruk'Luhn mountain range.

He allowed himself a rare smile—tight-lipped, cautious. Today was not only a celebration of victory but a rehearsal of devotion. He had ordered twelve crimson banners raised, each stitched with golden thread in the ancient Urdii tongue, hailing Thaarn as Aether's Final Sovereign. Dozens of slave choirs would sing odes to his supremacy, and the fountains would run red with incense-rich vapor. Drevvos had spared no expense. If Thaarn was pleased, perhaps he would bestow another medallion—or, more importantly, a moment of unburned regard.

Drevvos would never admit it aloud, but he feared Thaarn more than death itself—and to not please the Sovereign Flame was to invite dissolution.

His aides scurried about him, aligning timing rods and finalizing the aerial sequence for the skyfire drones. He waved them off with a bored flick of his hand. His mind was on the Pyrelance Legion—those merciless avatars of Thaarn's will—soon to take the streets. The sound of their synchronized steps was the sound of planets kneeling.

Veltharuun had been sealed shut. The city's enormous gates, each as tall as the towers of ancient Tyrrakel, were locked under aetheric bind-runes. No entrance. No escape. Over 300 million residents had gathered in the Avenue of Immolation, which stretched over forty kilometers through the heart of the capital. Towering spires of steelglass lined either side, their reflective surfaces showing back the frightened eyes of those who had gathered.

Drones spun in complex orbits above—not ordinary drones, but Rhyzopticon Wards, biomechanical sentinels with pulsating laser-eyes and dangling feelers that could sense the tiniest heart-flutter of dissent. Armed with ion-siphon talons and shriek-pulse emitters, they hovered ominously, sniffing for treachery.

Veltharuun's lower districts had been transformed into staggered bleacher tiers of citizens—some cheering, some weeping, some paralyzed with tension. Elites and loyalist families were given upper placements, while those deemed "unsteady" were pushed near the marching lanes. There, they'd be closer to the boots of the Pyrelance Legion, should any lesson in obedience be needed.

The march began with seismic reverberation. The ground itself shuddered. First came the Flameborn Heralds, adorned in platinum armor that gleamed in the open air. Behind them marched the Iron Ash Reapers, in cloaks of flayed banners and helmets crowned with spike antlers that curled like ram's horns.

Then came the Pyrelance Legion—formation upon formation, tens of thousands of mechanized warriors, their armor etched with branding glyphs, moving as if controlled by one sinister pulse.

Children screamed, either in awe or terror, as rhythmic war-chants pounded from the walls.

Elite guard units slithered between the crowds, their eyes hidden behind opaque lenses, each wielding a Vox-Spear—a weapon that could deliver command or death with equal ease. Overhead, the sky was slashed with trails of light as more Rhyzopticon Wards formed sigils in the clouds. Some burst into flame, drawing Thaarn's symbol for all to see. None dared look away.

From the sky descended the Throne of Conflagration—a floating chariot of blackened alloy and hovering gravity coils, surrounded by shimmering heat-mirage fields. Upon this monstrous platform sat Lord Xar'Vulek Thaarn, draped in full ceremonial armor and cape. His form was a tower of obsidian spikes and brutal geometry. His helm, crowned with jagged ridges and a burning central eye, masked his face entirely.

He seemed less a man and more a god of violence, forged in the crucibles of war. In his gauntleted hand, he held a Shaal'traven Disruptor Pike, its tip glowing with trembling white electric light. The crowd recoiled involuntarily—for it was said that even a whisper of its fire could end a hundred souls at once.

Beside him, lounging like a coiled nightmare, lay Vorrak—Thaarn's beast-familiar. Its skin shimmered with thick black silky fur that reflected no light, and its serpentine tail flicked lazily, venom glistening on the barbs.

Glowing orange eyes watched the crowd, slow-blinking like a predator that had already decided its next meal. Its forked tongue tasted the metal in the air, and every ripple of muscle beneath its skin spoke of ancient violence. This rare creature had been acquired by Thaarn as a pup, after a violent battle on the other side of the planet. It was his only partner in life.

Together, master and monster presided over the apocalypse of pride below them.

The parade moved through the sectors in waves. It lasted hours, crossing sixteen districts of Veltharuun. Music of ash-horns and blood drums filled the air. Through it all, above Thaarn's head, a massive aerial hologram projected a video on loop: the footage of the Skyraleon-class glider, struck by precision fire, spiraling in flames, smashing into the mountains of Tzuraan'dhel-Monkaar. A towering plume of smoke. A violent explosion of light. Silence.
Again and again, the death of Xa'rekthul-Yenu-Vaahn was played—each iteration drawing cheers, howls, and sobs. Children were made to watch. Civilians raised their fists in forced jubilation. Dissenters were silent—or vanished.

Veltharuun wept behind its smile.

As the final echoes of drum and march faded into the distant sectors, Drevvos Varn stood atop his private platform, shoulders slackened with relief. The parade had gone perfectly. Thaarn had not once looked displeased. The projected images, the pageantry, the utter saturation of obedience—it had worked. He felt it in his marrow.

Xa'rekthul was gone. The city believed it. The people feared it. And Thaarn, the Sovereign Flame, remained as unassailable as ever.

Drevvos exhaled and poured himself a glass of highly intoxicating Maarzrikk nectar. It trembled slightly in his grip—not from the wind, but from his own nerves beginning to uncoil.
If Thaarn had noticed even a single error, this night would have ended with screaming. Instead, it had ended with silence.

He gazed out upon the city, still cloaked in the scarlet light of dusk, the towers casting long shadows over the blood-colored streets. The people had returned to their homes, but the dread lingered. The silence was not peace—it was fear made thick, a fog of terror pressing into every doorway, every heart.

He smiled again, cold and tired.
In the era of Thaarn, revolution had no oxygen. Only ash.

And tonight, Veltharuun breathed none.

CHAPTER 25
SMOKE OVER STONE
A FATHER'S MISSION BEGINS.

They call this day a triumph, but to me, it stinks of fear disguised in the perfume of power. My name is Vaelik Dron'Shal-Mareth, and I walk among the fools of Veltharuun, wrapped in my dark gray robe with the hood drawn low over my face. I move with quiet purpose through the crowd that floods the avenue like an ocean of broken spirits, each one cheering, clapping, saluting, and screaming in praise of the Sovereign Flame. But I say nothing. I do not cheer. I only watch the parade of Thaarn.

My boots step over scattered petals—red as blood—that litter the stone tiles, crushed beneath the feet of millions. The sky above is crimson with a touch of pale bronze, dust-choked and filled with celebratory drone trails that loop in the heavens like electric serpents. Fireworks burst occasionally, thudding through the heavy air like distant mortar shells. To them, this is victory. To me, this is desecration. For I know what they do not.

I have stood beside Xa'rekthul-Yenu-Vaahn, my brother not by blood, but by oath. Years ago, we carved a scar into the heart of Lord Thaarn's war machine. We called it Operation Emberwake Upreach. While the world watched a false peace summit on the cliffs of Sur'vel-Kaarn, we infiltrated Thaarn's Prism Core Facility and ruptured its energy cell matrices with a cascade loop algorithm. The explosion took down over four hundred Pyrelance elites—and it was the first true victory of the First Alliance. We had no delusions. Every act of rebellion carved our names deeper into the Book of Death. Xa'rekthul led with fire, I followed with shadow. And now, they claim he is dead. But I do not believe in ghosts born of state-sponsored footage. He can't be dead. I just don't believe it.

Today, I stand at the fringes of the Grand Procession, the place where the black banners of the Pyrelance Legion stretch like the wings of vultures over the city. I wait, silent as ash, for the passing of Thaarn himself. The people around me chant, "SOVEREIGN FLAME, ETERNAL AND BLAZING!" Their voices ring in unison like the choir of the damned. I resist the urge to clench my fists.

The sky darkens slightly, the smoke from the drones and sky-pyres thickening. A bass rumble grows louder—there it is. Thaarn's obsidian throne-vehicle, massive and floating like a fortress in midair. It hums with gravitational stabilizers and emits a sinister glow from beneath, casting long skeletal shadows on the crowd. Atop it sits the monster.

Lord Thaarn's armor gleams like polished black bone, edged in spires that curve outward as if thirsting for blood. His helmet is horned, barbed like some apex predator of a forgotten age. In its center is a single burning orange eye that makes him look even more horrific than he already is. In one gauntleted hand, he clutches a Shaal'traven Disruptor Pike, an exclusive weaponized staff pulsing with white-hot energy. Next to his towering form lies Vorrak, his night-black-furred beast, venom-slick tail swaying lazily, serpent tongue testing the air. Their eyes are the same shade of glowing orange.

Above Thaarn's head, the same damnable footage plays on loop: the Skyraleon-class glider erupting into flame. The missiles. The mountain. The crash. The smoke. The so-called end of Xa'rekthul-Yenu-Vaahn. The crowd wails with elation every time the explosion blooms anew. But I stare not at the hologram—but at the cracks in its story.

I turn. I've seen enough.

Threading myself through the bodies, I push through the tide of limbs and sweat and cheers, deeper and deeper into the underlayers of the city where no floating throne dares hover. My breath grows easier the farther I go. Here, the alleys constrict. Here, the cheers are muffled. Here, surveillance is weak.

Veltharuun's inner warrens are a maze of decay. Buildings rise like jagged cliffs—crumbling but defiant. Trash fires smolder in metal drums. Children play with scraps of bio-plastene and coil-worm husks. Above, the sky is a narrow slit of crimson-grey light, and the enforcement drones fly too high to track faces. I move quickly, cutting through crooked corridors and rusted catwalks until I reach the narrow gap between two crumbling structures. My basement lies beneath.

I touch the door-sensor three times, pause, then twice again. A panel hisses open. A door, invisible to most, reveals old metal steps descending into darkness. I descend, sealing the entrance behind me. The scent of ancient iron and recycled air greets me like an old friend. Safe. At least, for now.

I remove my robe.

Underneath, I wear my true colors—muted yellows and a burnished orange tunic of the Shadraante silkweavers, long outlawed since Thaarn's rise. My body is battle-hardened, built for endurance. But it is my left eye that draws the stares of those who meet me. It glows faintly blue, then flickers red—cybernetic. A memory. A shard of psionic crystal embedded itself in my skull during an explosion at the siege of the Thaarnian Orbital Relay. The medics of the First Alliance pulled it out and replaced it with a cybernetic eye. And now that eye sees not just the visible, but also carries trails of artificial intelligence inside its core. In some ways, it's even better than the original.

"Father has returned! Yaay!"

I barely turn before I'm tackled by two small shapes. My son Virelooq and daughter Spaeya'Va leap into my arms. I hold them tight, heart pounding—their warmth more powerful than any weapon.

"You're home!" Spaeya'Va cries.

"Were you gone because of the parade?" Virelooq asks. "Did you see him? The monster?"

I nod slowly, a small smile pulling at my lips. "I saw him. And I thought of you both the entire time."

Their eyes—innocent and curious—look up at me with trust and hope. I kneel down.

"Remember," I say, cupping their faces, "we are not small just because they are big. We are strong because we know the truth."

They hug me again before I gently rise and move into the back room. This is my private area, and I never bring my children inside.

I shut the door and activate my comms array. Four blue lights blink on. I initiate a secure link. One by one, faces appear on my cracked, flickering display: Tullian Varro, mechanic and scout; Drava-Kei, former weapons engineer turned saboteur; and Yenn Vex, strategist and deep-code decryptor.

"I saw it with my own eyes," I begin. "The throne. The parade. The footage. They're making a theater of it."

Tullian leans in. "And you believe he's really dead?"

Drava-Kei shakes her head. "That glider exploded on Tzuraan'dhel-Monkaar. Why was Xa'rekthul even there? He said he'd never cross the border without us."

Yenn Vex folds her arms. "Unless it was a setup."

My jaw tightens. "That's what I'm thinking. Either he was lured there... or this death is staged. Something doesn't add up."

"Could be Thaarn playing god again," Tullian mutters. "Fake the death, declare a win, demoralize us. Classic authoritarian tactic. That's what I think."

"Then we need to be sure," I say. "I'm going to the crash site. I need to see it with my own eyes. If it's real, we'll mourn him properly. If it's not... then..."

Yenn Vex leans forward. "Then we take the lie and burn their illusion to the ground. We can expose their lie... if it is a lie!"

"I leave soon. Tell no one. I will give more instructions soon."

They nod. The screen blinks out.

I sit in the silence that follows, only the distant hum of the old water filter pulsing and hissing in the background. I lay out a small paper map, outdated but still accurate. I trace the route from Veltharuun to the Tzuraan'dhel-Monkaar ranges—miles across airless wastelands, patrol zones, and hostile territory. I'll need stealth, speed, and a damned miracle.

I fold the map.
My hands don't shake. I'm ready for anything.
The plan begins now. I must make haste.

CHAPTER 26

THE HOODED GHOST AND THE DIRECTOR'S DREAD.

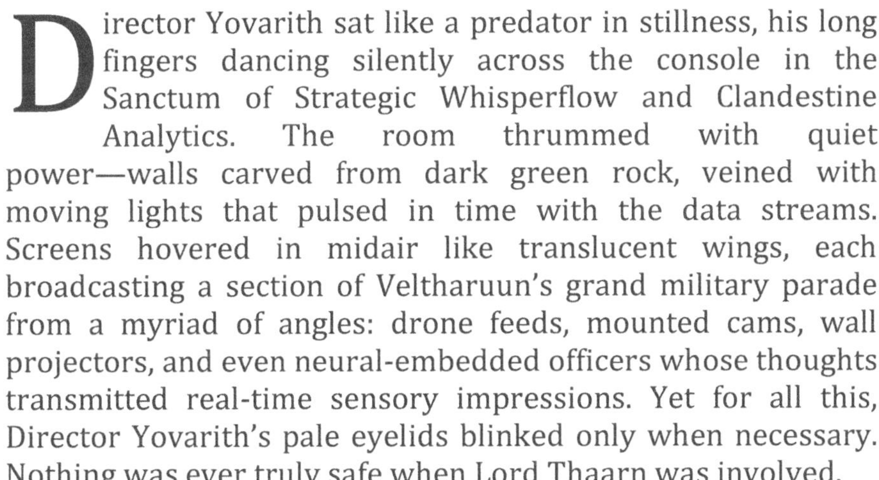

Director Yovarith sat like a predator in stillness, his long fingers dancing silently across the console in the Sanctum of Strategic Whisperflow and Clandestine Analytics. The room thrummed with quiet power—walls carved from dark green rock, veined with moving lights that pulsed in time with the data streams. Screens hovered in midair like translucent wings, each broadcasting a section of Veltharuun's grand military parade from a myriad of angles: drone feeds, mounted cams, wall projectors, and even neural-embedded officers whose thoughts transmitted real-time sensory impressions. Yet for all this, Director Yovarith's pale eyelids blinked only when necessary. Nothing was ever truly safe when Lord Thaarn was involved.

His jaw tightened as he leaned forward. One camera feed shimmered slightly—the edge of a storm cloud brushing the high atmosphere. He immediately redirected particle beam sentries to disintegrate a passing strael-wing, a small native and very noisy glider-beast whose leathery wings shimmered with anti-light. It vanished mid-flight in a puff of violet mist. The skies had to remain sterile. The crowd below must be protected. Not because they mattered—but because any disruption would reflect on him. And Lord Thaarn did not tolerate mistakes.

The Director exhaled softly. Fear was a constant companion. Thaarn was a monster in every sense—brilliant, merciless, and unpredictably cruel. But Yovarith was no fool. He had survived this long by being better than everyone else at seeing what others didn't. His entire being was attuned to anomalies, to the tiniest changes in behavior, light, or pattern. He had often boasted—silently, to himself—that he could detect a spy from ten thousand feet if their heartbeat fluttered oddly.

Hours passed. The parade thundered on—massive gliders flew in tight formations, elite ground troops marched like clockwork across the white-veined blackstone plaza, while Thaarn's image was projected onto colossal banners that flapped like living skin. Most of the crowd cheered with rehearsed awe. Yovarith remained unmoved.

Then he saw it.

A flicker.

One of the feeds—a mid-angle drone's vision over the eastern quadrant—caught a hooded figure.

He didn't blink.

"Zoom in 300 percent," he whispered.

The console obeyed. The screen widened. The drone camera focused on a lone figure, standing perfectly still. Cloaked in dark grey. Hood pulled far forward, face completely obscured. He wasn't clapping. He wasn't shouting. He wasn't moving.

He was simply... watching.

Yovarith's fingers tightened around a sensor-sphere, commanding the drone to hover lower. The man never looked up. Even when Lord Thaarn's grand floating fortress-vehicle passed by—ten stories high, oozing with crimson spotlights and wailing slave choirs—the hooded man only shifted slightly, turning just enough to watch.

And above Thaarn's platform, the looped hologram flickered again: the crash of a glider into the peaks of

Tzuraan'dhel-Monkaar. The death of Xa'rekthul-Yenu-Vaahn. The symbol of resistance, obliterated in fire.

The cloaked man stared. Then abruptly, turned and began to walk.

"Engage autonomous scout drone, type IX-Qri," Yovarith hissed.

A hatch opened from one of the exterior walls of a nearby building. A small, disc-shaped drone—smooth black metal with soft ripples of blue plasma—lifted silently into the air. The IX-Qri was no bigger than a small head. It could hide in shadows, adjust translucency, and emit no sound. A perfect ghost.

The Director took full control, breathing slower. The drone trailed the figure at a careful distance. Through alleys. Past monolithic pillars of rusted conduits. Across the fractured bones of ancient Veltharuun architecture. The drone remained invisible, watching.

The figure reached a near-forgotten quarter. Shanties stacked like termite hives. Roofs patched with scavenge-cloth and thermal glass. Old smells—spilled plasma, charred roots, metal-skin sweat—pulsed from every crevice. Towering buildings and long-dead structures loomed, mostly forgotten by new development. Then the man opened a ground hatch—barely noticeable—and slipped into a descending staircase.

The door closed.

Yovarith stood up.

His ominous eyes widened slightly. "First Alliance," he whispered. "You're not gone yet? I found you, little insect."

He reached for a secure channel. The screen shimmered.

A pale face appeared. Sunken cheeks. Eyes entirely black. Huge sacks beneath them, as if the man hadn't slept in years. He was tall, spindly, and still as death.

"Tzarron Vel-Kaith-Ruhl," Yovarith said, voice low. "Coordinates: Varnix-Delta-07. Grid eight of Lower Sprawl. Lock onto heat decay from hatchline 83-2J."

The spy nodded once.

Yovarith continued, "A cloaked individual descended into that structure. I want you to wait. Wait for anyone to emerge. Follow them. Do not engage. Do not be seen. If the individual moves, you track. If they speak, you listen. Spare no expense. Spare no mercy. I want answers and a highly detailed report."

Tzarron's voice came like wind over shattered glass. "Understood. Commencing infiltration. I shall remain unseen."

Yovarith leaned closer, eyes narrowed. "And Tzarron—if you fail, I won't need to terminate you. Thaarn will do it personally."

Tzarron gave a slow salute, hand over his chest in a curling motion.

The feed cut.

Yovarith sat back down. The room felt colder now.

He stared at the black hatch on his screen—the one the cloaked man had disappeared into.

His breath slowed.

His instincts, sharpened beyond all normal comprehension, screamed in silence.

This was no ordinary citizen. This was no lost rebel.

This was something important.

And if he was right—when he was right—then the chaos to come might be his golden chance.

"Councilor Drevvos is a bumbling mouthpiece," he whispered. "A child draped in power. Completely undeserved."

Yovarith leaned forward, hands clasped before him, elbows resting on steel.

"I should be Thaarn's shadow, not that fool Drevvos."

Outside, the parade thundered. Banners danced like flayed skin. Choirs sang the anthem of fear. The Director turned and faced the screens and holograms of the parade once again.

The game had changed.

CHAPTER 27
BENEATH THE HOOD, BEHIND THE EYES.

There are few pleasures in this world that match the crisp, clean trust of a superior who knows your true nature—and still finds use for it. Director Yovarith knows. He sees through the lies I wear like skin and recognizes the darkness buried in my marrow. Not everyone can handle what I do. They pretend to be above it—cleaner, more refined in their methods. But the Director? He sees me clearly. And that clarity, that understanding... it makes me feel valued. Useful. Powerful. A perfect blade in his arsenal. And if that blade must occasionally drip with blood or split a soul from its shell, then so be it. It's the cost of efficiency.

I don't pretend I need a cause. I have none. Not Thaarn's dreams. Not Yovarith's ambitions. Just my own need—to watch hope die behind a person's eyes. There is something deeply pure about pain—how it strips away pride, ideology, the clutter of identity. Only truth remains when someone screams. Their real truth. I savor that. The way some people enjoy the fragrance of rare flowers or the touch of sunlight. For me, it's agony. Theirs. And with each trusted assignment, I get to create more of it. And, of course, blood. Its drips make my heart beat.

There was one once—Yural Dro-Mentevk, a First Alliance rat who thought he could smuggle micro-filament signal ciphers through the kelp district to his sister unnoticed. I caught him mid-sprint and dragged him to my personal chamber beneath the Sanctum. Stripped him. Hung him upside down from the bone-hooks. And then I began. A thousand small incisions. One every ten minutes. Just enough to bleed him slowly—never too fast. His body stayed conscious through most of it. It's amazing how much blood one can lose and still beg for more mercy. I learned that when he started coughing up foam and still tried to whisper his sister's name. I took pleasure when *she* called my name, **Tzarron Vel-Kaith-Ruhl**, as she begged for her life. I gave her a mercy I never gave him. Instant death. There is no greater mercy in nature.

And now... now there's this one. This cloaked shadow who emerged from the undercity—unregistered, unrecognized, unseen before this moment. The Director sent me the coordinates with haste. Something about him felt off, enough to trigger Yovarith's instinct—which rarely fails. He didn't know who it was. That's my job. But something about the figure's presence on those surveillance feeds... the Director said it stirred something primal in him. And if it rattled him, then it must be worth killing. Or worse.

I've been here for hours. Stationed near the rusted grates of Sector 9-Zhurnil, on the fractured crust of a lower city junction near the Naruth Spillgrounds. Slums surround me. Leaking pipeways. Shattered arc-glass. Beggars missing limbs. I've been still for so long, I've forgotten what movement feels like. But I don't need comfort. I am comforted by the wait. The anticipation. A predator watches. A predator waits. And I am nothing if not a patient predator. I let my eyes drift toward the square hatch in the ground—disguised cleverly with molded debris. Most passersby wouldn't notice it. But I'm not most.

The Director's basic instructions are still in my skull: *"He'll come out. Follow him. Don't be seen."* I've lived by worse commands. The shadows are my kin. The stench of chemical runoff doesn't bother me. The shifting winds burn against my pale skin, but I don't flinch. I barely blink. I want to know who this figure is. I want to know what secrets he carries. And when I do... I want to break them out of him like cracking marrow from bone.

Something stirs.

The hatch.

A quiet hiss as internal mechanisms disengage. The cover lifts an inch—then more. I lower myself further into the rubble pile, narrowing my breath. From the dark interior of the under-basement emerges the figure. Same cloak. Same hood. Heavy fabric shrouds his entire body. I can't even glimpse a chin or hands. Whoever he is, he's gone to great lengths to remain a mystery. He closes the hatch softly, locking it with a motion I barely catch. Then he turns. Away from me. Toward the deeper parts of the city.

My pulse quickens.

The hunt begins.

He walks like someone who doesn't want to be followed—using alley shadows, broken stairwells, sewer-fed corridors. But I am better. I glide after him, my boots making no more sound than a feather dropped into snow. He moves fast, but not desperate. Not yet. We wind through burnt-out zones, past old steel bones of forgotten towers. The city shifts around us. Time blurs. I follow for over two hours. My muscles ache with the pleasure of pursuit.

Finally, I see where he's headed.

Thalmaruun Drift Anchorage.

A busy trading seaport. One of the few coastal entry points left near the boiling shores of the Drenneth Sea. The waters below aren't water at all—boiling nitrogen mixed with churning vats of liquid boron. The ocean itself glows faintly green, exhaling radioactive vapors into the air like breath from a dying god. Massive hover-ships—each shaped like angular spears—rest above the boiling ocean. They do not float by design alone. They feed on the electromagnetism produced by the molten minerals beneath the sea. Their turbine-inverted channellers siphon both energy and lift from the currents.

He approaches the boarding platforms and stands in line.

So do I.

I blend in—dressed like a dockworker. Grease on my gloves. Burn-scars on my sleeves. My forged ID is synced to a VeilTag on my wrist, a tiny black shard embedded with a pulsar-resonant chip. The boarding terminal pings it, reads my alias, deducts the fare in under three seconds. I move through without issue. But he... he's ahead of me. Just a few passengers up.

He enters the vessel.

Gone. He is out of sight.

I curse under my breath.

The line shifts again and I step forward—through the yawning gate and into the belly of the hover-ship.

The interior is massive. A sprawl of metal, glowing walls, and thousands of passenger tiers. My pulse spikes. Almost eleven thousand civilians packed in here. Faces. Voices. Shouts. The air smells of rust, sweat, and electrolytic coolant. I scan everywhere.

No sign of him.

Did I lose him?

Then—movement.

He's there!

Sitting far back, three sections behind me. And worse—he's looking at me.

I freeze. My spine stiffens. My blood drains to ice.

He knows.

For a second, I falter. Let it show in my face. Slight, yet obvious body language. The barest crack. But I recover. Slowly. Calmly. I take a seat several rows forward, cursing my mistake. I should have known better. But I didn't expect him to be watching me. *I didn't expect him to be watching me!* I have always been too perfect at this. How did I let this happen?

I glance back.

He's still looking. Still. Looking at *me*?!

Every few minutes, I try again. Careful. Subtle. Never enough to draw attention. But that hood never turns. Never shifts. It remains locked forward. Locked on me.

The passengers all board. The vessel seals. Engines charge.

And then—

We launch.

Not slowly. These mega-ships slice through the air like blades through silk. Over boiling seas, powered by the fury of planetary chemistry.

I grip the armrest tightly. Not because I fear the ride.

But because I don't know how to keep my eye on him anymore. I made a mistake. One that might cost me.

Should I inform the Director?

Maybe.

But not yet. Let's see where this goes.

Let's hope it's good news that I send the Director.

Let's hope.

CHAPTER 28
A PORTAL NOT YET PASSED.

The skies of Orulenthia churned with dark, surreal hues—a canvas of deep crimson and swirling violet beneath the never-setting red giant star. High above the surface, five figures soared gracefully on the wide, undulating backs of three Khyzraal Skharnuun—enormous, manta-ray-like creatures whose translucent wings shimmered with the colors of bloodstone and dotted glows. Omar and Ali rode with their companions—Ytelthuun, Nysha, and Vaan—gliding through volcanic thermals that rose from megastructures of magma and ash. The volcanoes were titanic, towering so high they pierced the cloud layer, crowned with glowing calderas that spilled slow rivers of molten gold. Down below, jagged obsidian mountains clawed at the horizon, broken occasionally by strange glowing pools, spiraling crystal groves, and scattered clusters of subterranean villages. These alien homes were half-buried in cliff faces or hidden beneath massive, moss-like structures that undulated with breath-like movement—alive in some semi-conscious way.

The Khyzraal glided above these vast wonders in silence, the only sound being the deep, thrumming pulse of their wingbeats echoing across the empty expanse. As the sun dipped ever so slightly, casting an eerie crimson glow over the valleys, the group spotted fields of bioluminescent fungi glowing from fissures in the rock and shimmering alien beasts with antlers like comet trails galloping along invisible ley lines of energy.

Slowly, the Khyzraal Skharnuun began their descent. Kshalriya—the lead Khyzraal and the only one with sentience and telepathic communication—lowered toward a flat plateau dotted with glinting blue crystals. In Ytelthuun's mind, her calm, wise voice echoed:

"This is the farthest we may travel now. We must rest. But we shall wait here until your return. Take your time."

Omar grinned wide as they landed, pumping his fist into the air. "That was the most awesome thing ever!" he shouted.

Ali leapt off his beast, high-fived his brother, and spun around with a yell. "I wish I had wings! That sky! Those volcanoes! Those antler thingies running around!"

"I thought we were gonna fall off when she banked left over that canyon! Dude, I think I saw a group of flying jellyfish right below us just before we landed!" Omar exclaimed.

"Those creatures were the Aezocpnidari," Ytelthuun chuckled, helping Nysha down from the creature's back. "They travel in large swarms and are extremely venomous—and highly aggressive. Best we stayed out of their way!"

"Unbelievable," Vaan said, smiling as his boots touched down.

Nysha nodded, her eyes wide with wonder. "That was like flying through a dream. That might just be my favorite way to travel through Orulenthia!" She laughed.

Still buzzing from their aerial journey, the group found themselves grounded atop a vast plateau of crystalline rock. A subtle wind passed through, carrying traces of sulfur, ozone, and something faintly floral. For a while, nobody spoke. Their adventure had lifted their spirits—but now the vastness of the world returned to them.

For the next hour, the five stood on the plateau, staring across the crimson land.

"So," Omar finally said, rubbing the back of his neck. "What now?"

Ali sighed. "We don't exactly have a map, do we? Or coordinates? Or even a clue where this Vault of Elders might be."

Vaan looked off into the distance. "Sometimes... sometimes dreams are the only maps we're given. Perhaps, if you slept again, something more may come. How about a nap, boys?"

"But we're not tired," Ali protested. "I don't feel even a little sleepy."

There was a pause before Ytelthuun—his eyes weary yet still glowing—turned to Kshalriya and telepathically asked, half-joking and half-desperate,
"Hey! What about you? Do you... know where we can find the sanctuary of Tzuraan'dhel-Monkaar? The Vault of Elders?"
He laughed aloud at his own joke.

For a moment, silence. Then, in Ytelthuun's mind, a gentle yet commanding voice spoke:
"There is a Tower. Sometimes called the Refuge of Crystalline Remembrance."

Ytelthuun perked up at once, his face growing serious.
"Wait, what?" Omar said. "She knows where it is, doesn't she?"

Kshalriya's long tail swayed as she gestured with her body.
"Across that rift. It waits."

They scrambled, following Ytelthuun as he pointed across the rocky cliff. There, just beyond a narrow land bridge spanning the canyon, stood a monumental structure embedded into the cliff's edge—within walking distance. Its crystalline form glinted with multicolored refracted light, its surface smooth like diamond, shifting through every shade of red, blue, and violet. The ancient spire shimmered with impossible beauty.

The walk to the Refuge was filled with growing awe. The tower was carved from a singular, towering crystal veined with ancient Ur'dii script that pulsed faintly with light. It dwarfed even the volcanoes behind them. As they reached the entrance, the massive doorway responded without resistance, creaking open in a slow, soundless motion. Inside, the air shimmered with strange energy. Light filtered through the walls like dancing fire, refracted into rainbows by the crystalline interior. Each step echoed through halls carved in impossible geometric shapes—shifting slightly when not looked at directly.

"This place..." Nysha whispered, eyes wide. "It's alive with memory."

Vaan ran his fingers along one wall. "The Sanctuary... or Refuge... was built by the Ancients before the sky burned. They used living crystal from the core of Orulenthia."

Every step echoed with reverence. The architecture defied human understanding—no visible supports, no wiring, no seams. The sanctuary breathed an ancient intelligence. They passed by alcoves filled with sculpted obelisks and silent chambers whose doors bore mysterious insignias.

The first room they opened was massive but empty, its tall domed ceiling rising like a cathedral above.
"Maybe a place for meditation," Nysha guessed.

Then came the second door.

The moment it creaked open, a vile stench burst out like a physical force. A combination of rotten flesh, sulfur, old sewage, and chemical decay invaded their senses. Ali gagged, shielding his nose. Nysha winced, tears forming in her eyes. Even the unflinching Ytelthuun visibly recoiled.

"It smells like something died and rotted in here a thousand years ago," Omar choked.

They moved forward cautiously, eyes squinting. Inside, shadows hung thick like old curtains. The room was huge, its ceiling lost in darkness. The air was thick and humid—every breath a challenge. They walked carefully down a long hallway lined with strange alien objects: floating illuminated orbs, various crystal arrays with black wires dangling, stacks of memory crystals, broken machinery, strange tubes full of murky liquids, glass tanks half-filled with iridescent gases, cracked screens embedded in the walls, coils and gears half-consumed by rust and time. Strange inscriptions and devices littered the space like a museum lost to history.

At the far end of the chamber, through a winding aisle of derelict tech and glowing relics, a throne sat beneath a canopy of broken crystal. And someone was sitting in it.

As they approached, their footsteps slowed. The figure was gaunt—barely alive. His face was a skull with parchment-thin skin. Cables ran from his chest, arms, and bald head into pulsing tanks of glowing blue fluid. Thick tubes snaked into his back. He wore a dark robe, frayed at the edges, his hood fallen halfway to expose a head riddled with scars, implanted wires, and embedded tech. Every breath was wheezing, mechanical.

Suddenly, a coughing groan rattled from the figure's chest. His head turned slowly, sockets barely able to focus. A weak, distorted voice rasped:
"Welcome... Omar and Ali... I... am Voraal Zenthir Kael... Keeper... of Kha'Len."

Ali gasped and fumbled through his satchel. "We have it! The talisman!" He ran forward, holding up the triangular artifact.

Voraal's eyes lit faintly.
"Yes... that is it. I have... waited..."

Omar stepped closer. "You've been entering our dreams. Speaking to us. That was you, wasn't it?"

The ancient keeper nodded slowly.
"Yes," Voraal rasped. "Too many... solar cycles ago...many centuries... the Kha'Len was stolen. I... remained behind. This Sanctuary... my prison and post. I connected my consciousness through memory conduits... each one linked to the talisman's

ruby node. Through telepathic wavelengths... transmitted by these crystals... I sent dreams. To whoever possessed the Kha'Len. Over hundreds of years... All those who possessed the Kha'Len ignored the dreams. Thought them... nightmares. But you two... you listened. I'm so happy you're here."
He tried to smile but lacked the strength or muscles in his face to do so.

"You've been doing this for centuries?" Omar whispered.

"Much more than that," Voraal wheezed. "Orulenthian centuries... several thousands of millennia by your world's measure. My artificial life-support system sustains me—viscous fluids... neurostatic stabilization. I am but barely alive. But each message... weakens me. Until... finally... you came."

Tears welled in Ali's eyes. "Then please, tell us now. How does it work? How do we go home? I just wanna go home!"

Nysha gently wrapped an arm around Ali as he cried. Voraal continued,
"The red crystal must be struck by a beam of pure light. Not any light—intense, focused. A particular intensity. Then... the portal opens. On the back... there are three control glyphs. Slide your finger across one of them. One for *Return to Previous Location.* One for *Select Random Destination.* And one... for *Choose Destination.* That last one... you must think your destination clearly into the ruby, and it will respond telepathically by opening the portal to that exact location."

Ali unzipped his backpack, pulled out a torch, and flicked it on. "Let's go. Right now. I'll use this torch's light to turn on the red crystal on the Kha'Len!"

Nysha and Ytelthuun cheered. But Vaan's face fell. His eyes clouded with conflict. "Wait," he said, pulling them gently aside. "Before you go... I need to say something."

He took a breath, voice trembling.

"You boys have changed everything. Our lives can never be the same. You gave us hope when we had none. You made us laugh again. Dream again. I never thought I'd care so much for someone from another world. I feel like we're family. I'm not afraid to say that I love both of you."

He looked to Nysha, who nodded and smiled.

"I want to ask two things. First... take the Kha'Len with you. Earth is safer. Hide it. Protect it. End the cycle. It has already been compromised here before."

He paused. "And secondly... I hate to ask this. But... would you stay? Just a little bit longer. Let me use its power—to bring down Thaarn. Then you go."

Omar stepped back. "What? No! We have to get home! Our parents—our lives!"

Ali shouted, "We helped enough! We almost died—like, multiple times!"

Vaan raised his hands. "I know. But please. Billions suffer here. If we do this... no more hiding. We end it. Then I'll send you home myself."

Omar looked at Ali. "Don't you think Allah would want us to be brave and help people in need? I won't force you, bro. Just... think about it."

Nysha stepped forward. "You're not being forced. You're loved. It is entirely your choice. We will honor your decision."

Silence.

Finally, Ali whispered, "Okay, Omar. Just... not forever. We do this for Vaan and our friends... then we go. Clear?"

They nodded.

"Alright," Omar said. "We'll help. Let's end this. We do this for Orulenthia. We do this for freedom."

Cheers, hugs, and Nysha kissed both boys on the cheek. Omar blushed.

Vaan approached Voraal.

"Respected Keeper. We have changed our minds. The Kha'Len is no longer safe here, and you are dying. We're taking it. To protect it. To end this suffering."

Voraal's eyes closed. Then opened faintly.

"Then... my purpose... ends. I will rest."

"No! Don't end yourself." Nysha said, but Voraal shook his head.

"I've endured enough... Let my memory... be peace. Please. Leave me now."

They bowed and silently exited the crystalline sanctuary, returning to the waiting Khyzraal.

"Kshalriya," Ytelthuun said telepathically, "take us back to the Valley of Crystals where we first met."

They mounted and rose once more into the crimson sky.

Below, the land waited for change.

In the hearts of five brave souls, hope ignited like a second sun.

CHAPTER 29
WHEN THE HUNTER GETS HUNTED BY THE GUY HE WAS HUNTING.

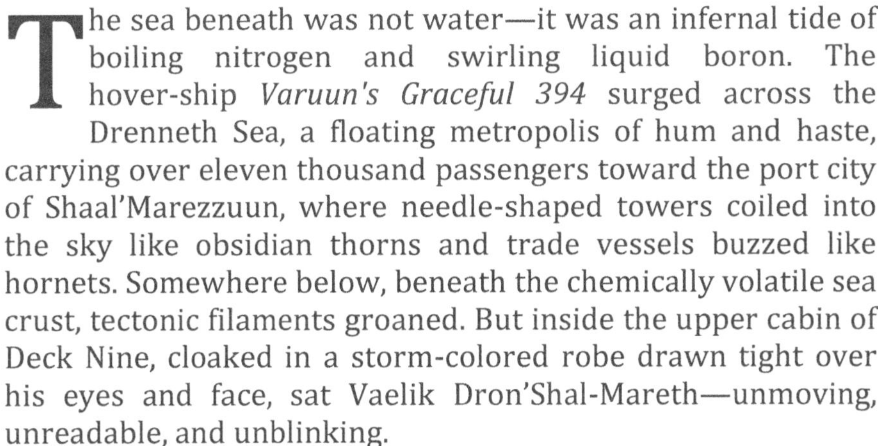

The sea beneath was not water—it was an infernal tide of boiling nitrogen and swirling liquid boron. The hover-ship *Varuun's Graceful 394* surged across the Drenneth Sea, a floating metropolis of hum and haste, carrying over eleven thousand passengers toward the port city of Shaal'Marezzuun, where needle-shaped towers coiled into the sky like obsidian thorns and trade vessels buzzed like hornets. Somewhere below, beneath the chemically volatile sea crust, tectonic filaments groaned. But inside the upper cabin of Deck Nine, cloaked in a storm-colored robe drawn tight over his eyes and face, sat Vaelik Dron'Shal-Mareth—unmoving, unreadable, and unblinking.

Three sections forward, past families of jewel-scaled Qerrathi merchants and a cluster of yellow-plumed pilgrims chanting praise to the Moon-Architect Zhyruun, sat a man who wasn't chanting. Wasn't sleeping. Wasn't breathing quite right either. His posture was relaxed to the point of theatricality, his tunic merchant-brown and crinkled just enough to fool the inattentive. But Vaelik had studied deception for decades. The man—unknown to Vaelik as Tzarron Vel-Kaith-Ruhl, top-tier operative of the Eyes Beneath—had a sliver of tension in the neck, the kind no spice trader ever carried. His face moved too smoothly as he turned. His boots were traveler's grade—non-slip soles for fast footwork, perfect for tailing in dense crowds.

Vaelik sat still but seethed with internal readiness. He had no name for the man, no proof yet—but everything in his instincts screamed *shadow operative*. It was a familiar feeling. And in his line of work, a familiar feeling usually meant someone wanted you dead by morning. The hover-ship would reach Shaal'Marezzuun in a few hours, and from there, Vaelik's plan was simple: acquire transport and head to the Tzuraan'dhel-Monkaar borderlands, the site of the infamous Skyraleon-class glider explosion in the Varruk'Luhn mountains. Rumor claimed Xa'rekthul-Yenu-Vaahn died there in the firestorm. Vaelik wasn't convinced. And if this stranger tailing him really was from Thaarn's side, the story smelled even more rotten.

The hours passed like melting iron. The air aboard the ship remained cool, perfumed by strange alien spices and the electronic tang of stabilizer coils buried beneath the decks. Vaelik's cybernetic left eye—itself a crimson glass orb seeded with Liranthian AI-nanocore tech—overlaid the world with data visible only to him: threat markers, micro-body heat trails, retinal ghosting, muscle movement analysis. He watched Tzarron's micro-gestures: the man scratched his right temple every four minutes. Twitched his finger when children cried nearby. He wasn't just watching Vaelik—he was analyzing him. Testing him. *Testing the tested*.

Vaelik rose with the smoothness of drifting mist, as if compelled by nothing more than restlessness. He glided toward the central stairwell, his robes swishing soundlessly despite the heavy traffic of alien passengers laughing, arguing, and snacking on skewered charrwuq-insects from the food vendors along the aisle. Through his augmented eye, he observed the spy moments later: the man rose too—precisely twenty-three seconds after him—slipping into the lower level's auto-stairwell, ascending. Red flags ignited in Vaelik's HUD. He didn't panic—he flowed. He exited the upper balcony and continued weaving through the ship's arteries: past crew pods, through maintenance galleries, beneath neon-spattered sky domes showing the flickering sea-sky above. Each turn confirmed the same: the man below wasn't losing him. But Vaelik was about to *lose* him instead.

A breath caught in his throat. If Tzarron had been following him since before *Varuun's Grace 394* even departed, then his home base—a hidden First Alliance node—could be exposed. Vaelik slipped into a maintenance alcove behind the mid-ship water recycler unit and pulled out a tiny square from his robe: a communicator no larger than a coin, encoded and triple-scrambled.

It chirped. A familiar face appeared—her face still as gorgeous as the first day he chose her as his lifelong partner.

"Vaelik?"

"Yurrintha-Lorae Vex-Mareth, listen carefully," he said. "The safehouse may be compromised. Evacuate with the children. Go to your brother's ridgehold. Immediately."

She didn't argue. She never did.
"And the base?"
"Activate the Zyrel-Va Corelock Sequence. Wipe the console of all files and maps. Seal it shut. No traces at all."
Yurrintha nodded once, expression carved from certainty and speed.
"Understood. I'll send word to the cell network. Be careful, my love."

The screen blinked out. Silence returned.
Only it wasn't silence—it was the war-drum thud of Vaelik's own heartbeat.
That spy would not make it off this ship alive.

He knew time was short. If the operative reported back to Thaarn or the Eyes Beneath Agency, it could spell death for not just his family—but the entire First Alliance's Southern Ring. Slipping through another crowd, Vaelik approached the rear hull passage near the electro-mag engine conduits, where the passengers thinned and the chatter grew distant. Massive cylindrical turbines hummed with energy drawn from the molten-metal mineral flows beneath the Drenneth. The ship siphoned raw magnetic lift through Turbine-Inverted Channellers, ancient Zothryan tech retrofitted for modern public transport.

There—behind a maintenance station, a bulky engineer's locker, dented and rusted with boron stains. He glanced around, then threw open the locker, yanked the uniforms out, and changed clothes at incredible speed. Robes off, mechanic tunic on. The work-mask, with its mirrored lens and breathing cowl, concealed his face. He left the robe stuffed inside the cabinet and emerged seconds later, hunching his shoulders like a worker exhausted from the conduits.

Tzarron came moments later, but too late—the hooded man was gone. The spy looked left, then right, tense now, hunting amid the crowd of engineers and midship tech-staff. Vaelik watched him from a distance now. The hunter was panicking. Tzarron scanned faces, every robed figure scrutinized. But there were none. Vaelik had vanished. The spy darted up to Deck Eleven—toward the open-air platform at the rear of the ship. Vaelik followed, staying hidden behind utility piping and sound-dampened ducts.

Outside, the wind screamed. Below, the boiling seas hissed in waves of chemical chaos.

Tzarron stood near the rail, wind whipping his hair and stinging his eyes. He activated his communicator with trembling fingers.

"This is Tzarron Vel-Kaith-Ruhl… reporting in."

The voice on the other end was like slime through cracked glass.
"You're late. I trust you have something useful, or should I begin drafting your obsolescence paperwork?"

Tzarron swallowed. "Sir… I… lost him."

Silence. Then: "You *what*?"

"I was tailing a suspect believed to be heading toward the Tzuraan'dhel-Monkaar region. He—he vanished. Changed clothes perhaps, disappeared into the crowd. I... didn't even see it happen."

"Ah," Yovarith purred. "So the Eyes Beneath's star pupil got outwitted by a stranger in a robe. What should I call you now, hmm? Blinky? Cloaky? *Captain Cloaklost*?"

Tzarron winced. "Sir, I—"

"Do shut up. I can feel the embarrassment you're oozing all the way from Veltharuun. Did he slip on your incompetence, or did you trip over your ego and fall into the sea?"

"I will continue the search—he may be heading to the Varruk'Luhn crash site. It's just a theory because it's a point of possible interest, but—"

"Oh good, a *theory*! How wonderfully useful. I'll have it engraved in my chambers."

Tzarron said nothing. His knuckles were white around the railing.

"Fine," Yovarith hissed. "I'm deploying interceptors now. Vrelkhar-class strikejets will drop squads near the Monkaar cliffs. They'll hide and wait to see who shows up at the glider wreckage—and then beat the information out of them. If this figure is heading there, we'll know soon. My interceptors will get there before he does. And you? *Do not fail me again.*"

The transmission ended.

Unseen behind a bank of fog-filter vents, Vaelik's fists clenched. The enemy was already reacting. He slipped away, disappearing into a side corridor, and activated another secure comm-channel to the First Alliance.

"Spies aboard the *Varuun's Grace 394*. Orders: increase perimeter scans. Eyes Beneath is moving. Be vigilant."

As the massive vessel cruised onward, Vaelik—now disguised as a quiet engineer—blended in with the river of life around him. Children chased mechanical hover-orbs. An overweight noblewoman sipped glowwine. Vendors sang songs to sell pastries filled with crunchy bugs. Yet inside, Vaelik was a storm. He sat in a new section of the ship, nowhere near his original post, his mechanical eye dimmed to passive mode. He was no longer being followed—he was unrecognizable to the spy now.

He thought of Yurrintha. Of the children. Of the families trusting him.
He didn't fear death—but he feared failure. The Alliance was bleeding, piece by piece, and spies slithered in like shadow-leeches.
He didn't know who else might be compromised, who else might be watching.
But one thing was clear.

The hunt had begun.

CHAPTER 30
WHEN ASHES SPEAK AND BLADES SING.

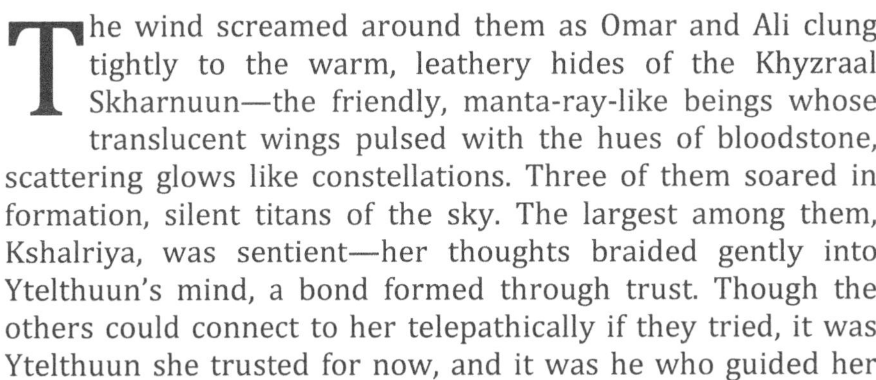

The wind screamed around them as Omar and Ali clung tightly to the warm, leathery hides of the Khyzraal Skharnuun—the friendly, manta-ray-like beings whose translucent wings pulsed with the hues of bloodstone, scattering glows like constellations. Three of them soared in formation, silent titans of the sky. The largest among them, Kshalriya, was sentient—her thoughts braided gently into Ytelthuun's mind, a bond formed through trust. Though the others could connect to her telepathically if they tried, it was Ytelthuun she trusted for now, and it was he who guided her with silent pulses of intent.

Beneath them, the world unfolded in a panorama of awe: chasms alight with molten fire, mountains vomiting slow streams of lava, and the shimmering horizon of Orulenthia's red sky, tinted with crimson hues unknown to Earth.

As the creatures glided over the spine of the Varruk'Luhn mountain range, the sheer grandeur of the landscape seemed to speak in tongues. Rivers of obsidian carved through silver-veined valleys, and far off, towers of glass-crystal forests reflected sunlight in impossible ways. Below, flocks of iridescent birds screeched and soared in unison.

Omar's heart raced with a mixture of wonder and dread; they were returning to a place where flames still clung to memory. As the Skharnuun began their descent into the crystalline valley, the temperature cooled, and the wind died down. The moment the creatures touched down, the group slid off their backs with reverent care. Each of them—Ali, Omar, Nysha, Ytelthuun, and Vaan—pressed their hands to the hides of their noble carriers, whispering silent thanks.

Kshalriya let out a low, harmonic chime that vibrated through the stones before lifting herself into the sky once more, disappearing into the blood-gold clouds.

The moment they landed, the group turned toward the scorched and twisted path leading to the wreckage of the glider that had crashed into the mountain. Though the glider had nearly become their tomb, it might still hold data caches, audio logs, or fragments of communication systems. More importantly, it could contain a working device capable of contacting any remaining First Alliance strongholds.

The decision to investigate was unanimous.

With the sun casting long, red shadows across the terrain, the five of them began their trek up the jagged slope. The air was dry and bitter, laced with ash and faint tremors from distant tectonic unrest. For hours, they walked, weaving through broken boulders, metallic debris, and dark streaks scorched into the earth from the glider's final descent.

Vaan was the first to stop. His black eyes narrowed. A dark shape zipped past the ridgeline above them, then another, followed by a third.

Without a word, he dropped to one knee and withdrew his combat binoculars—a sleek black device with auto-zoom and predictive tracking. Ytelthuun did the same.

Through the magnified lenses, they saw them—three Vrelkhar-class strikejets hovering like hawks above the shattered wreckage. But it wasn't just machines. On the ground, seven—no, eight—troopers stood in a rough circle. And in the center, two soldiers were hammering their fists into the bloodied face of a kneeling man.

Vaan zoomed in. The world fell silent around him. It was Vaelik Dron'Shal-Mareth. One of his closest allies.

His breath caught. "It's him," Vaan muttered, voice barely above a whisper. "By the fires of the Ancients... it's Vaelik."

The others turned sharply.
"Who?" asked Nysha.
"Vaelik," Vaan said, trembling. "One of my oldest brothers-in-arms. We fought a dozen battles together. If they kill him... we lose a mind too precious to replace."

Omar swallowed. "Then we help him, right?"

"Only Ytelthuun has a ranged weapon," Nysha said quickly, her voice cool but taut with urgency. "The rest of us have blades. Omar. Ali. You stay behind these rocks. No matter what. Don't follow us. I'll come get you soon."

She unstrapped six slender daggers found inside the escape pod's cabinets. She handed one to each person, including the boys. "For protection only," she said firmly. "Do not leave hiding unless everything goes wrong."

Vaan nodded. "We move like shadows. Quick. Silent. Kill fast. Be stealth."

Ytelthuun cocked his weapon—a compact orb-launcher, humming with latent energy. "Strike hard. Strike true."

The trio approached the site with deadly purpose. The terrain was rocky and cratered, littered with jagged outcroppings and sulfur-cracked roots. They advanced like specters, weaving between stones and using ridgelines for cover.

Vaan crawled low, blade in hand, eyes burning with vengeance. Nysha, agile as a hunting cat, took point—identifying patrol patterns and noting the soldiers' spacing. Ytelthuun stayed just behind, guarding their flank.

They were twenty meters out when Nysha raised two fingers. She was closest. One trooper had wandered slightly off to relieve himself near a bent girder. In a blur, she was upon him—a hand over his mouth, blade sliding beneath his helmet into the seam near his jugular. The soldier spasmed once, then collapsed.

She didn't stop. She spotted two more nearby, chatting. She darted forward, rolled beneath a beam, sprang up, slit the first one across the throat in a lateral arc, then buried her second blade into the third's temple through a helmet joint.

Now five remained. Two were still brutalizing Vaelik. The other three were moving cautiously now.

One looked up just in time to see Ytelthuun standing tall, orb-launcher glowing. A bolt of incandescent light fired—and the trooper's chest exploded, scattering metal and flesh.

The others shouted in alarm.

Vaelik fell to the ground, groaning. The soldiers left him and charged toward the direction of fire.

One more blast from Ytelthuun downed another trooper as he reached for his sidearm. Nysha dropped low and swept one attacker's legs, stabbing upward as he fell. Vaan leapt from a ledge and drove his dagger through the collar of another.

Screams filled the air. Explosions echoed.

The final trooper, chest heaving, activated his emergency beacon. "Commander Thaarn! We've found Xa'rekthul-Yenu-Vaahn! He's alive at the crash site! He's—"

He didn't finish. Vaan hurled his dagger. It buried itself between the soldier's eyes.

The man fell.

Above them, the jets screamed into a hard turn and vanished over the mountains, heading full-speed toward Veltharuun. They had taken video recordings of the entire fight and were returning to base with the data.

Nysha raced back to the boys, who had watched everything with wide, horrified eyes. She pulled them close. "It's over. For now. Come." She held their hands and led them toward the wreckage and took their knives back.

Ytelthuun and Vaan rushed to Vaelik, who was coughing blood, his eyes bruised and nearly swollen shut. He reached toward Vaan, who caught him and held him close.

A wind picked up, swirling dust as the jets' afterburn linger spun the grit into a haze. Vaelik rose unsteadily with Vaan's help, his grip tight, as if to confirm his friend was real.

"You're alive," he whispered, then laughed bitterly. "You're alive! Ohhhh!" He was in agonizing pain from the beating.

Nysha was guiding the boys around the dust clouds, shielding them with her cloak. Vaelik turned to greet them—and froze. His eyes, including the left cybernetic one, widened in pure horror. His face grew pale beneath the grime and blood.

"What in the abyss is THAT?!" he screamed.

His eyes bulged in raw, primal fear—the kind that claws its way up from the depths of the soul.

He scrambled backward on hands and heels, gaze fixed on Omar and Ali as if they were monsters from a nightmare.

"W-what are they?! No—no! Keep them away from me!" he shrieked. "Aliens! Demons from another world! Their eyes—they're not like ours! They don't belong here!"

He slammed into a jagged stone and convulsed with panic, froth forming at his lips. "I've seen monsters in my nightmares! They are the cursed ones! Get them away from me!"

"Vaelik, stop!" Vaan shouted, grabbing his shoulders. "They're not what you think—they're children! Flesh and blood!"

But Vaelik thrashed wildly, hysteria rising. "No! They wear skin, but it's a mask! I saw this—I saw this! The ancient prophecy warned us!"

Ytelthuun moved swiftly, pinning him with practiced force. "Be still, soldier. They are no threat. You shame your blood and your name. These are just young boys. They are harmless!"

Nysha stood in front of the boys, arms out like a shield. Omar and Ali stood frozen, faces pale, stunned as Vaelik's screams echoed across the crimson valley.

Ytelthuun held him still while Vaan gripped his arms. "They are with us," Vaan said. "They are friends. Not from Orulenthia, but friends. I need you to be calm."

Time passed. Two hours or more.

Eventually, Vaelik's panic subsided. The boys sat quietly beside him while Nysha tended his wounds and offered water. Vaan explained everything—the artifact, the legend of the Kha'Len, and how it might be their last hope against Thaarn.

Though shaken, Vaelik began to understand.

"Power like that..." he murmured. "Thaarn has nothing that could match it. To travel through space and time with a single device... incredible. Simply incredible."

They turned back to the wreckage. Much had been lost to the crash and scavenging beasts. Yet near the cockpit, Vaan recovered a battered communicator—its casing cracked, but the internal core mostly intact.

"I can fix this," he said, immediately working on it with his knife.

Vaelik stood slowly and turned to Omar and Ali. His expression softened with a deep ache of regret.

"Before we move forward," he said, voice rough but sincere, "I need to speak to you both. Omar. Ali."

The boys looked up warily.

Vaelik dropped to one knee, pressing a hand to his chest in the gesture of old Orulenthian reverence.

"I judged you as monsters. I let fear blind me. But in all my years fighting Thaarn, I've never seen such courage in ones so young—especially from another world. I'm totally embarrassed. I was wrong to act that way."

He paused. "When I was captured, I thought it was the end. But then I saw you. Aliens, yes... but not demons. Not invaders. Just boys. With hearts braver than mine."

He glanced at the talisman in Omar's hand. "And that artifact... it might be our only hope against Thaarn."

He looked at both of them. "I'm sorry. For the fear. The ignorance. The screaming. And... thank you. For your strength. Your mercy. Your friendship. If you'll have me, I'd be honored to fight beside you—not just as an ally... but as a friend."

He hugged them.

Then, laughing, he playfully punched their arms. "And come on! You've got those weird little eyes with white in them! Admit it—it's kind of funny! I may have a cybernetic eye, but your eyes are too peculiar!"

The boys started to smile, realizing he wasn't a threat. Maybe a little rude—but not dangerous.

Vaelik stood, taller now, resolve in his eyes. "We need to move fast. Thaarn knows now. We must strike first." He looked at the Kha'Len artifact, glowing faintly in Omar's hand.

Nysha stepped forward. "We'll need more than an army. More than weapons. We need something Thaarn can't predict."

Omar smirked, his eyes gleaming. "Then maybe... we should use the artifact now. Open a wormhole... and walk straight into Veltharuun."

CHAPTER 31
TO BLEED FOR MISTAKES BEFORE THE FLAME.

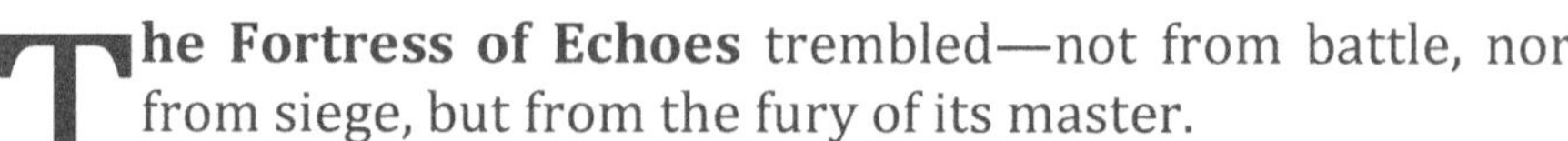

The **Fortress of Echoes** trembled—not from battle, nor from siege, but from the fury of its master.

Lord Xar'Vulek Thaarn moved through the citadel's obsidian-clad corridors like a force of nature unchained. His armored boots struck the polished stone with booming finality, each step reverberating like a death knell. The sconces lining the corridor flickered and hissed in their braziers, as if shrinking from his presence. Soldiers stationed along the route stood to attention but dared not meet his eyes. They had felt his anger before. But this—this was different. This was wrath untethered. Pure, seething, and seeking outlet.

When one soldier standing against the wall merely exhaled too loudly, Thaarn's eyes flared with bloody murder, and his gauntlet-clad arms blurred into motion. A single, merciless swipe caved in the soldier's chest, splintering ribs and collapsing lungs with a sickening crunch. The man's spine cracked audibly as he was hurled into the obsidian wall, his blood spraying in a fan across the black stone before he crumpled. Before the scream had even formed, Thaarn pivoted, seized a second soldier by the throat, and launched him into a towering black door forged from Onyxium—a hyper-dense void-alloy used in starcore containment units. The impact folded the soldier like cloth, and the door shuddered on its hinges with a groan that echoed down the corridor like a dying god's last breath. Thaarn then stomped his heavy boots into the already dead soldiers' skulls until they were mush.

No orders had been given. No provocations made. Death had not arrived with ceremony or cause. It had merely passed by in the guise of a tyrant—and chosen. Bones littered the corridor. Blood hissed as it hit the searing hot floor panels. The walls, carved with ancient war-sigils, bore fresh crimson marks that smeared downward like bleeding runes. Those who still lived dared not breathe. Dared not blink. For the Lord of Veltharuun was not a man. He was wrath incarnate—vengeance made flesh—and his rage had no appetite for mercy, only devastation.

The silence that followed was unbearable. A vacuum of sound born of collective fear. Those still living pressed themselves against the walls, their breaths held, sweat pooling beneath armor. None dared flee; to run would mean certain execution. And so they stood—trembling statues in a corridor that now reeked of scorched blood and ozone. The Lord of Veltharuun was marching, and the air itself seemed to recoil from his fury.

At the end of the grand hallway—carved from lava-rock and metal, veined with glowing crimson fissures—stood the immense double doors of the *Sanctum of Sovereign Flame*, a sanctified place of command, fear, and dominion. Without pause, Thaarn reached the threshold and, with one thunderous kick, sent both doors screaming open on their hinges. They slammed into the walls like collapsing towers.

Inside, Councilor Drevvos Varn and Director Yovarith stood beside a long obsidian conference table, which reflected the blood-red light of the room's central pyre. The flames licked skyward within a circular pit—an ever-burning reminder of Thaarn's dominion. Both men had been waiting, summoned by Thaarn himself, but now wished they had never come.

Councilor Varn flinched so violently at the explosion of the doors that his chair toppled behind him. He stood trembling, eyes wide with dread. Director Yovarith stood rigid, his pale face unreadable, but even he could not fully hide the twitch in his jaw.

Thaarn didn't slow. He crossed the sanctum like a thunderstorm on legs, black cloak trailing behind like the wake of a predator. With one colossal backhand, he shattered the conference table into a spray of molten shards and stone. Varn gasped but couldn't react before Thaarn's hand clamped around his throat and lifted him into the air as if he were a puppet made of twigs.

The wall rushed up behind them, and Varn's skull met it with a sickening thud. Once. Twice. A third time. Blood spattered across the flaming sigils engraved into the sanctum walls—and across Thaarn's bald head. Varn's legs kicked, hands grasping futilely at Thaarn's gauntlet, mouth agape but no sound escaping.

"Explain this... mockery of failure," Thaarn growled, his voice a furnace of hate. "You guaranteed me Xa'rekthul-Yenu-Vaahn was dead. You spat lies into my ears with the stench of certainty. Yet he stands! He breathes! On my world!"

Varn coughed violently, blood threading from his lips. "M-my Lord... I-I... the glider... it was destroyed. There were no... survivors presumed. No signals..."

"Do not insult me with coward's logic," Thaarn snarled. "You swore there were no doubts. You told me it was done—dead and buried beneath the mountains of Tzuraan'dhel-Monkaar."

"I... I was wrong. The sensors, they must have missed—"

Thaarn shook him violently. "Wrong? Do you wish to die in slow agony or in sudden fire? Shall I flay your mind with my Vorrak's venom before it eats your spine?" He gestured to the beast curled beneath his throne—a black smooth-furred nightmare of sheer muscle, whose tail twitched in eager anticipation of a kill.

"No, please!" Varn sobbed, clawing at Thaarn's wrist. "Spare me! It was not I who failed alone—Director Yovarith's scouts sent the report! They said the wreckage was unsalvageable! I trusted their word!"

From the shadows, Yovarith watched with sharp, gleaming eyes. He said nothing, but his expression darkened with a satisfaction he dared not show fully. This was a moment he had long awaited—a chance to see the mighty Councilor Drevvos Varn humbled. The director, meticulous and cunning, had ensured his agents recorded everything. And now, he would make sure Thaarn saw who truly served him better. He prayed Thaarn would eliminate Drevvos right here.

Thaarn bared his teeth. "Do not sling filth at others when the stain clings to your soul. You are the Councilor. It was you who gave the final word. Yovarith is part of YOUR team!"

Varn wept openly now, nodding desperately. "I will do anything to rectify this. Anything, my Lord!"

Thaarn hurled him across the room like refuse. Varn landed hard, coughing blood onto the scorched floor.

Breathing hard, Thaarn turned his gaze to Director Yovarith. He pointed an ominous finger at him.
"You! Show me the footage. Now!"

Yovarith, composed but tense, reached into his longcoat and pulled forth a thin disc-shaped device no larger than a coin. With a press, it unfolded into a tri-spined emitter. A shimmering veil of light expanded into a full-scale hologram. The room dimmed as a recorded scene materialized above the table's shattered remains.

The Vrelkhar-class strikejet's cameras played the combat footage in crisp detail. Thaarn leaned forward, his monstrous form settling into his throne as Vorrak stirred and hissed beside him.

The footage showed a red, rocky valley where a chaotic clash unfolded. The strikejet had intercepted a skirmish in progress, one in which three distinct fighters appeared. One was unmistakably Xa'rekthul-Yenu-Vaahn—his movements a seamless storm of flame and shadow, a deadly blur across the dirt. The second was a female, identity unconfirmed. She danced through the battlefield with twin knives, cutting down foes with haunting elegance—a specter amid the storm. The third, a tall man with a gun, was also unrecognized, but devastatingly efficient.

They weren't the aggressors—they were the rescuers. The footage revealed the object of their intervention: Vaelik Dron'Shal-Mareth, being brutalized by Thaarn's own forces. The troopers had surrounded and were savagely beating him when the trio erupted into action, decimating the attackers with terrifying precision. Eight elite soldiers fell before the storm ceased.

The footage looped—silent but damning. These were no chance allies. They moved as one—with history, coordination, and purpose.

EIGHT elite troopers. Dead. To three. How?

Yovarith swallowed his fear, expression carefully neutral. The Lord would likely want to know why eight highly trained troopers were annihilated so easily. As the video looped again, Thaarn leaned back and watched. To the director's surprise, he didn't ask.

"Slower," Thaarn ordered.

The playback slowed to half-speed, then quarter-speed. The trio's movements became clearer—lethal precision, seamless cooperation. Thaarn watched with cold intensity.

They zoomed into the girl's face. Unidentified.
"Who is she?" Thaarn asked.

"Unknown," said Yovarith. "Her genetic profile doesn't match any from Veltharuun. Possibly Vael'Sythrin Reach-born, or beyond. But she is skilled. Likely First Alliance."

"And the male with the gun?"

"Also unknown, sire. But certainly part of the same putrid faction. He seems to have military style training."

"Tell me more about the one our troopers were beating before the massacre."

Yovarith raised his head. "Vaelik Dron'Shal-Mareth. Former architect of sabotage, known to us since Operation Emberwake Upreach."

Thaarn turned slowly. "Speak."

"Years ago, during the peace summit at Sur'vel-Kaarn, the First Alliance—led by Xa'rekthul and Vaelik—breached our Prism Core Facility. Using a cascade loop algorithm, they ruptured our energy cells. Over four hundred Pyrelance elites were incinerated in seconds."

"Continue." Thaarn growled in rage.

"Vaelik commands infiltration teams. Cybernetic eye, likely augmented for thermal and signal spectrum. Our reports place him at attacks on the Iron Wards of Haldek-Karn, the Arkvault in Shaarn'yth, and two attempts on the Oriculium Mines. Almost always with Xa'rekthul. Always escaping."

"They mock us," Thaarn muttered.

"Yes, my Lord."

Thaarn said nothing.
He sat there. Brooding. Petting Vorrak.

Silence stretched.

Varn clutched his ribs, unsure if standing would provoke another blow. Yovarith stood tall, but tension tightened his jaw.

Finally, Thaarn stood.
His nine-foot frame rose like a tower. His cloak swirled behind him like smoke. His skin and bald head gleamed in the firelight.

"The city must fear."

"Councilor," he said, voice low and edged with razors. "Mobilize the armies. Every home in Veltharuun. Every dwelling. Ransack them. Tear stone from stone. I want every whisper hunted. Every breath interrogated. Mass infiltration."

Varn blinked. "M-my Lord, the population—"

"Billions of them," Thaarn said. "I know. I do not care. Search them all. No delay. No mercy."

Varn bowed, trembling. "It will be done. I swear. No failures. Never again."

Thaarn turned to Yovarith. "Director. Deploy every spy. Activate every drone. Every insect, every lens. I want eyes in every crevice of this city. Find them. All of them."

"Of course, my Lord. The Eyes Beneath Agency will not fail. I will get on it immediately."

"If you do fail," Thaarn growled, "I'll offer your bones to Vorrak as a toy. Be sure of that."

The doors groaned shut as the Councilor and Director left, steps quick, minds racing.

Thaarn remained.

He turned and beckoned Vorrak.
The beast followed. Venom glands pulsing.

They walked to the Grand Balcony—a vast, crescent-shaped expanse of obsidian, jutting from the edge of Mount Khurazh like a guillotine blade. The wind howled as it tore past the spiked parapets, laced with the scent of molten rock and iron. From here, Veltharuun unfolded like a living beast. Spires twisted skyward like claws, veined with glowing lava that bled through stone. Enormous plumes of steam rose from magma forges and vents, clouding the air with heat shimmer and sulfur. Crimson banners fluttered on mechanized poles, their edges scorched by drifting embers.

The sky was a living furnace, lit by a red giant star overhead. Clouds glowed like dying coals. The atmosphere trembled under the star's oppressive glare. Distant ridges shimmered with obsidian snow—a paradox of beauty and death.

Thaarn stood tall, the wind tugging at his cloak like it too wished to flee.
He felt the city's hunger—the desperation, the fear—and it fed him. Below, billions toiled, unaware of the fate he now prepared.

His lips curled into a cruel smile.

"They will obey," he whispered to the wind.
"Or they will bleed. They will all bleed."

Vorrak hissed and cuddled lovingly to his master.

The greatest threat to Orulenthia's security was about to be initiated soon.

CHAPTER 32
THE PORTAL TRIALS BEGIN.

The wind stirred dust and ash from the cracked plains, sending swirls of grit dancing like restless spirits around the crash site of the Skyraleon-class glider. The air still shimmered faintly with heat, and the blackened, twisted wreckage of the craft jutted from the rocky soil like the bones of a fallen giant. Omar squinted and raised a hand to shield his eyes, rubbing the grit from his lashes. The sky above was streaked with crimson-orange light from the eternal glow of Orulenthia's red giant sun, casting long, bleeding shadows across the scattered debris. Nearby, Ali leaned on a bent strut, his eyes wide with anticipation as Nysha pulled a cylindrical torch from her pack, its metal casing etched with old scorch marks.

Vaan stood silently before the Kha'Len, the ancient artifact resting in the crook of a stone pedestal they had erected from broken glider panels and loose boulders. Its triangular ruby core pulsed faintly—like a heartbeat in stone. The back of the artifact displayed three glyphs, their inscriptions glowing in Urdii script, unreadable to Omar and Ali. Vaelik paced nervously nearby, his eyes darting between the group and the horizon, his long hair rippling in the wind like frayed silk.

"This one," Vaan said, pointing to the first glowing symbol. "It means *'Return to Previous Location.'* If used, it will attempt to open a portal back to the last coordinates the Kha'Len registered. The second is *'Select Random Destination.'* No control over where it leads. Dangerous, but revealing. And this—" he tapped the third glyph, which was shaped like a thorned spiral, "—is '*Choose Destination*.' That one requires focus. Thought. Precision. We should try this one last."

Nysha clicked on the torch, sending a powerful white beam slicing through the swirling dust. She stepped forward, adjusting the torch's angle to shine directly onto the glyphs so Omar and Ali could clearly see what Vaan was pointing to. Her voice was steady, but her fingers trembled slightly. "You guys ready for this?" she asked.

Omar exchanged a look with Ali, who gave a quick nod. Their hearts thundered with excitement and fear, knowing they were about to pierce space-time itself.

Omar stepped forward, took a deep breath, and slid his finger across the first glyph.

The symbol flared to life in a flash of golden-yellow, etching glowing trails across its surface before sinking into the ruby core. Nysha immediately shifted the beam of her torch to the front of the Kha'Len, illuminating the red triangular crystal. The moment the light touched it, the crystal blazed with intensity, changing from a gentle pulse to a brilliant, radiant inferno.

With a crackle and a deep hum that resonated through their bones, the air in front of the artifact twisted inward. The space beyond the crystal folded like cloth sucked through a pinhole, then exploded outward into a swirling vortex of reds, golds, and blues. The center of the portal shimmered, then steadied—revealing the scrubby, open outskirts of Veltharuun.

Ytelthuun gasped aloud and stumbled backward, falling onto the dirt with a short yelp. Vaan instinctively stepped back, eyes wide and mouth agape. The sight was mesmerizing—a perfectly round gateway floating in the air, framing the exact terrain Omar and Ali remembered from when they had first arrived on Orulenthia. Sparse trees. Jagged hills. A familiar dust path.

"That's it! That's the place!" Omar shouted, pointing at the portal. He and Ali high-fived, their laughter bubbling up with the same childlike wonder they'd felt when they first discovered the talisman's power. Even Nysha allowed herself a grin, her fully black eyes flickering with reflected light.

Vaelik stood still for a long moment, jaw clenched. Then he whispered, "By the shadows of Khurazh... it works. It really works. A portal... A gateway to another space. This is brilliant!"

The portal shimmered for a few more minutes before the red crystal dimmed, and with a sigh like an exhaling storm, the gateway collapsed in on itself, vanishing with a soft flash.

Without hesitation, Omar reached out and slid his finger across the second glyph. Again, the script flared gold. Nysha redirected the beam, and once more the ruby ignited. This time, the air twisted into a different hue. The portal formed again—this time revealing a vast alien ocean under a violet sky. The waves rolled with a metallic shimmer, and bursts of lightning forked downward in lazy, electric arcs from thunderclouds shaped like spirals. This was a random destination selected by the Kha'Len by itself.

No one said a word.

They simply stared.

And then the ocean portal winked out.

They activated the random command one more time.

This time, the portal opened onto a vibrant, lush world teeming with life. Endless green canopies stretched across rolling hills, interrupted only by towering white structures that shimmered like pearl in the sunlight. Gigantic waterfalls plunged from impossibly tall cliffs, creating a chorus of roaring mist that sparkled like stars in daylight. Brightly colored creatures soared above the treetops in the blue sky, their wings like stained glass in motion. The air buzzed with the sound of thriving ecosystems—chirps, rustles, and songs echoing in a harmony of life. Everything pulsed with energy and serenity, as if the planet itself were a living, breathing garden.

Vaelik fell to his knees. "Wow! Look at that weird *blue* sky! *GREEN* plants? What?! This... this is power beyond measure," he murmured. "We could reach anywhere. Hide anywhere. Attack from anywhere." He was in complete disbelief.

A silence settled over the group.

Then Omar spoke. "Let's try the last one."

With careful breath, Omar pressed his finger against the third glyph. The script shimmered. The artifact thrummed. Nysha again aimed the torchlight into the ruby. But this time, there was no swirling vortex at first—only a slow, intense build-up of light inside the crystal, pulsing brighter with every second.

Omar closed his eyes.

He thought of Nysha's family farm. He remembered the small stone dwelling. The rows of pale blue crops. The silence. The safety. He recalled the way the breeze stirred the leaves in gentle rustles and how Luma would chase the shadows cast by the crimson sun. A sense of longing filled him—bittersweet and steady. He focused his thoughts like a sharpened arrow, pouring the image of the farm into the ruby.

With a roar of displaced air, the crystal ignited.

The portal opened.

There it was.

The quiet farmlands south of Vael'Sythrin Reach. The stone house. The neat rows. The breeze moving across the fields like ghost fingers.

"Well, here we go! Hope everyone's ready. Let's do this quickly." Omar was excited.

One by one, they moved toward the portal.

Vaan entered first.

Then Ytelthuun slipped through.

Vaelik followed with a cautious step.

Nysha turned to the boys. "Let's go home."

Ali grinned and went through. Omar took one last glance at the red sun above.

Then he stepped forward.

The sensation of travel through the portal was like being unzipped from reality and stitched into another. A current of raw, electric air wrapped around them as if they were wind-spirits diving through the veins of a living planet. Time fractured. Shapes bled together. Gravity forgot its laws. Their breath caught in their throats, not from fear, but from the sheer alien force pulling at the fibers of their being. The sensation was both painful and sublime, like being burned and healed in the same moment. Light had taste, sound had texture, and their thoughts shimmered in colors they couldn't name.

Omar felt his body stretch and compact all at once. Patterns danced across his vision—maps, memories, starlit fractals spiraling into and out of each other. He could hear the pulse of Orulenthia itself, a heartbeat of molten rhythm beneath the vibrations. His arm turned into spaghetti stretching forward into the unknown.

Ali's voice echoed somewhere near and far. "This... this is insane!"

The portal roared.

Then everything fell away.

Omar and Ali landed gently this time—not jarring or breathless like their first experience. Probably because their bodies were now adjusted to the gravity and air of Orulenthia. The landing was a soft glide into familiarity. Nysha let out a breath she hadn't realized she'd been holding, her eyes wide with disbelief and joy. Vaan gave a low, breathless laugh, clapping Vaelik on the shoulder.

"It actually worked," he whispered, half in awe.

The relief was palpable. After so many near-deaths, misfires, and cosmic unknowns, they had arrived safely—exactly where they had intended. Luma, Nysha's fluffy creature, popped its head out of her backpack and gave a delighted squeak. Everyone laughed. This was a joyous occasion.

They were back at Nysha's family farm.

The soft hum of the crystalline grid pulsed in the soil beneath them. The house looked untouched, serene amidst the alien rows of crops. Pale blue leaves waved as if welcoming them home.

Inside, they activated Nysha's grid console. Vaan, Vaelik, and Ytelthuun immediately began speaking through comm-crystals, reaching out to nodes across Orulenthia. Transmission lines opened to secret Alliance outposts—coded messages, anxious voices.

After nearly two hours of frantic communication, the full weight of the situation emerged.

Veltharuun was no longer safe.

Thaarn had begun a full sweep of the city, twisting it into a living nightmare of paranoia and dread. Once-bustling markets now lay hollow and abandoned, their stalls overturned and splattered with black ash. The streets echoed only with the crunch of boots and the wail of aerial drones—sickle-winged machines that screamed through alleys, scanning everything with harsh crimson beams. Homes were not just searched—they were violated. Doors exploded inward. Walls were ripped open with sonic charges. Infants were torn from cribs while parents were forced to kneel under gunmetal muzzles. Every shadow became a potential traitor. Every whisper, a crime. Thaarn's elite enforcers—cloaked in flowing black exo-robes and bristling with neuromagnetic weaponry—marched from block to block, dragging the innocent away for "questioning."

Public squares became makeshift theaters of terror. Loudspeakers blared crackling warnings in Thaarn's voice: *"Confess, and you may serve. Hide, and you will burn."* Steel platforms were erected, and the promise of daily executions—though none had yet occurred—hung over the populace like the stink of rot. People began disappearing. Families woke to empty beds. Friends vanished mid-sentence. And always, always, the red sun glared down, casting everything in a feverish glow, as if the city itself were bleeding from invisible wounds.

But no rebels had yet been caught.

And that made Thaarn angrier.

But it was only a matter of time.

"Everyone's talking about you, Vaan," said a voice through the grid, fuzzy but emotional. "You're alive. You've returned. That gives us hope."

Hope.

But fear too.

Thaarn's forces were mobilizing in every district. They were hunting the First Alliance with a fury.

The transmissions finally ended. The grid dimmed.

They were all exhausted beyond belief. It had been too long since anyone had last rested or slept.

Omar and Ali curled up together on a soft patch near the console, with Luma wriggling between them, nestling against Ali's chest. Nysha and Ytelthuun slumped on a nearby bench, boots off, legs sprawled, breathing slow.

The red sun above burned endlessly, but the room felt dark with fatigue.

Only Vaan and Vaelik remained upright, huddled near the Kha'Len resting atop a crystal stand. The device no longer glowed—it pulsed with quiet purpose, waiting.

"I've got ideas," Vaelik murmured. "We could open portals near Thaarn's prison complexes. Get our people out. Move them to remote sites. Hit targets. Vanish. Keep repeating."

"Every use of the Kha'Len leaves a trace that we have a technology they don't," Vaan said. "We can never allow them to know we have this power. Everything has to be done as quietly and neatly as possible. They cannot record us or else it's over. Our attacks need to be as mysterious as possible."

They planned and brainstormed for a while, sketching out imaginary operations on a transparent data-slab. But soon, even they could no longer stay awake.

They laid down beside the others.

And for the first time in days, silence took them.

Only the hum of the distant fields remained.

And far, far away—in the iron towers of Veltharuun—Lord Thaarn sharpened his knives against the civilians of the city.

CHAPTER 33
FROM DOORSTEPS TO DUNGEONS – VELTHARUUN'S DESCENT INTO HORROR.

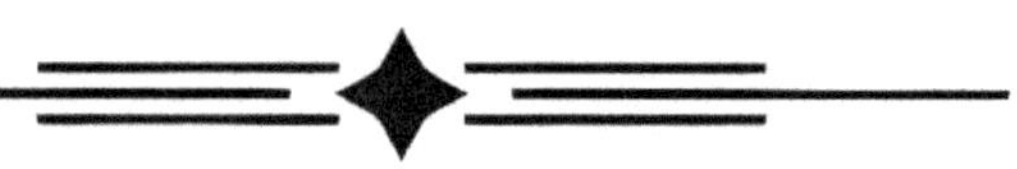

The city of Veltharuun had become unrecognizable in just a few solar cycles. Once teeming with neon-lit markets, winding crystalline streets, and the thrum of a thousand voices from every walk of life, it now groaned beneath the iron boot of Lord Xar'Vulek Thaarn's regime. Entire districts lay in ruin. Homes had been ransacked by cloaked enforcers who tore through personal sanctuaries like predators among prey. Doors splintered under the assault of steel-booted soldiers, while walls bled dust and memory into the streets. Families were dragged into the crimson glare of the red giant sun—fathers accused of conspiracy, mothers beaten for silence, children left wailing beside the charred husks of their vehicles. Shops that once sold artisanal wares now stood gutted, the proprietors either executed or taken—no one dared ask which.

Along the River Spienalyynt, once famed for its iridescent blue lightflows, corpses had begun to drift. Thaarn's enforcers had found several traders harboring encrypted messages, and for that, they were beheaded and tossed into the waters as a warning. High above the skyline, drones patrolled like vultures, scanning for heat signatures and voice prints. Any anomaly, any hesitation, any stray whisper against the regime—even behind reinforced walls—was logged and reported. Deep in the heart of the Aurelianeq Sector, two entire housing complexes had been leveled with seismic charges after a suspected First

Alliance sympathizer was discovered to have once lived there. No survivors. Not even the elderly or infirm were spared.

Fear was omnipresent—in every alley, every glance, every unspoken word. The shadows of Veltharuun were no longer just darkness—they were haunted with the knowledge that at any moment, anyone could vanish. This was not merely a city under occupation—it was a crucible of paranoia, where loyalty was currency bought with blood, and silence the only proof of innocence.

Director Yovarith stood hunched over a vast console in the Eyes Beneath Agency's subterranean control chamber. Banks of holo-screens hovered around him in shifting orbit, casting ghostly light over his gaunt, angular face. Dozens of spectral-blue eyes glowed on each screen—feeds from spider-like reconnaissance drones skittering through ventilation shafts, beneath floorboards, and even inside household reservoirs. Invasive audio siphons latched onto windows and walls, recording whispered conversations and dream-induced mutterings. He watched as one feed captured a woman humming a lullaby—an old resistance tune. With a flick of his wrist, a crimson sigil branded her home as suspect. Moments later, the drone released a spore-pulse beacon to signal a strike team.

Every breath taken by the city was archived. Every meal cooked, every pattern of sleep, every fluctuation in tone—all of it fed into the Khyreth-Net Sovidome, the sentient surveillance matrix that funneled suspects into Yovarith's growing database. From that artificial intelligence network, names emerged like condemned ghosts: architects, engineers, schoolteachers, street performers. To Yovarith, innocence was an illusion—statistical noise. His left wrist vibrated. An incoming transmission.

"Director. Report to the Sanctum of Sovereign Flame at once."

Thaarn's voice cut through his mind like a brand. Without hesitation, Yovarith deactivated the display and swept from the chamber, cloak trailing like living ink.

Meanwhile, Councilor Drevvos Varn stood in the Grand Cartographic Hall, surrounded by a flickering dome of holographic terrain—a three-dimensional rendering of Veltharuun and its surrounding outlands. He gestured toward key sectors, assigning squads and air-drones with grim precision. The vox-chambers on his belt echoed with incoming battle reports, and his eyes—cold, black shards—watched with surgical focus. He had divided the city into quadrants, placing shock troops near marketplaces and elite siege units around potential data centers. The southern ward had been isolated, its communication pylons vaporized by targeted plasma bursts. Even emergency frequencies had been muted.

He watched the map cycle through simulations—raids, blockades, entrapment strategies. In one, a decoy broadcast lured suspected rebels into a clinic before sealing it and flooding it with nerve mist. Varn paused, considering the variables. The ends always justified the means. This was war. War against the First Alliance—and anyone else who stood in the way.

A notification pulsed at the edge of his vision—Thaarn's mark.

"Report to my Sanctum. Now."

Councilor Varn closed the map with a sweep of his hand, grabbed his glaive-helix, and strode into the torch-lit corridor, steps silent but seething.

At the apex of the Fortress of Echoes, in the volcanic sanctum of the Sovereign Flame, Lord Xar'Vulek Thaarn stood before a brazier of molten crystal. The chamber pulsed with ambient heat, red-orange light flickering across obsidian tiles and golden fire-etched walls. Above him, gargantuan effigies of conquered worlds loomed in alien metal, mouths eternally agape in horror. His dark robes flowed like thick oil, and the armor beneath shimmered with veins of arc-light.

He had summoned them. The Director. The Councilor. Their efforts had been acceptable—but Thaarn hungered for more. Every hour that passed without the fall of the First Alliance was a personal insult. His clawed control-glove hovered above a console inlaid with crystal and ruby. One touch, and the cells below would ignite with agony. He smiled.

They arrived.

Director Yovarith entered first, kneeling low, head bowed until the tips of his tall headpiece scraped the steps.

"My lord."

Then came Varn, slower, but equally reverent.

Thaarn did not rise from his elevated throne. His voice cracked the silence like a monstrous thunderstorm.

"Tell me, Director. How far have your shadows crawled? What secrets have they unearthed from this city's dying whispers?" His voice was a haunting growl.

Yovarith rose slowly. "My lord, the Khyreth-Net Sovidome has rooted itself in every vein of Veltharuun. We've deployed proximity-lurkers in all high-density housing sectors. Whisper-probes have been installed in temple walls and civic statues. We intercepted three memory-crystals containing future attack coordinates targeting your transit hubs. We traced encrypted vibrations from musical instruments in Resistance-frequented districts. Disguised empath drones have infiltrated pleasure houses and child-learning domes, sniffing out rebellious sentiment before it blooms. Over two hundred and fifty confirmed rebels have been executed for choosing to fight. One hundred and eighty-six more are captured and under interrogation. More... will follow."

Thaarn leaned forward, lips parting in what might have been a smile. "You have exceeded my expectations, Yovarith. A rare feat."

The Director bowed again, eyes wide with quiet ecstasy. This was a special moment. Praise directed at him—and not at the councilor—was a prize. He hoped Thaarn found Varn lacking.

Thaarn's gaze snapped to Varn. His voice dropped further.

"And you, Councilor? What of you? Have you tasted even a sliver of success, or must I again reflect upon your failure to eliminate the traitor Xa'rekthul-Yenu-Vaahn?"

Councilor Varn swallowed and stepped forward. "My lord, I've begun to redeem the stain. My squadrons have unearthed six hidden weapon caches, five underground meeting halls, and three encrypted signal transmitters buried beneath faux gardens. We've dismantled over seventy percent of rebel comms infrastructure in the outer city. I've flooded the eastern sectors with neural screamers, driving potential insurgents to madness. Any caught aiding the afflicted are taken—alive if possible, but often not. All have been delivered to your dungeons for further clarity extraction."

Thaarn stared, unreadable.

Then: "Satisfactory. Satisfactory, Councilor."

He rose—monumental, dreadful.

"But this is not enough. The city must be purged. Not cleansed, not pacified—purged. Continue the siege. Break them in their homes, their souls, their dreams. Tear open walls. Burn their food. Poison their water, if need be. Rip secrets from their throats. Every scream must serve a purpose. I want the First Alliance dragged from every rock and root."

He stalked the room, shadows dancing across his face.

"And when we find them—when at least three hundred rebels lie within my reach—then begins the spectacle. You will build a platform above Mawe'Porozqq Plaza. I will call it, 'The Pinnacle of Judgment.' It will broadcast to every corner of this planet. From its blood-slick surface, I will execute them one by one, while millions watch in person and billions via hologram."

Thaarn turned and smiled.

"I shall wield the Fal'Korynth Reaper—my execution scythe forged from the severed spines of the four Threximaar kings—and beside me, my Vorrak will feast on rebel remains. When this is done—when the world sees me slaughter their hope—none will ever defy me again. Never. Ever."

He burst into a maniacal and uncontrollable laughter. Not amusement—something volcanic and mad. It echoed into every crevice of the Sanctum, freezing the spines of even his most loyal servants. The Director and the Councilor shivered in horror and awe.

They left to initiate his will.

The solar cycles passed like bruises blooming across flesh.

Spy drones swept the streets like mechanized locusts. Shadow squads burst through homes without warning. In the Pazl'Eruuq Temple District, an entire family was drowned in molten silicate because a child muttered a rebel anthem. A supply shop was incinerated for using symbols resembling the Alliance's crest. An old man's arms were shattered and his skin flayed for refusing to name his granddaughters. They killed him anyway.

Food was withheld from apartment towers until someone spoke. False tips earned coin and amnesty. Neighbors turned on neighbors. The noncompliant were branded with searing sigils and displayed in markets—still breathing, still screaming. Hospitals closed. Schools became interrogation centers. Fire-slicked drones and hover-ships patrolled the skies, dragging prisoners by their arms in harnesses.

In the south, artists painted murals of hope. Thaarn's enforcers turned the neighborhood into a crater. His fury was absolute.

And in the Fortress of Echoes, it grew worse.

The dungeons overflowed with a density of suffering beyond comprehension. Bodies lined the obsidian corridors, some twitching, others frozen in twisted agony. Screams were the native tongue—raw, endless, echoing as if the walls themselves mourned. Rebels, suspected or not, were suspended in acidic plasma that stripped skin and memory alike. Others were impaled beneath thought-drills, minds pierced by psionic agony until secrets—true or not—were extracted.

One chamber housed bio-cubes that looped each prisoner's most traumatic memory. Another contained cages suspended in air, each holding someone whose body had been replaced piece by piece with fireglass that burned brighter with every scream. The Path of Untruth forced captives to crawl on bleeding limbs across electrified grates, confessing to crimes they'd never heard of. Execution chambers designed not to kill, but to break, dripped acid drop by drop, carving confessions into flesh.

Even the guards trembled. Some whispered of a wing so dark even Thaarn seldom entered it—where walls held the souls of the screaming dead. It wasn't a prison. It was a cathedral of agony.

Some prisoners were impaled through the shoulders and left to hang until they begged to confess. One woman had her limbs turned to crystalline stone, then shattered while Thaarn applauded.

A group of rebels sent a final message: "They're torturing everyone...even the innocent... run while you still can—" It cut off. Their heads now sat on pikes outside the fortress.

Veltharuun's walls bore a single message:

THE PINNACLE OF JUDGMENT – TOMORROW

Three hundred would die.

Children were taught to cheer. Billboards displayed the Fal'Korynth Reaper spinning beneath the red sun. Vorrak snarled in anticipation.

There would be no mercy.

Veltharuun was no longer a city. It was a carcass—hollowed by fear, rotting under despair. Streets once filled with music were now mute, scattered with ash and old blood. The red sun burned like a festering wound. Children didn't cry anymore. Silence kept them alive. Even the wind dared not howl.

Holograms looped the same grim mantra:
Tomorrow, they die. Your silence will be rewarded.
Smoke rose not for warmth, but from funeral pyres. The soil grew nothing but bones and sorrow.

In the Fortress of Echoes, Lord Xar'Vulek Thaarn prepared—not with blade, but with a hunger so absolute it gnawed at the fabric of reality itself.

The city braced for the massacre.

And in the silence, hope cracked—
and turned to dust. Only misery remained.

CHAPTER 34
THE RED SKY WAITS FOR HEROES.

The pale blue rows of Nysha's family farm shimmered gently under the dull red light of the ever-constant sun. The symmetrical crops stood in obedient lines, swaying lightly in the wind as if unaware of the world's collapse just a continent away. The house—a small stone structure laced with crystalline panels—was quiet, yet heavy with tension. Inside, Nysha sat curled in a corner, her shoulders trembling, her face streaked with tears. Her black eyes, red from weeping, stared blankly at the flickering hologram hovering above the room's central console. The transmission played on loop: Thaarn, looming before a massive crowd, announcing the event that would become etched in infamy—The Pinnacle of Judgment. She choked out a sob as the images showed First Alliance rebels being dragged by chains, their eyes wide with terror, bruised and bleeding, their fates already sealed.

Vaan stood beside her, torn. He wanted to rip the console from the wall and hurl it across the room, to scream at the sky until his throat gave out. But all he could do was place a trembling hand on her shoulder.
"It should've been me," he muttered again and again, his voice cracking under the weight of guilt. "If I had just surrendered... maybe this wouldn't have happened."
His shame wrapped around him like a shroud—thick and suffocating. But Ytelthuun, ever the calm in their storm, stood firm before him.

"No, Vaan," he said sternly, his one organic black eye filled with resolve. "Thaarn's wrath is not born of you alone. He was always going to bring ruin. You are not the cause of his madness—you are simply the excuse."

Plans had been drawn, discarded, revised, and drawn again. Before Thaarn's rampage, they had dreamed of using the Kha'Len to open targeted portals—into the dungeons, the surveillance towers, the prison caravans transporting captives under cover of night. They would slip in, liberate, vanish. A perfect retaliation without blood. But none of it had come to pass. Thaarn's blitz on Veltharuun had struck before their schemes could solidify. The executions, the citywide raids, the endless screams—those had come first. The blood had begun to flow, and now all they could do was find a way to damn the flood.

Outside, a wind picked up, tossing fine dust into the air like ash from a funeral pyre. The red sky roared faintly, like the growl of some distant god. Vaelik stood by the edge of the field, staring into the horizon where nothing moved but dust and regret. He clenched his jaw as he watched the newsfeed replay Thaarn's speech. Three hundred to be executed. The whole world watching. And the tyrant would be the executioner himself. Hope, once so stubborn, now clung to their hearts like the last ember in a dying hearth.

It was Ytelthuun who finally broke the silence.
"We can't just sit here. Not anymore."
His voice rang like tempered steel in the quiet room. He looked at the others—each one frozen in fear and pain, their minds scattered like debris in a storm.
"We have to do something."

Vaelik rubbed his temples.
"Do what, Ytelthuun? Take out Thaarn? You think it's that simple?"
He gestured toward the floating feed of the Fortress of Echoes.

"He's hidden in that mountain fortress like a god on his throne. Even if we open a portal inside, we don't know which room he's in. That entire structure is crawling with drones—drone swarms, pulse cannons, flame beacons, motion mines. Anything not tagged to their system gets shredded in seconds. Before we even find the right room, we'll be obliterated."

"But we do know where he'll be tomorrow," Ali said suddenly, his voice quiet but firm.
The youngest of them all, he now stood near the console, eyes fixed on the execution announcement.
"He'll be on the execution platform. At The Pinnacle of Judgment. We know the time. We know the place. That's something. Isn't it?"

Everyone turned to him. The silence that followed wasn't dismissal—it was awakening.
Vaan stepped forward, nodding slowly.
"He's right."

Ytelthuun's eyes widened, the gears in his mind already turning.
"Yes... yes! That might actually work. A direct portal. Right onto the stage. Mid-execution. According to the holo-news, he'll be alone on the platform as he executes the rebels. His military won't be far, but he'll be isolated on that stage."

Vaelik exhaled.
"That would be madness. But also... brilliant."

Omar spoke up.
"If we opened a portal at just the right moment... he wouldn't be expecting it."

"We'd have one chance," said Nysha, her voice raw but steady.
"One heartbeat to strike before the drones register our presence."

"The people will be watching," Vaan added.
"If Thaarn falls before their eyes, it could ignite everything. Fear may finally give way to fury. They'll rise. That's for sure."

"Even if we fail," said Ytelthuun, "even if we don't make it out alive... the signal we send will echo. That the fight is not over—not even in a situation as bleak as this."

They sat together, building the idea like architects of rebellion. Vaan proposed timing the portal to open precisely when Thaarn stepped forward to begin the executions. Nysha offered to amplify their chances with a signal disruptor she had scavenged months ago. Ytelthuun began listing coordinates and mapping escape portals in case any of them survived. Vaelik detailed drone sensor delay times and how they might hack a delay loop for just three seconds. Every mind was on fire. Ali and Omar watched, awed, as the impossible took shape before them.

And in that moment, hope did not flicker—it roared.

The hours before battle are always the heaviest.

Vaelik knelt beside the Kha'Len, whispering to it as if it could understand his pleas. He double-checked the glyphs, the red triangular crystal, and the shimmering patterns that only revealed themselves under the right wavelength. Nearby, Ytelthuun was preparing remote bombs—cloaked detonators that could be tossed into a drone nest. Each one no larger than a thumb, yet powerful enough to punch a hole through a fortress wall.

Nysha stood at a tall, narrow workbench beside her home, checking the signal jammer she planned to wear on her arm. It hummed faintly, its surface glowing with alien script. She adjusted the dial carefully, praying it would buy them the seconds they needed. She also packed her torch, so she could light the red crystal of the talisman. Across the room, Vaan packed supplies—first-aid stimulants, energy cells, crystalline explosives, and the last of their food ration bars. He paused only once to stare at a faded picture of himself with a woman—his mother—before sliding it into his vest.

Omar and Ali helped where they could, mostly tasked with watching. Both had learned not to get in the way, but neither could stop their racing hearts. Ali kept twiddling the edge of his shirt, while Omar rubbed his fingers across the Kha'Len's surface, as if trying to memorize its feel. The room buzzed with quiet motion—people moving, preparing, building toward a moment where everything could change.

And beneath it all was fear.

Ali finally broke the silence.
"So… what about us?"

Omar turned to Nysha, who was adjusting one of her pulse-rings.
"Do we… go with you? Or…?"

Nysha's face crumpled. She dropped everything, ran to them, and wrapped them in a tight, sobbing hug.
"I'm so sorry. I'm so sorry we didn't think— with everything that's happened… we should've planned your way home."

Vaan stepped forward, nodding solemnly.
"You two have risked everything just by being here. After this… once the attack on Thaarn is done—no matter the outcome—we'll open a portal. You'll go home. You'll be safe."

Ytelthuun placed a hand on Omar's shoulder.
"We promise. The Kha'Len is yours to command. We'll make sure you reach your world again."

"Inshallah," said Ali softly.

"Inshallah," echoed Omar.

Vaelik stepped close, eyes glimmering.
"You two are stronger than most warriors I've known. You've earned peace. And you'll have it."

Omar swallowed hard.

"Just… thank you. All of you. I never thought we'd meet people like this—like you. You guys have become like family to us."

Ali wiped a tear.

"I'll miss Orulenthia. Even if it's scary, even if it's broken right now… it's also beautiful. And… you made it feel like home."

Omar nodded.

"If something happens tomorrow… and we don't get to say goodbye again… know that we'll never forget any of you. Not ever. You changed our lives. We'll follow you to Thaarn's location so we can quickly leave after your attack. We can't risk staying here on this farm… in case… well, in case you guys don't make it back. Then we'd be stuck here without the talisman, with no hope of ever returning. We still have a chance if we come with you and stay with the talisman."

The room went quiet, heavy with emotion. For a moment, nothing moved. Then Nysha pulled them into another hug—longer, tighter, filled with a sorrow that had no words. She felt genuinely sorry for the boys, who didn't deserve any of this.

They lay down that night in silence.

The red giant sun still hung above, casting its eternal crimson glow across the farm. The pale blue crops swayed gently, unaware of the war being planned just meters away. Omar and Ali lay side by side on sleeping mats, their hands clasped together beneath a thin blanket. Ytelthuun leaned against a wall, eyes open but unfocused. Nysha curled on her side near the doorway, clutching her signal jammer like a child's toy. Vaelik sat cross-legged near the Kha'Len, eyes closed in meditation. Vaan stared at the ceiling, fingers tapping the hilt of his blade, his mind lost in the battle to come.

No one really slept. Their thoughts raced like stormwinds through a canyon, howling with what-ifs and dread. The sky above seemed lower than usual, heavier, closer—as though

Orulenthia itself were holding its breath. The red hue wasn't warm. It felt cold. Watching. Waiting. Even the stars had dimmed, smothered by the ever-burning curtain of crimson. Each breath felt weighted, as if the very air had thickened with the promise of violence and loss. They could almost hear the distant echo of drums—phantoms of the execution to come—beating in their minds like war rhythms heralding the end. The farm, for all its quiet and isolation, felt like a fortress besieged by anxiety and time. And no barricade could keep the future from arriving.

They lay there, hearts hammering in silence, as if the ground beneath them might vanish at dawn.

Tomorrow, they would challenge a tyrant.
Tomorrow, the world might change—or burn.

CHAPTER 35
THE EXECUTION HOUR BENEATH A DYING STAR.

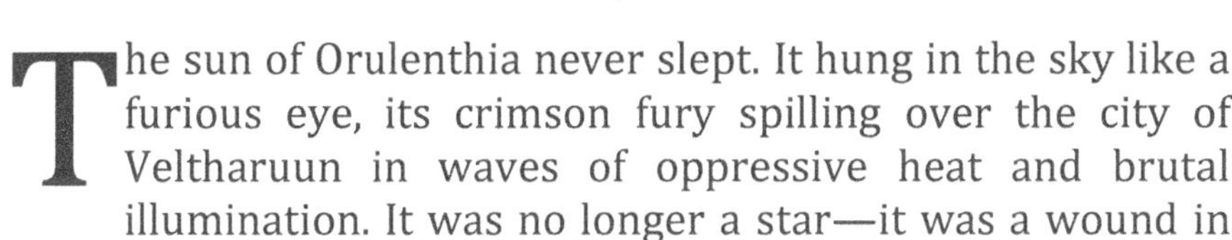

The sun of Orulenthia never slept. It hung in the sky like a furious eye, its crimson fury spilling over the city of Veltharuun in waves of oppressive heat and brutal illumination. It was no longer a star—it was a wound in the heavens, bleeding fire across a planet that had long since forgotten mercy. Today, it glared with malignant anticipation. The Execution Hour had come.

Councilor Drevvos Varn stood at the edge of a high-tiered viewing platform, several meters beneath the obsidian execution stage. His gloved hands gripped the railing, the polished metal trembling faintly beneath his fingers—not from fear, but from excitement. Director Yovarith stood beside him, his obsidian armor reflecting the arterial glow of the sky, eyes flitting across streams of tactical data scrolling over his augmented retinal visor. They had reviewed every detail a dozen times. The magnetic pulse-grid perimeter. The anti-personnel pulse turrets, hidden in plain sight to manage a shaken crowd. Even the dispersal pattern of crowd-control drones had been recalibrated. Nothing would go wrong. This was Thaarn's special day.

Above them loomed the execution platform—a jagged stage of brutalist black alloy laced with crimson veins of molten circuitry. Towering above the Mawe'Porozqq Plaza, it was shaped like a massive, jagged crescent. On it knelt 300 rebels of the First Alliance—defiant freedom fighters, broken down to bleeding husks. Their arms were restrained by binding coils made of alien biotech that slithered like living chains, holding each rebel in place. Every prisoner was blindfolded by memory-suppression metal mesh—a shimmering band that dimmed cognition and drowned dreams. They knelt in perfect formation—ten columns, thirty rows. Three hundred in total. Each line was separated by narrow alleys, wide enough for the executioner with a Reaper's scythe to walk through.

And upon a grotesque throne forged from lava and hardened metals, etched with suffering and empire, sat the executioner himself: Lord Xar'Vulek Thaarn.

Clad entirely in glistening black armor that devoured light, Thaarn sat without his usual ceremonial helmet, his pale skull bare and gleaming. His pitch-black eyes glowed like coals in a corpse's sockets. Resting across his lap was the Fal'Korynth Reaper—his long-awaited execution scythe. Forged in the distant gravity wells of Lporii'Restil-Faz, its quantum-edge shimmered with spectral flames. It had never been used. Today, it would feast.

At his side, lounging like the shadow of death made flesh, lay Vorrak.

Its fur was thick, black as pitch, almost metallic in sheen. Its face was angular, lizard-like, with glistening eyes of molten orange. A snake-like tongue flicked from between rows of jagged fangs, tasting the scorched air. The creature's long, barbed tail—dripping venom—swayed hypnotically. Vorrak was still—for now. But the crowd, the guards, the world—they all knew it needed but a whisper from Thaarn to become carnage incarnate.

Above them, camera drones—called Zeydril Orbs—hovered in ghost-silent clusters, their mirrored surfaces transmitting high-resolution footage to tens of millions of hologram displays across the planet. Today was declared the Triumph of Dominion. But it was no celebration.

It was horror masquerading as theater. A blood-drenched ballet. A planet-wide crucifixion of hope.

Nearly four hundred million citizens flooded the Grand Plaza of Dominion and its surrounding sectors—shoulder to shoulder, scaling rooftops, hanging from balconies, clinging to antenna towers. Children sat on shoulders; elders leaned on canes. They had come not for justice, but out of fear—obedient silence disguised as support. The stage was lit. The audience assembled. The executioner sharpened his blade with every heartbeat.

All that remained now—was time.

The moment of reckoning approached. Councilor Varn's gaze locked on the huge sky-clock mounted above the execution platform—its dial read: 3rd Compression of the Rhuz-Val Pulse, the planetary time-division marked by the rhythmic contraction of the red giant's solar core. It was precisely at this moment that the horn would sound.

The Torr'garaksa Horn, an impossibly massive instrument carved from the fossilized trachea of a sky-behemoth, was raised by a towering six-armed guard clad in scaled armor. With a breath that shook the tectonic plates beneath the plaza, the horn unleashed a sound that felt like the apocalypse. It didn't just pierce the air—it shattered it.

The crowd erupted. Flags of blood-red unfurled across the wind. Cries of "LONG LIVE THAARN!" echoed in countless dialects. Children cried. Parents wept and cheered. The noise was not joy. It was hysteria.

Lord Thaarn stood.

He lifted the Fal'Korynth Reaper above his head with one hand, the other raised to beckon the worship of billions. The metal of his armor hissed with kinetic activation. He drank in the noise like a beast inhaling steam. Every movement he made was echoed in the screens surrounding the city, reflected back at him in fractal infinity.

He walked the edge of the stage, arms outstretched. Director Yovarith clapped until his armored gloves cracked. Councilor Varn shouted "GLORY TO THAARN ETERNAL!" through a pulsing voice-projector.

The tyrant moved like a dark prophet in the firelight. He paused, looked down upon his prey, and smiled.

Then, he approached the first prisoner. A woman—face battered, lip split, nose crushed—but spine unbroken. She raised her blindfolded head and screamed, "FREE ORULENTHIA! FREE ORULENTHIA!"

The crowd gasped.

Thaarn pointed his scythe at her.

He took a step back. Twisted his body, winding the strike like a predator about to pounce. He raised the Reaper above his head. The crowd held its breath.

And then—something happened. A glimmer. A light. A shimmering circle began to grow wide.

A burst of impossible light crackled a few meters in front of Thaarn. The air tore apart with an audible hum. A portal spiraling outward like the center of a storm, surged into being.

Thaarn froze mid-swing. His arms trembled. His scythe hung suspended in the sky.

From the portal exploded six figures:

Nysha landed first, slamming down a veil of electromagnetic dust that shimmered with static and shielded their flank. Ytelthuun followed, his body crackling with psychic charge. Vaelik stormed out like a thunderbolt. Then came Omar and Ali, stumbling behind the veil, ducking low behind the others. And finally—Xa'rekthul-Yenu-Vaahn.

Vaan emerged in a single bound, sliding forward, blade already drawn, eyes locked on Thaarn like an avenging god.

The crowd went silent.

Then chaos.

Thaarn's mouth twisted in   utter disbelief and black eyes widened. "Xa'rekthul-Yenu-Vaahn," he snarled, the syllables warping the air.

"TRAITOR! INSECT! YOU DARE COME HERE?!"

Nysha wasted no time. She flung crystalline explosives from her utility harness over the edge of the platform. They detonated in fractal shockwaves, sending blast pulses into the viewing terrace below. Councilor Varn and Director Yovarith were thrown like dolls against the walls, slammed unconscious, or possibly killed dead, by the concussive waves.

Vaelik reached for his EMP weapon—the Zhauric Pulse Talon, a construct of sleek metal and electrified veins. He took aim. His cybernetic eye targeted precisely. He fired at the sky. Bolts of blue crackled upward, and within seconds, the Kynerath Drones—the kill-programmed hunter orbs—sputtered and died, falling like burning meteors into the crowd. Screams followed. Panic erupted.

But the Zeydril Orbs—the harmless video-recording drones remained.

The world would see this. They needed to.

Behind some prisoners, Omar and Ali crouched, hidden and terrified. The screams of millions thundered around them. The rebels knelt unmoving—still blindfolded, still bound, unaware of the chaos unraveling.

"I WILL END YOU, XA'REKTHUL!" Thaarn roared. "You festering little jhaern-worm! Vorrak—TO ME, MY BOY!"

Vorrak stood seething in anger. It rose like a horror from myth, tongue flicking, tail arched, fangs glistening.

"I'll handle this," Vaelik growled, eyes never leaving the beast.

Nysha grabbed his arm. "Vaelik, that thing has gutted entire battalions—don't you dare underestimate it!"

"Then I'll die a soldier!" he barked, pushing her aside.

He hurled a small incendiary sphere at Thaarn. The explosion flared at the tyrant's feet. Smoke. Fire. BOOM! And yet... no damage. Thaarn stepped through the flames like a demon, laughing. His armor was too strong. The bombs had no effect. His armor was impenetrable.

Vaelik's hand closed around his blade—a Khar'Zeth Fang, a machete made from the volcano-forged metals of Wyr-Knig.

Vorrak lunged towards them.

Vaelik screamed, "FREE ORULENTHIA!" and ran to meet it.

The impact was monstrous. Disastrous.

Vaelik's war cry echoed as he met the beast mid-charge. With both hands clenching the hilt of his Khar'Zeth Fang, he drove the blade downward in a savage arc just as Vorrak lunged. His cybernetic eye calculated the precise point to strike. The machete—jagged, bone-ridged, and forged to pierce the hides of monsters—slammed down with a wet, splitting crunch into Vorrak's skull. Resistance met him—sickening pressure pushed back—then cracked like stone under divine judgment. The blade sank deep, cleaving through black bone and sinew, splitting the monstrous head nearly to the jaw. Gore sprayed in arcs of black ichor, speckled with sparks as the Fang scraped something hard inside the beast's skull.

But Vorrak's death strike had already begun.

With savage instinct, the creature's barbed tail whipped forward. The spike—slick with venom—slammed into Vaelik's chest with the sound of shattering bone. It burst through his armor like paper, punching through his sternum and out under his left shoulder blade. A stream of green toxin hissed from the barb, searing his lungs from the inside.

Vaelik gasped—a wet, guttural sound—as foam bubbled from his mouth. He vomited involuntarily with blood and bile surging from his throat. He staggered; hands still locked on the blade buried in Vorrak's skull. As he fell to his knees, he gave one final wrench, splitting the beast fully down the center, until its head cracked open like a grotesque fruit. Vorrak's death-shriek echoed through the bones of everyone present.

Then both warrior and beast collapsed together, still locked in mortal embrace—the barbed tail protruding from Vaelik's twitching body, and the shattered skull of Vorrak steaming beside him.
It was done. The damage was irreversible.
"VAAELIIIK!" Nysha screamed.
Ytelthuun howled. Ali sobbed in tears. Omar buried his face.
Vaelik's body twitched, then went still. His eyes shut and his cybernetic eye turned off forever.

Thaarn looked down at the fallen creature—the only love of his life.
"You insects," he snarled. "My Vorrak's life was worth ten thousand of yours! You horrible murderers! How could you... Vorrak!"

Nysha charged, eyes burning with fury and tears.
"FREE ORULENTHIA!" she cried.
Ytelthuun followed, staggering but raging. Vaan, blade drawn, charged beside them.

Thaarn spun his Reaper like a cyclone. The butt of it slammed into Ytelthuun's head. He dropped to the hard floor.
Nysha lunged. Thaarn swept her legs out with the scythe. She fell, and he struck her skull with the blunt side.
Vaan skidded to a stop.
Now it was just him—and Lord Thaarn.

"ENOUGH!" Vaan shouted. "Orulenthia has bled enough! The First Alliance has suffered enough! Your madness, your empire, your lust for conquest ends here! Orulenthia will once again be free! Free from you!"
Thaarn grinned.

"You're just a corpse who forgot to die. You and your pathetic friends will rot in the dust of my legacy. Orulenthia belongs to ME. You will never stop me!"

Thaarn raised the scythe high.
"Come on, then," Vaan growled, eyes blazing.

The crowd began to chant.
"XA'REKTHUL-YENU-VAHN! XA'REKTHUL-YENU-VAHN!"
Thaarn's face twisted with rage. The crowd was chanting his enemy's name. Intolerable. This was too much for him.

They circled each other, never breaking eye contact—each waiting for the other to strike first.
Ytelthuun rose again—barely—and lunged. Thaarn struck him down with a gauntlet punch that shattered bone. Blood sprayed from Ytelthuun's head.
"STAY DOWN, INSECT!" Thaarn barked.

Vaan screamed, "FREE ORULENTHIA!"
He charged, wielding his blade.
Thaarn spun with terrifying speed, cutting the scythe across Vaan's chest in one swift move. He sliced easily through skin, muscle and bone.
Blood exploded out of him.
Vaan collapsed to the hard floor, gasping for breath and coughing up blood. His chest and stomach were split open, blood soaking the platform as he cried in agony.

Nysha screamed, "NOOOO!!! XA'REKTHUL-YENU-VAHN!"
Thaarn laughed maniacally, triumph gleaming in his black eyes as he planted his heavy boot on Vaan's chest and turned to the crowd.

Omar and Ali crouched low behind one of the kneeling rebels, their bodies pressed against the scorched platform. The molten veins beneath them pulsed like a heartbeat—angry and ancient. Around them, the screams of millions roared like a tidal wave of terror and awe. The air was thick with acrid smoke and the stench of blood and ozone. Holographic banners shimmered above, projecting Thaarn's cruel face in dizzying, surreal loops.

Ali's small frame shook beside Omar. His fists trembled, and his wide, innocent eyes were locked in panic. He peeked from behind the rebel, then recoiled instantly.
"He's—he's standing on Vaan," he whispered, voice cracking. "He's laughing. Vaan's gonna die! We're gonna die! What do we do, Omar? We're gonna die!! He'll come for us next!"

Omar swallowed hard. His throat was dry as ash. He dared a glance. Thaarn stood triumphant, foot on Vaan's chest, scythe slick with blood. Behind him, Vorrak's carcass coiled in death beside Vaelik's slumped body. Nysha's cries echoed beneath the monstrous noise.

"What do we do?" Ali whimpered. "We can't fight him. We'll die, Omar. We'll die here. This is our end!"

Omar couldn't answer. Every part of him screamed to run, to cry, to disappear. They were just kids from New Jersey. What were they doing here, on a dying planet beneath a bleeding star, watching a monster kill their friends?

His thoughts spiraled—until something surged up inside him. Not courage. Clarity. Like a star breaking through storm clouds.
That's it.
The talisman.
The glyphs.
The phone.

His breath caught. The pieces clicked.
He turned to Ali so fast their shoulders bumped. "Ali," he said, locking eyes, "Gimme your iPhone. NOW!"
Ali blinked, confused. "Wha—what? My—"
"Your PHONE!" Omar hissed. "Toss it now!"

Ali fumbled through his pocket and pulled out his cracked iPhone. The screen was filthy, the battery at 11%. But it would do.

He tossed it underhand. Omar snatched it midair with trembling hands. He swiped the screen, thumb moving with desperate speed. The Kha'Len glyph interface shimmered, glowing softly.
There it was—*"Select Random Destination"*—etched in the flowing Urdii script.

He slid his finger across it. It pulsed—gold, bright, alive.
The talisman buzzed with energy. Its red triangular crystal flared dimly. No time to think. No time to pray.
Omar flipped on the iPhone's flashlight.

A focused beam of white light shot out. He angled it toward the red crystal at the talisman's tip.
The moment the beam hit, the gem lit up with infernal radiance.
Omar pointed the crystal at Lord Thaarn.

A vibration surged through the platform. The world gasped.
And then—
A portal ripped open behind Thaarn. He hadn't noticed. Too busy gloating over Vaan. Too busy enjoying the fight.

Ali focused his thoughts and spoke to Vaan telepathically: *"Vaan! Get up! Look behind Thaarn! There's a portal behind him!"*

Vaan looked up, bloody and shaking. His breath came in ragged gasps, pain exploding behind his eyes. Blood matted his hair, copper in his mouth. Through blurred vision, he saw the portal behind Thaarn.

With every ounce of agony, Vaan twisted beneath the tyrant's boot. His blood-slicked hand grabbed Thaarn's ankle—and shoved. Just enough to push it off.
But not by his strength alone. By something unpredictable.

From Ytelthuun's satchel, a blur exploded—small, furious.
Luma.
The tiny, cuddly, fur-covered creature had stayed hidden. But

now, sensing danger, he pounced. His eyes blazed. He launched onto Thaarn's face with maximum and unexpected ferocity.

Thaarn staggered, roaring in shock. Luma's claws dug deep. His fangs latched onto the soft flesh beneath Thaarn's eye and crunched. Then sank into his nose—blood gushed. He thrashed like a demon, tearing skin from bone. The wild anger coming from this cuddly animal was incredible and overwhelmed the dictator completely.

Thaarn flailed and yelled in agony, trying to rip the beast off. His boot lifted off Vaan's chest in a blind panic as he tried to save his face and bald head from being torn off by the sharp razor-like claws and teeth of Luma.

Vaan rolled to the side. Elbow to the floor. He rose—slow, agonizing. His armor cracked. His vision swam. But he stood.

He roared. A final scream. "FREE ORULENTHIA!!"
He lunged forward tackling Thaarn with all his might and weight pushing him into the open wormhole.

Luma was still savaging Thaarn's now bleeding face as Vaan slammed into him. The three figures—vengeance, fury, disbelief—hurtled into the pulsing portal to another point in the universe.

And vanished.

The portal slammed shut.
Thaarn. Vaan. Luma.
Gone.

"XA'REKTHUL-YENU-VAHN!" Nysha cried with tears. "Luma!! They're gone!"
The crowd panicked. Voices rose. Ytelthuun blinked. "Wh... what happened?"
Nysha grabbed him. "We have to go. NOW."

They sprinted to Omar and Ali who were still crouched and hidden behind the kneeling rebels.
"You have to leave. Activate it. Go HOME! Take the Kha'Len

with you. We don't have time! If the crowd notices aliens on the platform, their fear and prejudice will turn into punishment."

Tears flowed. Hugs were fierce. Nysha kissed both boys' foreheads. Ytelthuun, bloodied but upright, placed a heavy hand on their shoulders.

Ali: "We'll never forget you. Good bye!"
Omar: "Thank you... for everything. I love you, Nysha!"
Nysha: "Go. Before they see you... Wait... What did you say?"

Omar slid his shaking finger across "Choose Destination." The Urdii letters glowed. The red crystal pulsed. He imagined home—Old Bridge, New Jersey.

He flashed the phone's torch back into the crystal. A portal opened wide.

They didn't waste time. One last look. A wave. A smile.
Omar grabbed Ali and jumped.

They were ripped from Orulenthia like threads from a tapestry. No air. No direction. Only force.
They spiraled through space-time. Lights, geometries, memories spinning.

Omar could hear taste and see smells. Ali's grip was tight. They were fragments of humanity, drifting through cosmic veins. Their bodies stretched to unimaginable lengths towards the light in front of them.
The brightness became unbearable.

Then—
They were spit out.

A thud. Cold asphalt. Old Bridge, New Jersey. Silence.

No war. No screaming. Just crickets.

Omar groaned. Sat up. His G-Shock blinked: 11:03 PM. The same day that they disappeared. Earth had barely noticed their absence. Orulenthia had aged through several weeks of blood and fire. It had been only a few hours on Earth since their disappearance.

Ali crawled up beside him, wiping tears. They stood, staring at their home—normal, glowing softly.

Omar couldn't speak. Both the boys breathed the New Jersey air into their lungs like it was something new and alien. Their eyes adjusted to the darkness, which they were no longer used to, because of the perpetual red giant sun of Orulenthia. Their heads shifted around in every direction looking at everything, just to be sure they were back on their beloved planet.
Ali whispered, "We're home…? Are we really back?" His legs shivering from the change in gravity.
Omar nodded. "Yeah. We're home, little brother. We actually made it."

And for the first time since crossing the stars, they felt small. Irrelevant.
But safe.
And overwhelmed.

The quiet night wrapped around them like a blanket stitched with peace. They could hear distant honking of traffic and the sounds of American TV shows coming from the nearby windows. They were home. They were actually back. It was over.
Above them, the stars shimmered.
But none were red.

They stumbled towards their front gate trying hard to keep their legs balanced and their heads straight. There was nothing but smiles on their weary faces.

CHAPTER 36
THE KHA'LEN SLEEPS, BUT NOT THEIR DREAMS.

The living room was chaos—but it was the kind of chaos born from relief so overwhelming it couldn't contain itself.

Their mother stood in front of them, chest heaving, sobs spilling from her mouth like she was exorcising weeks of grief in a single breath. She smacked Omar's cheek, then Ali's arm, but each hit was followed by a wild, trembling kiss to their foreheads. Then back to more tears, more frantic words, more flailing hands. Her hijab had fallen down around her shoulders, her hair disheveled—and she didn't care.
"NEVER—never!—disappear on me like that again!" she shrieked between choked breaths. "Astaghfirullah! What if something had happened to you? What would I say to Allah? What would I do?" Her voice cracked into something raw and animal. Then she pulled them both into her arms again, pressing their faces into her chest as if to make sure they were still real. Her tears soaked into their dusty clothes, and her perfume—rosewater and sandalwood—clung to their skin like a sacred veil of comfort.

Their father stood a few steps behind her, his face a taut mask of control. His eyes, bloodshot but alert, shimmered faintly with restrained emotion. He didn't say a word at first—just stared at them both as if they were miracles. Then a smile broke across his face. Not a small one. It was full, proud, relieved—a fatherly smile that stretched into something holy. He walked forward slowly, placed one large, calloused hand on

each boy's shoulder, and gave a gentle squeeze.
"Alhamdulillah," he whispered, as if afraid even Allah might snatch them back if he spoke too loudly. "My sons are home."

The atmosphere in the room was thick with a cocktail of raw emotion—relief, disbelief, confusion, and love. The boys felt it wrap around them like a warm storm.

"What do you mean there was no signal?" their mother was saying now, wiping her face with the edge of her scarf, her voice still cracking but returning to something softer. "No signal, no calls, nothing? Your father even called the police! I was about to—Astaghfirullah—I was about to think the worst!"

"We're sorry, Mama," Omar said gently, his voice hoarse and his eyes low. "We just went walking in the woods. We didn't know it was that late. There was no signal out there. And we got... lost. That's all. After walking aimlessly, we finally found our way home. That's all, I swear."

Ali nodded quickly beside him. "We tried calling, but nothing worked. Then we found the main road again and walked all the way back home. We're really sorry it took this long."

Their father stepped closer, sniffing the air with a mock expression of disgust that cut through the heavy tension like a blade.
"You two smell like you've been camping with skunks for a month," he said, half-laughing. "What were you doing out there? Rolling with raccoons? And what are these weird clothes you're wearing?"

Omar grinned sheepishly. "It was... a weird part of the woods. We fell into the dirt a few times. It was dark! Uhh... we were rehearsing for a play and had to dress like this. Drama class stuff. You know how it is."

Ali added, "We're just really, really tired. Can we go upstairs now? Please?"

Their mother, still trembling, wiped her nose, kissed both of their cheeks again, and then stepped back, trying to compose herself.

"Go upstairs," she said firmly, pointing toward the hallway. "Take long showers—hot water. Scrub every part of yourselves. Then come back down. I made Moroccan roast chicken. Couscous. Salad. Laban. And I swear to Allah, if you don't eat properly, I will lose my mind."

The boys climbed the stairs, and the familiar creaks beneath their feet felt like a lullaby of normalcy.

Inside the bathroom, Omar turned on the faucet. Hot water thundered into the porcelain tub. He stripped away the alien-stained layers he'd been wearing since Veltharuun—clothes stiff with dust, ash, dried blood, and the scent of battle—and stepped into the downpour. The water hit his skin and it was like being born again. Heat spread through every bone, every bruise, every cell. He tilted his head back and closed his eyes as citrus-scented shampoo bubbled through his hair and down his shoulders. This wasn't just a shower—it was a ritual cleansing. A return. A resurrection.

But beneath the peace, memories surged.

Nysha's laugh—how it echoed in the cave beneath the crystal spires. The scream of Vaelik as Vorrak's tail struck him. Vaan's voice in the wind—his sacrifice, his fury, his final dive into the portal with Luma clawing at Thaarn's face. The way Luma—a tiny, sweet creature—had transformed into a frenzy of raging vengeance, launching out of Ytelthuun's bag like a fur-covered comet of wrath was unbelievable and unexpected.

He clenched his fists as the water pounded his scalp. They were gone. And yet... Orulenthia lived. Orulenthia was free of Thaarn. What would happen there now?

Ali was in the adjacent bathroom, soaking under jets of water so warm they felt like silk, wrapping his tired muscles in waves of comfort he hadn't felt in weeks. He scrubbed every inch of his skin, lathering thick clouds of fragrant bodywash that smelled of mint and eucalyptus—like walking through an ancient forest at dawn. The steam curled around him, wrapping his vision in a dreamy haze as the alien soil, dried blood, and phantom residue of Orulenthia's red dust slid away down the drain. His fingers moved slowly, reverently, tracing scars and bruises that were still tender, as if through each careful scrub he was whispering farewell to the chaos they'd survived. He closed his eyes, letting the water cascade down his face, and for the first time in weeks, his heart felt light again—as though with each droplet, a burden lifted from his soul.

He thought of Vaan too—how he had taught them strength, how he believed in them when they didn't believe in themselves. He remembered the sky beasts—the Khyzraal Skharnuun—and the way their manta-like wings caught the thermals above the mountains, gliding over dark forests and floating monoliths. He remembered Orulenthia's red giant sun, and ghostlight casting long shadows across silver lakes. Earth felt... small now.

They dressed in soft cotton pajamas. Omar's were navy blue with tiny white rockets. Ali's were forest green with pixelated dinosaurs. They laughed at each other—two boys, finally clean, finally safe.

Then they raced downstairs.

The aroma of roast chicken met them halfway down.

Their mother was waiting, already placing dishes on the table. Before she could say anything, both boys rushed forward, wrapping their arms around her. They kissed her cheeks. She laughed, swatting at them affectionately.

"Sit down, sit down, before I lose my mind again!" She couldn't help smiling.

The table was a mosaic of color and warmth. Bastilla sat at the center—golden, flaky pastry dusted with powdered cinnamon, its savory scent wafting like perfume. Omar grabbed a piece before it was even set down and moaned into the first bite. The minced chicken and vegetables inside melted on his tongue, seasoned with saffron and other aromatic spices.

A massive plate of couscous steamed beside it, piled high with tender roasted chicken—skin crackled and glistening—and a medley of carrots, zucchini, potatoes, chickpeas, and cabbage. The vegetables, kissed with olive oil and slow-steamed to buttery-soft perfection, glistened in the warm kitchen light. The scent was intoxicating—earthy spices mingled with the sharp sweetness of caramelized onions and the savory depth of cumin and turmeric. Their mother poured laban from a chilled jug, its creamy tang slicing through the richness of the meal. The glass pitcher fogged with condensation, and the boys could hear the gentle clink of ice cubes swirling inside. Even before the first bite, the entire kitchen felt wrapped in warmth and the promise of nourishment.

There was salad too—fresh greens, cucumber slices, ruby red tomatoes, olive oil, lemon, a pinch of black pepper. It crunched with life.

The boys didn't speak. They devoured. Their parents stared in stunned silence as they ate like starving wolves. Plate after plate vanished.

Upstairs, peace settled.

Their parents, finally able to rest, had gone to bed. Their father closed his eyes first, his muscles relaxing for the first time in hours. Their mother lay beside him, her hand resting over her chest, repeating "Alhamdulillah" until she fell asleep.

Omar and Ali returned to their shared bedroom. The walls were plastered with familiar comforts—NBA posters, vinyl decals of spaceships, and the worn calendar still stuck on the day they left. But those once-cherished symbols of normalcy now looked strangely hollow, like souvenirs from a life they no longer fully belonged to. The colors were the same, the layout untouched—but something within the boys had shifted irreversibly. The air itself seemed different, too still, too quiet, as though the room were holding its breath in awe of the young travelers who had crossed galaxies and survived chaos. Every item whispered of a past untouched by wonder and war, and now those memories clung to the edges of their perception, reshaping the room into both sanctuary and relic of an innocence forever changed.

Omar looked at his Sony PS5, still untouched. His Kendrick Lamar poster stared down at him, framed by blue LEDs. He grinned. But he wasn't ready to game. Not yet.

Ali grabbed the Kha'Len and they removed their translator devices from their ears and wrapped it all into old shirts—soft, forgotten ones from soccer camp and middle school. They placed this bundle into a small box and buried it beneath a mountain of comic books and winter coats in the closet's darkest corner. Nobody could know about the Kha'Len.

Then, pajamas rumpled and bellies full, they climbed into their beds.

Ali passed out first. He couldn't stay awake any longer. He started snoring gently and rhythmically.

Omar lay awake.

The moonlight filtered through the blinds, silver bars cast across the room. Outside, crickets sang. Inside, it was silent.

His thoughts wandered like drifting smoke through the caverns of memory. Vaan's voice echoed in his heart, not just as sound but as presence—a calm force of wisdom and strength that still wrapped itself around his soul. He could see the Skyraleon glider cutting through blood-red skies, the wind slicing past their faces as they soared between floating mountains like arrows through ancient air. The waterfall where Nysha had splashed him danced again in his mind's eye, droplets catching the violet sunlight like shards of crystal. The first time she kissed him—her lips trembling slightly—it felt both like a whisper and a promise.

But more memories surged. Vorrak—the towering monstrosity, its breath rancid and hot, its black, furred, muscular body a pinnacle of evil creation. Its venomous tail whipping forward in a blur of death, striking down Vaelik with a sickening crunch and a scream that tore the very air apart. Vaelik's red cybernetic eye flashed one last time in fury and pain before darkness claimed him. Omar winced—the memory a knife he didn't want to pull out.

He remembered falling from the sky, hurtling in a metal pod toward jagged cliffs below, the landscape spinning wildly outside the small porthole. The impact had been thunderous—a bone-jarring slam that left his body vibrating for minutes. Somehow, they had survived—more than once. Again and again. Their allies had hidden them, risking their lives to protect them not only from Thaarn's brutal forces, but from the public too, shielding them with cloaks and courage.

It was all still so raw, so enormous. A galaxy of feeling pressed into the tiny shell of his bedroom. The stars might have been millions of light-years away, but the fire of that world still burned behind his eyes.

He cried, softly. Not from grief. From gratitude. He missed his friends and would forever remember the bravery of Vaan, Vaelik, and the cute little dangerous monster, Luma.

He turned on his side.
Smiled.
Then Slept.

The following day, school was normal. The bell rang. Students bustled. Lockers clanged.

But for Omar and Ali, nothing was the same.

Lyndsey waved at Omar. He waved back automatically, but her smile—once something that would have made his stomach flutter—now felt like a pale echo. It didn't reach his heart. The hallways, once full of harmless chaos, now felt sterile—untouched by the wildness he had come to know.

The fluorescent lights above buzzed quietly, flickering over white linoleum and rows of identical lockers. There was no scent of ozone from a portal's wake. No shimmer of foreign stars peeking through broken ceilings. The air felt too thin. Too bland. Too Earth-like. He missed the scent of burning elements in the wind, the way the crimson sky pulsed with life, the sound of rebels shouting freedom beneath a red giant star.

Every face here belonged to someone who hadn't seen the crimson clouds of Orulenthia or stood beneath Thaarn's shadow. They didn't know what it meant to run for your life with a glowing artifact pressed to your chest. They didn't understand the weight of sacrifice. The taste of courage. Everything had changed.

They walked to class, each step feeling like a dream half-remembered. The corridor lights were too bright, the walls too narrow—everything felt artificial compared to the vastness of Orulenthia's open skies. Teachers handed out worksheets that felt trivial—meaningless scribbles to boys who had spoken Urdii. Classmates joked about TikTok trends and cafeteria rumors, but the boys only half-heard, as if the language no longer fully registered. Everything was too loud, too colorful, too simple. Life went on—but not the same life.
The echoes of Orulenthia hummed in their bones, like a forgotten song waiting to be sung again.

The boys had been permanently changed. Their minds could never accept the normality of Earth again.

There was a hunger in their souls. A spark.

At lunch, Omar whispered, "Dude, I can't stop thinking about Orulenthia and our friends. Do you think... there's more? I mean more out there?"

Ali smiled, eyes gleaming.
"We haven't seen anything yet. I'm sure of it."

They were finally back on Earth. They were finally safe.
But the yearning had only begun.

Though the boys had buried it in familiar clutter, The Kha'Len's presence refused to be silenced—humming like a dormant heartbeat, waiting.

And it was only sleeping. It was awaiting reactivation.

What other worlds might it open next time?
Who would they meet?
What evils would they face—and what wonders?

Would this be Omar and Ali's last adventure?
Was this the end?

As they slept, they both knew—
This was only the beginning.

THE END (?)

❖ *"When redlight fades to hearth-born flame / and crystal drinks the blaze again / the way shall open to names unknown / where stars remember and stones have flown." –* ***INSCRIPTION ON KHA'LEN*** ❖

ABOUT THE AUTHOR

Adil Bhatti is an American-Pakistani writer whose global experiences across countries like Türkiye, Morocco, Dubai, Japan, the USA, and England have deeply shaped his storytelling. Passionate about travel, diverse cultures, and great food, he writes with heart and imagination—always inspired by the love of family. For inquiries or connection, reach out at **ALPStudioLLC@gmail.com** or through social media **@6MillionRupeeMan** (Instagram and Threads). ❖